FEARS FROM THE PAST
FOLLOWED HER TO PARADISE.

It seemed inevitable that these two men should be on opposite sides, dominant males of most species usually were, but she hated the idea of being the female in the middle. And she knew she had made it worse by turning to Kyre with such obvious relief. His words confirmed it.

"I will take on the pleasant duty of making sure you are not alone with Winston St. James again. Alone with me is another matter," he whispered.

The words should have been gratifying to her, but they were not. They carried an unmistakable threat. The urge to escape rose in her again, the urge to escape both of these men. . . .

SUFFER A SEA CHANGE

SUFFER
A
SEA CHANGE

Celeste De Blasis

BANTAM BOOKS
TORONTO • NEW YORK • LONDON • SYDNEY • AUCKLAND

All the characters in this book are fictitious, and any resemblance to actual persons living or dead is purely coincidental.

SUFFER A SEA CHANGE

A Bantam Book / published by arrangement with the author

PRINTING HISTORY
First published in 1976
Bantam edition / October 1986
3 printings through August 1988

ISBN 0-553-27750-2

Published simultaneously in the United States and Canada

Bantam Books are published by Bantam Books, a division of Bantam Doubleday Dell Publishing Group, Inc. Its trademark, consisting of the words "Bantam Books" and the portrayal of a rooster, is Registered in U.S. Patent and Trademark Office and in other countries. Marca Registrada. Bantam Books, 666 Fifth Avenue, New York, New York 10103.

PRINTED IN THE UNITED STATES OF AMERICA

O   12 11 10 9 8 7 6 5 4 3

Full fathom five thy father lies;
   Of his bones are coral made;
Those are pearls that were his eyes:
   Nothing of him that doth fade
But doth suffer a sea-change
Into something rich and strange.
Sea-nymphs hourly ring his knell:

—SHAKESPEARE,
The Tempest

ACKNOWLEDGMENTS

I wish to acknowledge the invaluable help I received from J. S., senior special agent, United States Department of Justice, drug enforcement administration; the public relations department of the Metropolitan Police at Scotland Yard; and A. L., special detective, Birmingham Police Force, England. All gave freely of their time and expertise. The authenticity of the hunters and the hunted in *Suffer a Sea Change* is due to their efforts on my behalf, and I am very grateful.

I would also like to thank my dear friends, Geoffrey Parker and Michael Lowe, who served as my liaisons with the London Metropolitan Police Force and the Birmingham Police Force; David B. Wingate, conservation officer, Bermuda, who shared his rich store of ornithological lore with me; and Brian Goble, who mitigated my ignorance of sailing with his love and knowledge of the art.

And my deepest gratitude to Pat and John Draper, who invited me to accompany them to Bermuda in 1972, and to my parents, who made it possible for me to go.

1

No harm.
I have done nothing but in care of thee,
Of thee my dear one, thee my daughter, who
Art ignorant of what thou art, naught knowing
Of whence I am.

THE TEMPEST

Jess hung up her coat and put her hat away carefully, clutching the small box tightly in her hand. The typewriter kept up its ostentatious speed, a sure sign Larry had heard her come in. She squared her shoulders and walked into the common room. The typewriter stopped with a key-jammed clatter, and Larry swung around to frown at her, condemning her for not paying tribute fast enough to his savage industry. A wave of impatience swept over her, and her plan for breaking the news gradually was washed away. She was amazed to hear herself saying calmly, "Larry, I'm trading you in on a trip to Bermuda. You can find another place to rent while I'm gone."

His expression was so ludicrous, Jess had to swallow convulsively to keep herself from laughing. "Well, we agreed, didn't we, that if my house proved too small for both of us, you would find something else?"

She saw it in his face. He had always thought he might move if he found something better; he had never even considered that she might ask him to go.

"It's that old lecher, isn't it?" His craggy face was

contorted with anger and suspicion. "Uncle Arthur's giving the good little girl another prize for virtue and getting rid of his rival at the same time. Very neat. Are you traveling together or will he just meet you there as a surprise?"

She knew she ought to be insulted, but she wasn't. She was amused by the extraordinary picture of herself and Arthur Barton as lovers, and at the same time she was saddened by the sudden clear image she had of something she had suspected for a long time—Larry was just as piecemeal as the rest of her friends. She was addicted to outcasts. Among all her friends, only Arthur was whole. The rest were all in or out of uneasy marriages or mired in loneliness, in shambles mentally or physically. Pity was only a minor motive. Her compulsion to protect arose out of the conviction that society, the great "they," was geared more and more efficiently to obliterate those who did not measure up. And then a year ago, Uncle Arthur had come into her life, intact, unoppressed, and not an uncle at all.

The memory of the day was vivid. She had had a tidy sum for the drawings done for Larry's current play book. She left the worry of her car at home and rode a bus into Boston with a distinct plan in mind—to buy a hat and then to enjoy an outrageously expensive lunch. The hat hadn't been difficult; she had found it at her favorite boutique. It was hers instantly, a great brooding affair of black felt with a brim big enough to shelter tears, unwise laughter, or a mysterious alter ego. She wore it, pleased with the half darkness it cast on her face, warning the cloudy sky not to drop so much as one wet pellet on her vulnerable treasure.

She thought the hat a strong enough omen to decide her dining place, and she went to the restaurant without a qualm. Within a few minutes, she had a new title for another of Larry's books—Suzie and Bill Go to Lunch Together Because Suzie Isn't Welcome by Herself. The restaurant had had its share of trouble from the ACLU and from women's organizations, but apparently an unescorted woman was still taboo. The maître d' wore a plastic smile as he told her there was no room, patently untrue since she could see the empty spaces.

She was debating whether to argue with sweet reason or to be uselessly but satisfyingly obscene when a voice behind her said with quiet authority, "The lady is with me," and then kindly, "I am sorry to be late, my dear."

The maître d's face turned tallow, and the snobbish lift melted into such obsequiousness that Jess was speechless as the man burbled, "Of course, Mr. Barton. Please accept my apologies. If the young lady had only told me . . . but no, it is my fault. Right this way."

She whirled around, mouth open to ask what was going on, but she checked at the sight of her benefactor. Tall, lean, white-haired, at least in his seventies, face lined, mouth thin-lipped and nose beaked with age, the man had the brightest blue eyes she had ever seen outside of her own family. His expression was as correct and disciplined as his British accent, but his eyes danced with unabashed mischief and enjoyment, plainly asking her to share the joke on the man who so richly deserved it.

Her normally husky voice was a trifle squeaky, but she managed to say, "Actually I'm early. I finished shopping well ahead of time."

"I can see that. Your hat is quite fetching," he replied as they followed the maître d'. Jess nearly laughed aloud at the realization of how she must have been preening. Like most women, she found it impossible to wear a new hat casually, and the old gentleman was well versed in the nuances of feminine behavior.

The table was in a good location, and the waiter was beside them instantly, obviously pleased to see Mr. Barton. The two men greeted each other with the ritualized courtesy of mutual respect. Jess recognized it because her father had had the same talent for acknowledging the dignity of those who served him.

"Do you wish to make your own selections, or would you allow me to order for us both?" The bright eyes were amused at this tricky juncture of the conspiracy; food preference was basic knowledge shared between friends, but as far as he knew, she might think bouquet garni was some sort of fish.

"Please, you order. I always enjoy whatever you

choose." The slightest blue wink paid her tribute. She was safe; her brother, Sean, had once threatened to base a scientific thesis on her, claiming she was the only truly omnivorous creature he had found. The only thing she couldn't abide was raw oysters, and the only thing which worried her now was the cost of the lunch—she had planned to be extravagant, but not quite to the degree which the growing order of dishes indicated. But she had to wait until the waiter left before she could broach the subject, and then she was forestalled by Mr. Barton.

"Quickly now, before he returns. 'My dear' is very nice, but he will be insulted if I don't introduce you properly."

She didn't even consider giving a false name; lying to Arthur Barton was unthinkable from the first. "Thank heavens, Jessica Banbridge is a fine name," he said. "It is rather horrid that the one thing we carry all of our lives is decided by someone else. I would have hated to introduce you as Gertrude such and such."

The waiter returned with a bottle of wine, and he and Jess were introduced by Mr. Barton, who apologized smoothly for having forgotten they had not met before. A surreptitious glance at the bottle and her first taste of the wine told Jess she simply had to mention the cost.

"Sir, ah, Mr. Barton. This has been lots of fun, and I do thank you for rescuing me, but I must insist on paying for my lunch, only if I eat all of the things you've ordered, I don't think I'll be able to, to pay that is." Good lord! She sounded just like a child before the principal. It had something to do with the blue eyes watching her so intently.

"Miss Banbridge, I never allow young women to pay when I kidnap them for luncheon. And this is hardly the place to stage a hunger strike. Nor would it be kind of you to walk out and leave my reputation as a passable escort irreparably damaged. Now, having disposed of your options, I consider the matter closed." His voice was severe, but his eyes were not, and Jess smiled back and surrendered.

The meal progressed from one tempting dish to the next; the wine flowed freely from white to red; and the conversation flowed as easily. But suddenly Jess stopped in mid sentence, realizing Mr. Barton had effortlessly found out almost everything about her while giving only the barest account of himself. She knew he was still actively head of his London-based import export firm, that he also had a branch in Boston, which he visited frequently, and that he was very wealthy; but beyond these impersonal facts, which could easily be gleaned from a credit-rating sheet, she knew nothing. And she had been in the middle of telling him about the loss of her parents and Sean, a subject still so nightmarish she had spoken little of it to anyone.

She shook her head as though coming out of a trance and suspicion was clear in her eyes and voice. "What's going on? I've just handed you my life story on a platter, and I don't even know why you want it. I feel as though I am being interviewed for a top-security job."

"Forgive me, my dear. I am an old man. I have no children. My wife died ten years and more ago, and my life holds little chance of surprise. I fear I have become terribly curious about other people's lives. But I assure you, my curiosity is harmless. I won't make any indecent proposals—I am much too old and too tired."

Jess laughed at that; no one as vital as Arthur Barton could be called too old and tired. But she felt reassured nonetheless. Only a certain look which had flashed across the lined face when she mentioned being interviewed for a job still had her puzzled. She thought it had been the kind of look you have when someone has stepped into your brain for an unexpected instant of knowing precisely what you're thinking. But she couldn't be sure and dismissed it, positive that whatever else he was, he wasn't dangerous.

She felt afterward that she hadn't had any choice anyway; she had been intrigued by him from the first, and more than that, even by the end of that first meeting, she found that she liked him very much, much more than she had liked any human being for a long time.

In spite of her claiming the reliability of the public transport system, he had insisted on giving her a ride out to Lexington. His car was large, black, chauffeur-driven,

archaic, and perfectly suited to him. He said he preferred
to drive himself, but not on the right-hand side, thank you
very much.

It did not even bother her that he was probably
giving her a ride so that he could find out where and how
she lived. But she had a twinge of panic at the idea of the
inevitable meeting between Larry and Mr. Barton, and
the feeling was justified, for the two men loathed each
other on sight. Larry saw the car drive up and shot out of
the house like an enraged watchdog. "What goes on, Jess?
I demand an explanation," he barked.

Jess barely restrained herself from telling him to shut
up and quit acting the fool. Instead she introduced the
two as civilly as she could—her association with Larry was
a demerit, but it put something right that at least he was
not her husband.

There had been no question of inviting Mr. Barton in
with Larry so openly hostile, and Jess had felt a sense of
loss as the car pulled out and disappeared. But that feeling
eased with Larry's questions about the man, his sly accu-
sations about what they were up to. Larry would not have
liked to know that his possessive bullying made Jess
strangely sure she would see Mr. Barton again.

A month had passed before they had their next meeting. Mr. Barton called her at home one evening, chatted
pleasantly about his last few weeks in London, asked her
how her drawing had been going, and then invited her to
a weekend performance of the Royal Ballet in Boston. She
accepted with alacrity and no thought of Larry until she
hung up and found him standing behind her.

"Lord Pip Pip and all that. Jess, I won't have you
going out with that antique bastard. There are some very
suitable names for men like him."

Jess hated getting angry; the rushing blood, the
shouting, the clenched muscles always made her feel ill,
and she often chose to back down rather than make a
scene. But she couldn't do it this time. Her friendship
with Arthur was already too precious. She tried to keep
her voice even, but it still had an ugly, menacing note.
"Larry Foreman, you don't own me. You rent part of my

house, not part of my soul, and you will not tell me what to do. Mr. Barton and I are just friends, but I don't like my friends called foul names. I've never said a word against your seeing Pauline Stracey. I don't expect to be the only woman you know. So you'd better get your head screwed on straight about Mr. Barton."

Larry had mumbled something about Pauline being strictly a business contact, but he had backed down enough so there wasn't an obvious row everytime Jess went out with Arthur. But the dislike between the two men never eased. Mr. Barton included Larry a couple of times, but neither event was a success. At one point during an aftershow supper, Arthur, tired of Larry's sullen behavior, said with mocking politeness, "I assure you, Mr. Foreman, my interest in Jess is purely avuncular. If it makes you feel easier, please call me 'Uncle Arthur.'" Larry had scowled openly; Jess had burst out laughing and had adopted the name.

Arthur had become more and more a power in her life. She received letters and small gifts from England when he was there and always a call when he returned to Boston. He took her to marvelous plays, dance recitals, art shows, and fine restaurants, and she ceased to feel guilty about it. Her humble turnabouts—picnics, leisurely birding walks, dinners at home when Larry was out, foreign film festivals in Cambridge and tennis matches—were received with deep gratitude by the old man. And he did his best not to tamper with her private life though sometimes his concern got the better of him, and one night he said bluntly, "I do not understand how a woman with such superb taste in the arts can have such profoundly bad taste in men. I begin to think Larry Foreman is your albatross, but I can't think why you should be condemned to carry him."

She was startled by her reaction; she felt no fierce urge to defend Larry, only a need to define her own motives. "After my family... well, up 'til then I hadn't minded being alone, I guess because knowing they were close by meant I wasn't alone at all. I had an apartment in Boston then, but I spent a lot of time at the family's house. But then I just couldn't bear it. And Larry came along when I needed him most. I met him first as a business contact, a new client for my drawings. They're mostly for children's books, you know, and Larry writes those play books which are quite popular. I was buying the house, and it was big enough for two people to have virtually separate apartments upstairs while sharing the rooms downstairs. He needed a place to rent. I needed a tenant. The house is sort of isolated, and he seemed to offer more protection than a woman. Neither of us demands much beyond the security of knowing we have a place to come home to that isn't empty. Neither of us gives much either. I wouldn't call what we have love. I think it's more like a habit."

For the first time she saw deep sadness in the blue eyes. He shook his head slowly. "What a very poor substitute that is for loving." Then his gaze had sharpened, the expression completely changed. "Will you be able to break that habit?"

She hadn't known then; she knew now. And she knew that whatever Arthur's long-range plan was, it was nearing completion. She had been manipulated by him from the first, chosen for a specific purpose. She had realized and accepted it early in the game. She was willing to go along with him because she was curious, because she was becoming more and more restless, but most of all because she trusted Arthur to plan only for her welfare, never to harm her.

She clutched the box in her hand as if it were a talisman, hearing Arthur's words as he had given it and the trip packet to her. "I am flying back to London tonight. You are going to Bermuda next week." She had been so stunned she hadn't made a sound. "You may make useless protests if you wish, but nothing will change my determination that you go, and you will never deal me a worse hurt than if you refuse. You will be going with a group of amateur tennis players who are going to have a tournament there. Your unending enthusiasm for the game will find a fine outlet. I also expect you will find numerous subjects for drawing and many species of birds you've never seen before. I mention all of this to tempt you, of course. But my major purpose is to get you away from that man. That is my condition. He must not be waiting for you. You must break the habit before you leave."

Then he had handed her the box. "This is not to be opened until you arrive home tonight, and it is never to be returned. It has been in my family for years, now it is yours. All I ask is that you wear it as a token of my deep love and respect for you."

He had escorted her to his car, giving his driver instructions to take her home. He had leaned in, kissed her gently on the forehead, and said softly, "I trust 'uncle' will still be a proper title in the future, but I could not love you more were you my own daughter."

She didn't know what the words really meant though she heard them again and again on the silent trip home. She thought perhaps she was in shock. She hadn't protested his plans; she felt as compelled to finish what he had started as he did.

Larry must have been talking for a long time, but the words penetrated slowly. "You haven't heard anything I've said. I hope it's worth it, whatever memory is giving you that glassy-eyed stare. I think that old man is mad. I think you both are."

Not one word of love or loss. There never had been. "I think you might be right," she said and heard the front door slam with Larry's angry exit. She didn't worry about where he was going; good old Larry wouldn't hurt himself on her account.

She opened the box slowly and stared at the contents for a long time, not touching the ring. She felt the tears on her cheeks, and she could see Arthur clearly, smiling gently to himself before he settled down to sleep out the flight to London. This too he had planned, this touching to make her feel something. He had worried that her calm existence with Larry was killing her ability to feel anything. He was probably right. She hadn't cried since . . . no, she hadn't cried that day either, so it wasn't Larry's fault. He had simply done nothing to end the frozen calm. Her tears stopped abruptly; she wasn't sure she could handle really thinking about it and letting go, not yet. She blanked the image of the cold waves breaking from her mind.

There was a small white piece of paper curled in the circle of the ring. She took it out and knew before she read it that it would be cryptic, not to be understood until later. It said: "To my Jessica, who will, I hope, become his Miranda and suffer a sea change into something rich and strange."

She knew the reference. She had played an exasperated Miranda to a chronically nervous freshman Ferdinand in a collegiate production of *The Tempest*. She got out her battered copy and found the stray bit of information in the introduction to the play—in spite of Shakespeare's references to the Mediterranean, the play was most certainly based on the wreck of an English ship on the Bermudas. One line even mentioned "the still-vex'd Bermoothes." Arthur was sending her to the islands and had cast her as Miranda, the innocent and unworldly maiden; he himself could be no other than Prospero, father of the girl, sorcerer of the islands—he had been so since he first found her, first began the spell. But who then was Ferdinand, the prince, and would there be a Caliban, a monster? And what of Ariel, the spirit in bondage to the sorcerer's will.

"You are far too clever, old one," she murmured aloud as she picked up the ring for the first time. She loved jewelry and knew something about it from her art classes, but she had little beyond a few modest pieces left by her mother. Never had she thought to have anything like this, yet she felt no surge of pride in ownership. She felt something akin to fear of a sorcerer's power, as if putting on the ring would mean the final acquiescence to Arthur's will. She wished her childhood had been bare of tales of magic rings.

She had promised, promised to finish what Arthur had started for her and somehow for himself. She put the ring on. It fitted perfectly on the ring finger of her right hand, and even that did not surprise her. The gold setting was heavy and ornate to support the large stone, an emerald carved with strange patterns—a mermaid with tiny features and a curving tail and above her, a ship with sails forever full in the wind. Perhaps not so strange if Arthur's family had long been in merchant shipping and proud of it. She wanted a rational explanation, but it was no use.

She looked at herself in the mirror. She was the same, yet not the same. The same long, deep-blue eyes looked at her from dark lashes under clearly defined brows. The angular facial bones and straight nose, the generous mouth, the whole face surrounded by a cloud of black hair. Everything was familiar. Everything was changed. The shutting down, the still set which masked any emotion, the careful control of the past two years was slipping. It was not by her volition, but she could see it had begun. The eyes which had been so full of mute acceptance were now expectant, demanding something happen. The mouth was curved, ready to be happy. The whole face was softer, younger than her twenty-six years, younger than her experience, vulnerable again. Only by recognizing the transformation could she see what had been. The first of the sea change here, away from sight or sound of the tide.

The wind was blowing by the time she went to bed, and the house creaked loudly. Before the uneasiness of the old timbers would have become part of her, making her nightmare return, making her desperate to have someone close. But this night sleep was not like drowning, and she was glad Larry was not in the house.

He did not return until early morning. He didn't look at her, just mumbled about packing and wandered aimlessly, gathering up his possessions. Jess felt pity mixed with scorn. Poor Larry, he never lived a day without feeling guilty about something. It was a wonder such a hulking bear body of a man could be inhabited by so timid a boy. She made breakfast for both of them, using food as a lure to make him sit down for a moment.

"Larry, this is ridiculous. You've paid rent on your half for the rest of this month, and I'll be gone for most of it. You've got a lot of time to find another place. I'm not throwing you out today."

His words were muffled by a piece of toast, but she

heard them clearly enough. "Have another place already. Spent the night there. Polly's a nice girl."

As opposed to me, thought Jess, trying not to smile. She knew she was missing her cue; Larry was finally looking at her, glaring actually. He was waiting for her to be jealous, but it just wasn't there. "Oh, I'm awfully glad for you. I think the two of you are well suited," she said sweetly, trying to keep the relief out of her voice. His response sounded something like "humph!" as he stalked out of the kitchen.

By the time she got home from the library with some books about Bermuda, the house was empty. Nothing of Larry remained except the door key he had used and a note saying that while their personal relationship was ended, he hoped their professional one would continue.

Jess sat down and laughed until tears stung her eyes. Practical Larry, he didn't really mind losing her, but he couldn't face losing those stupid drawings of fat-legged children with bright yellow trucks and redheaded dolls for his *Suzie and Bill* play books. It made her feel a great deal better about the whole situation. "Bad taste in men is right, Uncle Arthur," she said to the empty air.

Beyond a trip into Boston to buy some new beachwear, she had little to do to get ready, so little it was frightening to discover how rootless she was. The house was hers, purchased with money from the sale of the Marblehead home she never wanted to see again. She wouldn't really miss Larry's nominal rent. Her family had enjoyed what they had and had not saved much, but there had been enough left even after buying her house so that she would not starve if she were not able to sell her art work for a while. She was fond of her house in an abstract way because it was spacious and had a well-lighted room which worked perfectly as a studio. But it had never really become a home. She didn't have a cat or a dog to worry about; even that commitment had been unwanted. All she had to do was take a few plants to the neighbors', lock the house, and turn a set of keys over to them.

2

...Hear the last of our sea-sorrow.
Here in this island we arrived; and here
Have I, thy schoolmaster, made thee more profit
Than other princesses can that have more time
For vainer hours and tutors not so careful.

The tour was to meet at a parking lot in Marblehead to avoid the confusion of Logan airport. Cars would be left there, and a bus would take the group to the airport. Since the bus would be leaving at eight in the morning, Jess had to start long before it was light.

It was what she considered a depressingly typical late October Monday, dripping a cold rain which made you feel damp no matter what you were wearing. Not until she was well on her way, her Volkswagen making dogged sputtering noises as it took the slick roads, did Jess consider what it was going to be like to be in Marblehead, even for a short stop. She had been so set on Bermuda nothing else had registered. Now she wished she had planned to meet the group at the airport, in spite of the hassles it would have involved. The queasy feeling grew until she had to remind herself severely to keep her attention on her driving. Suddenly she heard Arthur's words from months ago. "But, my dear Jessica, you must have left many friends there. Places are just places, only the mind fills them with ghosts, gives them the power to haunt."

Now she understood. Most of the people on the tour

would be from the Marblehead area. Some of them would have known her family. Some would remember her. "This too?" she whispered softly as she pulled into the meeting place. She had no trouble finding it; the whole area was forever etched on her brain.

She froze as she got out of the car. It was there, right beyond the line of darkness, swirling, sucking on the rocks, filling her nostrils with the salt-creature smell. She swallowed the sickness in her throat. What in the world was she doing, going to a place visibly surrounded by her implacable enemy? She could get back in the car, go inland, flee to safety. And never suffer the full sea change. She hesitated too long.

The kind voice, its English accent only slightly altered by years and marriage in America, welcomed her. "Jess, how good to see you again! Glad you could manage this ghastly hour. I think you know some of the others, but I'll introduce you anyway."

"Mrs. Allenby, I didn't know you were involved in this." But I'll bet Arthur knew, she added silently, realizing she had sounded ungracious and accusatory.

Mrs. Allenby missed it or ignored it; her voice lost none of its friendliness. "Involved is hardly an adequate word! Jane Crowl and I started the business last year. You know, children practically grown, time on our hands, dreadful danger of becoming dull old ducks. We call the company 'Jet Sets'. We run small tennis trips to various places. Tennis is so popular now, and it's a good excuse to travel. Of course, we only deal with amateurs, keeps things friendly, but we have had good players on every trip so far, so you won't lack for some stiff games. By the way, please call me Rose, Mrs. Allenby is far too formal."

Jess smiled in the darkness. The awful tension was dissolving, helpless against Rose's enthusiasm. And her amusement increased when she got a closer look at the people standing near the bus. The sky was lightening enough so that she could see what an incongruous picture they made. Tennis rackets are difficult to pack, and most of the people were carrying theirs, cradling them protectively against the damp. Jess could pick out those with gut because they were acting as if even the plastic covers weren't enough to prevent limp strings. One man was wearing his racket inside his coat. Jess stifled a giggle; anyone seeing them all bundled in winter wools and overshoes and sporting tennis rackets would judge them mad.

Before she began the introductions, Rose whispered, "Don't worry if you can't remember the names. We're going to pass out lists which will help sort everyone out. There're seventeen of us in all."

Jess was hopeless about memorizing names on the first try, but usually something in every face stuck in her memory, a habit learned for future use in drawings. The overall impression with this group was that everyone was well-to-do, well-dressed, well-groomed, country club set, hardly unexpected with people going on a trip such as this. She was relieved she did not know that many of them. Dr. and Mrs. Cranston, and Jane and Will Crowl had only been casual acquaintances, as had Harry and Rose Allenby, and they all greeted her warmly but with no awkward intensity. The only hurdle came when she heard a soft voice saying, "Jess?" and turned to face Sally Carlson, tall, slender, blond, brown-eyed Sally. There was a horrible silence as it all rushed back—laughing, loving, shy Sally, not shy at all with Sean because his confidence was contagious, Sally who might have been with him that day had she not been visiting her aunt in Boston.

Sally did the best thing. She hugged Jess and kissed her on the cheek. "It's okay, Jaybe, it's got to be. He left such good memories," she whispered, using the nickname which had been Sean's and through him, Sally's private property.

Sally turned away for a moment, and Jess swallowed hard and managed a smile when Sally introduced, "My friend, Tom White. I think maybe you two have met before."

"Yes, of course, nice to see you again, Tom," Jess said, offering her hand. She remembered him quite well because she had had such a rough time of it, and the whole town had known it. His wife had been a vicious drunk who caused a scandal every other week. But because he adored his two children, he had been unbelievably patient, trying to keep the family together. Obviously that had changed, because, though he had to be somewhere over forty and Sally was only twenty-five, they were clearly more than friends. His face had been prematurely aged by what he had borne, but when he looked at Sally, the lines softened. He was a good man, and Sally deserved that. Jess hoped Sally would tell her how they'd gotten together. With a sudden sense of wonder, she recognized a new change— she hadn't had any curiosity about other people's lives for a long time, and here she was, hardly able to forebear asking Sally a thousand questions. She felt the insistent weight of the ring on her finger.

Once everyone was on the bus, Rose handed out the lists and sat beside Jess, making a face across the aisle at her husband. "I never get to sit beside him," she complained with mock anger. "Once he's squeezed his bulk and then all his camera equipment into a seat, there is never any room for me. We've been married for twenty-five years, but I always travel alone."

Harry beamed placidly at them before burying his face in his newspaper again. He was over six feet tall and weighed over two hundred pounds, and Rose was so tiny she made him seem even bulkier than he was. An odd combination, yet perfectly suited to each other.

Jess studied the list, and Rose started to give her a rundown then stopped. "I'll just muddle things. You'll know everyone soon enough. Tennis has a way of doing that."

Jess felt very much at ease with Rose, and they chatted about all manner of things on the bus ride. The only subject which was carefully avoided was Jess' family. At one point, hoping she sounded casual, Jess asked if Rose knew Arthur Barton.

"I don't know him well, though my parents are most fond of him. They still live in England, and though they're both terribly old and frail, Arthur visits them quite frequently. Though I'm sure the drawings you did for his firm were superb, wasn't it kind of him to give you this trip?"

"Yes, it was very kind," agreed Jess weakly. Drat his cleverness! She had thought to pry his plan out of Rose, but Rose didn't know a thing about it. He had said just enough to provide a reasonable excuse for giving her the trip without damaging her reputation.

When they arrived at the airport, there was the inevitable confusion of transporting seventeen people and their jumble of luggage and rackets, but Jane Crowl and Rose managed to get everyone to the proper gate in plenty of time.

Though the men had to empty their pockets and the women had to open handbags and overnight cases, the guards' inspection was cursory—there wasn't much chance of people bound for the tennis courts of Bermuda wanting a side trip to Havana—and there was little delay in boarding. Jess found herself sitting on the aisle seat, nice not to have to look down on hundreds of miles of open sea. She was beside Rose and an older woman.

She was a good traveler. She liked the sensation of flying, and she felt safer in a plane than in a car. Before, she hadn't even minded looking down at the ocean. But then, everything had been different before. She and Sean had gotten to travel a great deal from the time they were small. Her father's typical reaction to a good architectural fee had been to pack the family and take off on some adventure. Her mother had gone along with it whole-heartedly, adding most of her salary as a teacher to the projects. Both parents had believed the experience gained by seeing new places far outweighed the value of money in the bank. Jess still agreed, and the memories of her first summer in Europe when she was eleven, and Sean was thirteen were still vivid.

She shook her head in protest. She was not going to let that happen, that sure turning of pleasant memories into grief. Whatever else he had planned, she was sure Uncle Arthur had meant her to go forward not backward in her life.

Rose touched her arm and asked in concern, "Are you all right? You look a bit off-color."

Jess smile at her. "I'm fine, thanks, I really am. I think the excitement just got to me for a moment."

"You think you're excited! Let me tell you, I have palpitations every time we start out on one of these jaunts. Jane makes an ideal partner. She's so calm. I'm always sure we're going to lose half of the group en route or that there won't be any room in the inn when we arrive, despite months of planning. By the way, take out your list and mark 'sat by her on the plane' beside Mrs. Stanley Clinton's name. Mrs. Clinton, this is Miss Jessica Banbridge."

They shook hands across Rose, and the older woman spoke first. "Now that is ridiculous. My name is Elsie."

"And mine's Jess. Rose, I think you did that on purpose. Typical tour director's trick to make formalities sound silly."

Rose nodded without a trace of guilt. "I'm learning."

Jess felt an instantaneous sympathy for Elsie. She was probably no more than sixty, and she was as immaculately groomed as her Boston Brahmin accent, but social position had done nothing to soften the years. Her face was lined, and what once had been finely drawn features now looked small and crumpled. Her mouth was touched only by light color, but her skin was so pale, it looked garish. Her eyes were dark and alert, but the whole effect was one of great strain.

Feeling she'd seen too much, Jess looked away and met the cool blue eyes of the woman across the aisle. She heard Rose hiss in her ear, "Mrs. Jonathan Cooper." Her nod and her, "I'm Jess Banbridge," were met with the barest of nods and a curt, "Elizabeth Cooper." She felt the blood rise in her cheeks and wished she had learned how to deal with rude people. But then she had a curious sense of double vision. Elizabeth Cooper was very much like Elsie must have been thirty years before—a tall, perfectly shaped blond woman, sure of beauty and position, not having to care much about what strangers thought and not caring much anyway about anyone outside of her circle. The comparison made Elizabeth seem peculiarly vulnerable and not at all threatening. Jess looked at the list and wondered where Mr. Cooper was. The Jonathan in the name meant they weren't divorced, but it didn't mean he was still living.

She turned her attention back to her seatmates. Rose and Elsie were talking, or rather, Elsie was talking and Rose was adding an occasional kind murmur. Jess began to get a clear idea of why Elsie looked as she did, and the tale was made all the more poignant because the voice wasn't asking for pity. It was just giving the sordid facts one by one.

"I wish I could blame it all on Stanley, but I can't. Other families survive the parents' difficulties without falling to pieces. Somehow I failed my only child utterly. My God, if you could see the man Janet's living with! She's been caught stealing for him and much worse. I'm quite sure they're both on some drug. I tried to help for a while, but it wasn't any use. Maybe I was too old when I had my child; maybe I just didn't have the right kind of love to give any more. I'm telling you this because I know how people talk, and I'd just as soon have it out in the open as to listen to hushed whispers."

"Please, Elsie, you mustn't feel that way! All of us with children have had some problem or other. I'm sure you heard that business about our son Richard being arrested for the results of an illegal drag race. He completely wrecked the car and broke a few bones. We were lucky he didn't kill himself. For days after I couldn't face anyone. Then I decided I'd done all I could. Children are, after all, separate people." Rose was doing her gallant best to reassure the other woman, but there wasn't much comparison between the daredevil escapade and the horror story of Janet. Jess suppressed a shudder. How ghastly to know you had produced such a child.

When Elsie excused herself and left her seat, Rose whispered hurriedly to Jess, "Poor woman, she has had a bad time of it! Her husband was ghastly. He married her for her money, and then he proceeded to gamble it away. He was compulsive. I think the heart attack which killed him was a blessing, if a grim one. But it's taken her a long time to recover. She doesn't even play tennis, but I hope the company and the climate will be good for her."

As Elsie moved back to her seat, the pin on her suit jacket fell off into Jess' lap. Even though it was only a costume piece, it was cunningly made—a golden hummingbird with a large red stone for its body—and Jess exclaimed over it as she handed it back.

Elsie thanked her and explained, "I haven't any sense when it comes to bird motifs. I have bird plates, figurines, jewelry, all sorts of things."

Jess laughed in delight. "I'm even worse than that. I'm a chronic bird-watcher, which is like admitting to a touch of madness, and I even check figurines to see if I can identify the bird and if it has been colored properly. I packed my binoculars, and I can hardly wait to go birding in Bermuda."

Much of the tension eased in Elsie's face when she smiled. "I'm only a beginner, even at my age, but I brought my glasses, too, and I'd like very much to go with you, if you could bear my slow pace."

Jess knew she had acquired another outcast, and she didn't mind at all. She turned in time to see Elizabeth Cooper's expression of disdainful amusement, and she considered committing the social outrage of making a face at her. Instead she gazed at her steadily until the blond's look shifted uneasily away.

When she turned back she found Elsie staring at Arthur's ring. "I need more than binoculars. I just noticed it. It's quite magnificent. Wherever did you get it? Or is that an impertinent question?"

"No, not at all," Jess assured her, but she had no intention of explaining where it had come from. "I'm awful about admiring people's jewelry. I assume if they wear it, they want people to notice. This was given to me by an old family friend." Only a small lie. She wondered how she could have been so dense. The ring was unique and eye-catching. Arthur had been insistent that she wear it. She had thought its purpose was to remind her of their friendship; now she saw it might very well be a signal to someone else. She resisted the impulse to take it off and stop the spell. It made her feel vulnerable and blind, as though it would tell someone else a great deal while sharing none of the secret with her.

She was relieved when the puppet voice announced that the plane was beginning its descent and all seat belts must be fastened. Dwelling too long on Uncle Arthur's possible motives made her dizzy and helped not at all.

The plane angled for its approach, and Jess gasped as she caught her first glimpse of Bermuda. She had seen the pictures in the guidebooks, but nothing had prepared her for the vivid colors of the world beneath her. The water melted around the land like stained glass—turquoise, green, Madonna blue, and lavender studded with dark patterns of coral. And the land itself was lush with myriad shades of green and the surprise of predominantly pink, pastel houses with gleaming white roofs.

Rose said softly, "I envy you. I am still amazed at the beauty, but I've been here before, and nothing is quite the same as the first time."

In a daze Jess gathered up her purse and tennis racket and waited her turn to deplane. With the first touch of the warm, humid air, she wished she could shed her wool clothing right there. She could hardly believe that only a few hours before she had been at the beginning of a cold autumn day. Even though the air was tainted by the smell of jet fuel, the scent of the land came through, rich and spiced by a thousand growing things.

She didn't even mind the delay for gathering luggage and going through customs. The people around her were so fascinating, she wanted to drop everything and take out her sketchbook. Bermuda shorts, of course, but it hadn't occurred to her that they would be the standard uniform of the officials. Bermuda shorts, knee socks, well-polished shoes, shirts, ties, and pith helmets. Oh, lordy, she thought, only the British could wear such outfits with dignity.

The evidence of the colony's racial mix was even more fascinating. The faces ranged from the whitest English cameo carefully guarded from the sun to every shade of black from pale tan to ebony to faces touched with the copper gleam and prominent bones of Indian ancestors who had been brought as slaves from North America to Bermuda centuries before.

Jess tried not to stare rudely, but there were several faces she wanted to remember in detail for drawings to be done later: an official whose blue eyes blazed in a face tanned by years of foreign service and disregard for the elements, whose mouth was held sternly in line to prevent the twitches of laughter which threatened him as he listened to the complaints of a fat woman in a flowered tent; the woman's face, puffy and discontented, and probably easily placated by a chocolate; a taxi driver beaming genially at passersby and asking if anyone needed a lift; a young black man, his body as slim and as rigidly held as a lance, eyes wide and face gray.

Jess dropped all pretense of politeness and stared openly at him. It couldn't be anything else. He was terrified. The chill of the morning touched her spine again. She followed his gaze. He was staring at Rose Allenby and most of the Jet Sets group. He turned in her direction suddenly and nearly knocked her down as he bumped into her. She put her arms out instinctively to steady him. He paused for an instant and then broke free and was quickly out of sight. Close to, his fear-glazed eyes had looked blind, and she had felt the tense cording of his muscles, yet she knew he had focused on her for an instant, had seen her clearly.

Her first impulse was to run after him, but then she realized how futile that would be. Even if she caught him, she could hardly ask a perfect stranger what he was afraid of. She looked back at the group and felt relief. Of course, she had focused on the people who were important to her, ignoring completely the fact that there were others, including some non-tourists, behind them. The young man must have been looking at one of them. She searched the faces carefully, disappointed to find that no one was gazing in the direction the young man had taken, and no one had followed him. But that didn't mean anything. Perhaps the enemy hadn't seen his victim. It was an uncomfortably clear conviction that the young man was the prey, not the hunter.

She ordered herself firmly to stop speculating. It was as useless and frustrating as always when a slice of a stranger's life drops into your lap—a conversation overheard in a restaurant, an incident on a bus when the people suddenly got off so you never would know who had done what to whom. Jess had found the best way to quit wondering was to imagine the ending of the story so completely that you believed it. But she found she didn't want to imagine the end of this one at all.

Rose was calling to everyone like an anxious mother hen, reminding them not to leave anything at the airport, to set their watches ahead one hour for Bermuda time, and to follow her to the proper line of taxis. Jane Crowl was assuring Rose that everything was going smoothly. Jess shrugged off the last of her tension and followed the herd docilely.

There was a lot of good-natured laughter about fitting several pairs of long American legs into the small British cars. Jess saw Elizabeth Cooper slip gracefully into the car ahead just as she herself blundered into her allotted space beside Elsie.

The last person to get in with them was Ann Armstrong, and she said there had been some confusion and her friend, Dana Grant, was in one of the other taxis. Their husbands worked together, Ann explained, and then she added on an oddly defensive note that she and Dana had left husbands and children at home.

Her brown hair framed her face like a cap of short, soft feathers and made her dark eyes look even larger than they were. Her skin still held some summer color. Her features were too regular to be called beautiful, but she was attractive. And in spite of the faint shadows under her eyes, and a certain tautness in her face, she looked quite young, much younger than she was. Jess knew that for sure because her mind had just flashed on Ann's children. The resemblance was too close not to mean the same family. The oldest boy must be over twenty now.

"Pardon me," she said, "but didn't a couple of your children take tennis lessons from me one summer? It was just a recreational program run by volunteers for a few weeks, but I seem to remember a Timmy and a Margaret Armstrong, nice kids and good players besides."

Ann's face relaxed at the mention of her children, and she nodded. "Yes, those are two of my brood. Then you must be part of the Banbridge family that . . . My God, I'm sorry!" She lit a cigarette and inhaled nervously.

"Don't be," Jess said. "It's natural to connect the name. Yes, I'm from the same family." She was grateful Elsie didn't ask any questions. If she were curious, someone else would tell her.

Everyone had been accounted for, the taxis pulled out, and conversation in Jess' car dwindled to pure tourist talk and cries of delight. Both Elsie and Ann had been to Bermuda before, and they pointed out so many things that Jess felt as if she were going to unscrew her head if she turned it around any faster. She was overwhelmed by what she saw. The car crossed a rickety-looking metal causeway onto a narrow road, and Elsie explained that actually Bermuda was a series of islands connected by various bridges. Whatever it was, it was extravagantly beautiful. Everything was covered by masses of greenery, vegetation of incredible variety. At some points stone walls made the road so narrow that even from her middle seat, Jess could see into the hearts of purple morning glories. The maximum speed was only twenty miles an hour, a mere fifteen in the towns, and she was glad the driver obeyed because the road was overrun with people on bicycles and motor scooters. She gulped, wondering which would provide the best transportation with the least danger—she'd have to rent one or the other because there weren't any cars for drive-it-yourself hire in Bermuda.

If Arthur had wanted her to face the sea, this was certainly the place for it. It was so all pervasive she would have to wear a blindfold to keep its liquid light out of her eyes. But here it wasn't the same. It wasn't icy cold and beating relentlessly on jagged rocks. She probed carefully, but she did not feel the wild rushing terror she had so long associated with the sea. No, not so long, two years. Here the water looked calm and welcoming, warm, washing up on brilliant beaches. Bermuda pink houses and pastel pink sand. Here and there a pale blue or green house. Everywhere the white roofs, utilitarian, treated with lime to purify the rain water fed into cisterns in this land of scant fresh water, but still looking as frivolous as frosting on a cake. For a moment, she had the cynical thought that the whole place was a Disney set, lines and colors courtesy of the cartoon department. It was reassuring to notice narrow strips of land, carefully cultivated, asked to produce, a woman hanging out laundry, children tackling each other in a small yard. People did live, work, and procreate here in spite of the appearance of a gingerbread world.

Ann had shared her feeling because suddenly her voice was bitter. "That Dana, I never should have let her persuade me to come! I need a place to think, not never-never land. Sweetness and light are her bag, not mine." It was such a young, aggressive remark for a middle-aged housewife with three or four children that Jess couldn't think of a thing to say.

Luckily Elsie didn't share her inhibitions. "My, my, times they are changing. Here I am, an old woman willing to be enchanted, and I end up with two youngsters who can't stand a pretty place. Don't deny it, Jess, I saw the shutter come down on your face, too."

Her good nature was hard to resist, and by the time they drew up at the Queen's Gate, they were both teasing her with squeals of, "Oh, Elsie, isn't that pretty, pretty!" Jess suspected their driver would be very glad to be rid of his crazy passengers.

3

'Tis a villain, sir,
I do not love to look on.

Jess thought the Queen's Gate quite perfect; even the pervasive pink was beginning to look good to her. It was situated in Paget Parish at the closed eastern end of Hamilton Harbor. Looking across the water she could see the road leading into Hamilton and the outskirts of the city. It would be a pleasant walk, and she wouldn't have to risk the traffic on a bicycle or scooter.

The main building was an old manor house. Rose explained the meals would be taken there and there was a pub on the ground floor, an announcement met with appreciative murmurs from the crowd milling on the narrow drive. The guest accommodations were in cottage units around the manor, and Jess was relieved to learn her roommate would be Sally Carlson. Elizabeth Cooper would be rooming with Elsie Clinton, and Jess thought the older woman would be well able to handle her.

The salt-water swimming pool and five tennis courts were set in formal gardens in back of the manor, and Jess persuaded Sally that if they hurried, they would have good time for some exercise before they had to clean up for the five-thirty gathering in the pub. Sally complained good-naturedly she was probably the only one who had been condemned to rooming with a true fanatic.

Their room was one of the two on the lower level of a

four-unit building fronted by a small cement patio and a gentle grass slope which ended at the water's edge. Ann and her friend were checking into the other room, and they accepted the challenge to a friendly doubles match.

Dana was about the same small size as Ann though her hair was red and her skin freckled, but their expressions were totally dissimilar. Dana's face was open and carefree, making Ann's look even more troubled by comparison.

Though not overly spacious, the room was comfortable, and Jess thought it a delightful touch that there were two new cans of tennis balls on the bureau, compliments of the management, and so much more useful than fruit or flowers. She and Sally unpacked quickly, collected Ann and Dana, and hurried to claim a court before everyone else got the same idea. They were in such a rush, they nearly collided with a man who was coming up the narrow stairs from the gardens. He was making slow work of it, leaning heavily on a cane.

Jess hoped he hadn't heard her involuntary "Oh!" of pity, though she feared he had. But not even that could account for his strange reaction. She saw his eyes widen and narrow again in the instant before he moved politely to one side to let them pass, meeting her smile and thanks with an abrupt nod. But his eyes remained intent on her; she felt them boring into her back even as she continued on her way. She was sure she had never seen him before, yet there was nothing impersonal about his stare. His first stunned disbelief at the sight of her had been followed by the piercing inventory of his eyes. She felt as though he had taken her in all too quickly, questioning, doubting what he saw—an odd response from a stranger. An odd man all in all—she wasn't blind either. Over six feet, height diminished by shoulders hunched to lean on the cane, probably not forty yet, hard to tell in a face so lined and bitter. But even with life etched so clearly, it was a very handsome face framed by thick, dark brown hair. The bones were good from high cheekbones, well-defined brows and arrogant nose to the firm, even-lipped mouth. But his eyes were his most arresting feature; large and compelling, they were a deep, smoky blue-green, a color which could be so warm, and they had frozen into watchful stillness at the sight of her.

"Not exactly Mr. Friendly, is he? Glad he isn't part of our group," Ann said, and Jess nodded agreement, making no comment. Maybe he wasn't Mr. Friendly, but he wasn't indifferent either, at least not to her. Uncle Arthur? The thought rose unbidden. No, surely not, not a man who looked as though he never smiled. And then she remembered Caliban, crippled in mind and body. A warning with the promise? The cold crept over her flesh, and she made an effort to return to the business at hand. There wasn't much difference between a too-active imagination and insanity.

Though the far courts were occupied, probably by resident members of the club, the other three were empty. They chose the center court because of fewer shadows from the surrounding foliage. The courts were of reddish brown composition, and Jess guessed they would be fairly slow, something she liked because it cut down the power of a serve and made long rallies more possible. Ann said the stuff was called Laykold, and the way she said it made all four of them giggle at the obscene possibilities of the word. Jess thought it sad Ann was under such a strain, for she judged her to be one of those people who normally finds humor and enjoyment in even the most humdrum days.

They started out slowly, warming up plane-cramped muscles, and Jess was amused as always by the sly testing of each other's skill. She and Sally hadn't played together for over two years, so it took them a while to find their rhythm again. Dana and Ann obviously played often together, and they were good, but they tended to be competitive over shots which were clear calls for one or the other. Jess winked and Sally caught it—the place to put the shots was down the center where both would battle for it, then catch the alley on either side on the next one. It worked with fair consistency until Ann yelped, "Damn it, Dana, they've psyched us! Call 'em!"

They were changing sides, and Jess was checking

Uncle Arthur's ring anxiously to make sure it was still whole and thinking it wasn't very comfortable to play tennis wearing it, when someone hailed them. Looking up she saw three figures simultaneously, momentarily motionless in a Greek frieze—a tall man with a tennis racket, and to the right, the crippled man, leaning on his cane, watching them, and further to the right, beyond the dark opening of the pub, standing in the service break of the wall, body still tense and ready to flee, the young man from the airport. Even at the distance, Jess knew he was the same one and was sure he was looking at her as intently as she was at him. So he had seen her earlier when he had nearly knocked her down, and he recognized her now, her and someone else? She heard another call, shifted her glance and saw Tom behind the tall man. When she looked back at the wall, it was without hope; she knew the man would be gone.

Sally's arm around her, Sally's voice. "What?" asked Jess vaguely.

"I said, 'You look terrible.' What in the world were you staring at?"

Tell Sally, nice, no nonsense Sally? Tell her what? She heard a noisy chattering and saw the pair of birds sitting on a branch, large, brightly colored birds with yellow breasts, rusty wings and black and white-striped heads. "It must have been the heat, you know, with the humidity it had me reeling back to summer for a moment. And then I caught sight of those birds and forgot everything else. I'm quite sure they're flycatchers, Great Kiskadees to be exact. I've read about them. They were imported from Trinidad to control one pest, and they've become pests in their own right since. But aren't they spectacular?" Her voice was a hollow ramble in her own ears, but apparently it sounded all right to Sally who responded with, "Now look, I know how you are about birds, and I wouldn't have you put away for it, but you won't be any use to me at all on the court if you go winging off like that, excuse the expression."

"Okay, promise, everything is back in place, eyes and brain included." Good, sounded very normal.

Jess got her first good look at the stranger when Tom introduced him as Kyre Tarkington. "We're in luck, Kyre's been here for a couple of days, and he's longing for a game, swears he's an amateur like the rest of us. I'm going to take him to Rose Allenby as a prize trophy. We men in this group are outnumbered; we need recruits."

Sally made a face at him. "You've never complained about having too many women around before. I know what it is. You're afraid you'll lose to an all-woman team."

Jess was thankful for the chatter which covered her confusion and gave her time to get her breath back. Kyre Tarkington was one of the most handsome men she had ever seen. He was at least three or four inches over six feet, even taller than the man on the steps, but he wasn't rangy at all. He was broad-shouldered and muscular, and his tan showed deep against his tennis whites. He was one of those men who stay fit until they die, never giving age a chance to add one extra ounce, for he was probably over forty. His features were as strongly molded as those of a Roman emperor; the heavy brow, cheek, nose and jaw lines all bespoke power. His hair was thick, tawny, and sun-streaked with gray at the temples. His eyes were a strangely light-filled golden brown, sharp and knowledgeable. His eyes betrayed his age more clearly than the faint tracery of lines on his face. Jess' mind went involuntarily to the man on the steps. The difference in the two was radical. The man with the cane was cold, still, inward looking in comparison with Kyre. Kyre radiated power like some sleek and dangerous animal. Doubt of his manhood or indeed any form of self doubt would be alien to him.

She found herself standing straighter, watching him with keen cat's eyes. She couldn't help it. He drew the feline response from her easily with the attention he was paying her. Though he was talking to the others, his eyes were telling Jess that he found her an unexpected delight. Ann asked what he did, and his answer made Jess' pulse quicken. He had his own import-export business in Boston. He dealt heavily in antique jewelry.

"That, for instance, is a very fine ring you are wearing, Miss Banbridge," he said. "May I have a closer look?"

Her slender hand was in his large one before she quite knew how it had gotten there. He admired the ring, turning her hand so that the light caught in the carved stone, commenting on the size, color, and probable age. But she knew he was teasing and testing by touch things which had nothing to do with his expertise in the jewelry field. She felt the blood rising in her cheeks as she withdrew her hand.

It finally fit. Kyre and Arthur were in the same business, and jewelry no less—the ring was easily recognizable. Though Kyre hadn't mentioned Arthur as a mutual acquaintance at the sight of the ring, maybe he soon would. And then again, maybe Arthur, alias Prospero the sorcerer, hadn't let Kyre in on his plan either, trusting geography and biology to complete it. It seemed to be working. To have met both Caliban and the prince in such a short space of time—the spell was moving too swiftly, and she wondered if she could keep up. No man could be more opposite to Larry, and knowing how Uncle Arthur detested Larry, his choice of Kyre made even more sense. But Jess was not sure she could handle a man like Kyre. His magnetism was tangible, but she was not so naïve as to overlook the fact that his power to hurt would be equally strong.

She heard Sally asking sweetly, "Does your wife play tennis, too?" and she could have kicked her for the transparent question.

"I'm not married, but if I were, that would be my first requirement," he said, smiling at Sally, but his eyes flickered to Jess again, saying plainly that was one barrier down.

Jess was relieved when Tom called a halt to the chatter. "If we don't start playing soon, we won't get any exercise at all today."

"My friend, Mr. Physical Fitness," Sally muttered, but they headed for their respective courts.

Jess tried to concentrate, and she got most of the hard shots, but she kept missing the easy ones, and she and Sally were beaten six-three, six-four. "I'm sorry, Salky," she apologized and realized too late she'd committed

Sally's previous sin by using Sean's nickname. She heard his voice clearly, warbling his silly song in a terrible falsetto, "Some say that sulky is sexy, but sweet Salky has the key to my heart." Salky, Sean's Salky.

For a moment Sally's face was rigid save for the huge, hurt eyes, but then she smiled, and softly so that only Jess could hear, she said, "We'll both have to admit remembering, Jaybe, otherwise we'll be scared to death to say a word." Salky and Jaybe, bound together by Sean's special names, Sean's special love. It wasn't nearly as painful as Jess would have thought.

She and Sally stayed to watch the men play while Dana and Ann retired to their room with warnings that there probably wouldn't be any hot water left in the whole place once they'd showered. In spite of his height, Kyre was quick and handled ground shots very well. He was in fact very good. Sally saw it too and said, "Tom's no slouch either. If you and Kyre were a team, we could give you a good run for the money." But when the match ended with Kyre a handy winner, Sally sighed, "I guess I'll just have to let Tom get more rest."

Tom heard and scolded, "I'll choose my own activities, thank you, young woman." He asked Kyre something and then spoke to Sally again, this time including Jess. "Why don't you two scat to the showers and meet us at five in the pub. We'll play the gentlemen and buy you something tall and cool before we have to drink some gruesome friendship punch with the group."

Jess thought ruefully that it was a good thing she found Kyre attractive since there was already a conspiracy afoot to pair her with him—Uncle Arthur seemed to be getting help from unexpected quarters. As Sally agreed for both of them, Jess chalked one up to Tom's balance that he could still offer a woman a cocktail in spite of the problems he'd had with a drunken wife.

Sally yelled, "Beat you to the hot water, whatever's left of it," as she scrambled up the stairs and raced for the room. She won easily because Jess stopped in the middle of the road between the manor and the cottages, bending down to correct a nonexistent problem with a shoelace.

She looked up and down the road; there wasn't a sign of the airport man.

The mocking voice startled her so that she nearly fell over. "Untied laces. Very dangerous indeed. Damned good way to break your neck."

She straightened and spun around, guessing who it was before she caught sight of him staring at her from the second-level balcony of the manor. She stared back at him, feeling her anger rise. Caliban, the misshapen one, the lower nature of man, even his poetry had been a beautiful yowling of rude, bloodthirsty thoughts. But somehow the image did not quite fit, and she spoke sharply to cover her confusion. "Look, I don't know you from Adam, and I don't care to. And I make it a habit to stay away from people who suffer from the unfriendlies. It's contagious, and I don't need it!"

His inexplicable response was a puzzled frown swiftly erased by a cultivated blankness. Only his eyes remained alive in his still face; bleak and wary, they watched her until she rounded the corner of the building out of sight.

Sally peeked out of the bathroom when she came in. "What kept you, get run over by a scooter crossing the road?"

"Nope, ran into limping Caliban again." The image was out, and she wasn't sorry; it would keep those smoky green eyes from affecting her.

Sally caught the reference, but she said, "Maybe he just can't bear seeing healthy people. What a place to be when you're locked to a cane."

"Quit it, Salky. You and your damn sweetness! You'll have me feeling sorry for him in a minute." She couldn't explain and didn't try that his reactions seemed much more personal than that. It didn't make any more sense than the here and gone again man.

They rushed to get dressed, and Sally groaned, "I have a feeling I'm going to need a vacation after this. I bet every day will be one long scramble."

"Probably, but at least you've learned. I remember when you were never on time for anything," Jess teased, amazed at how easy it was to share old memories with her now that the first ice was broken.

"Tom cannot abide tardy people. And don't look like that. You won't have to think of clever ploys to make me tell you about him. It isn't any secret that I'm crazy about him. When there's time, I'll tell the whole thing. But right now, turnabout's fair play. What do you think of Kyre? Isn't he a doll?"

Jess pulled a sad face. "No, actually I think he's terribly ugly, poor man. You wouldn't be playing match-maker on the first court, would you?"

Sally threw a pillow at her. "You'd better appreciate all the work I'm putting into this. I love 'love' games, and I think that man is spectacular. He likes you, too."

"Your puns are revolting, Salky, but okay, I'll admit things are looking up in Bermuda." Caliban was forgotten as she thought about Kyre. Away from him, her doubts were strong. That power which emanated from him, it was overwhelming, and she had never had to cope with it on a personal level before. Her eyes gleamed suddenly—even so, the hunt might prove exhilarating.

"Hello, I think we've been disconnected. Where have you gone?" Sally asked and then added, "Never mind, don't tell me. I'm a decent girl. And where we're going now is to meet Tom and Kyre." She moved suddenly and gave Jess a hug. "I'm so glad you came on this trip! I've missed you, but I knew you didn't want to see anyone who would remind you, especially someone who would remind you of Sean."

"I'm glad I came, too," Jess agreed steadily. "I'm beginning to learn that reminders of Sean can be very beautiful."

The men were waiting for them, and Kyre jumped to his feet and swept them an elaborate bow. "Well met, fair maidens, surely the fairest of them all. Tom, the light for thee, the dark for me. And that is the extent of my glib pub patter."

They laughed at his foolishness, and Jess felt easier in his company. She couldn't help feeling pleased with their appearance—Sally, nearly matching Jess' own height of five nine, straight and slender with her soft blond beauty accentuated by a long black skirt and lacy white blouse, and herself in a long halter dress which fitted without a wrinkle and matched the sapphire of her eyes. Her hair was wound in a smooth ebony coil on top of her head, and her only ornaments were a pair of gold hoop earrings and Arthur's ring. It gave such a nice shot of confidence to know you were put together as well as you could be and that the effort was appreciated.

Appreciated by most anyway. Jess' eyes had been roving, taking in the quaint details of the pub: the low, heavily beamed ceiling and meandering L space, the framed prints of knights in armor to fit the pub's name, The Queen's Knights, the solid wooden tables and chairs, everything looking as if it had just been transported from an English village.

She had a hard time swallowing. He was there, his cane leaning against the table, his eyes staring unblinkingly at her from the shadows at the back of the pub, blue-green eyes touching her as surely as a hand.

She choked a little and her eyes watered. Kyre asked solicitously, "Shall I pat you on the back or something?" She shook her head and managed to gasp, "Who is that man?"

Kyre followed her gaze, and his narrowed eyes belied the lightness of his words. "Oh, him. I was curious too, so I asked. He's one of the major shareholders. Three or four Englishmen own this place, and they take turns coming out to check on it. If you ask me, I expect it's probably a good expense account gimmick or something like that, vacation paid by business. I'm all for it, but it's sure wasted on him. Grim fellow, isn't he? Not good for public relations at all, excuse the pun. Has he been rude? Shall I go punch him in his aristocratic nose?" In spite of the bantering words, there was an aggressive note in his voice.

Jess' tension eased and still staring at the man, she laughed. She was pleased with the result; his face flushed angrily. He knew they were talking about him. Still watching him, she said to Kyre, "I know it's unkind, but he deserves it. I call him Caliban," and all four of them laughed, though Sally's lacked enthusiasm. "Sweet Salky," oh, Sean, she hasn't learned yet how to be cruel, not even for an instant, isn't that miraculous?

She didn't know which of them would have won the staring contest because suddenly the room was full of Rose, Jane, and the rest of Jet Sets, and she lost sight of the man in the screening crowd.

Tom's dire prediction of a punch bowl proved to be correct, but the drink was so well laced with rum that there were few complaints and enough refills to make things lively. Ann and Dana came over with promises not to gloat over their victory more than once every ten minutes. The difference in the women was further emphasized by their evening clothes. Dana was conservative in a long, tailored shirtwaist, while Ann was flamboyant in a swirling gypsy skirt in layers of orange and brown. Though the style was young, it looked fine on Ann, but Jess couldn't help thinking it was one more statement of defiance, and she wondered what exactly Ann was trying to say.

Elizabeth Cooper was another story altogether, and Jess turned to look at her when she heard Ann sneer, "If it isn't the red queen."

Elizabeth was wearing a halter dress too, but there was no similarity between hers and Jess'. Elizabeth's was cut so low front and back that it looked as if one careless shrug of a shoulder would reveal all. The material was a shimmering second-skin red. A huge ruby pendant dangled between her breasts, and she wore matching earrings. The way the light made the gems burst into crimson fire assured Jess they were genuine. The dress was spectacular, and the woman had the figure for it, but it was all wrong for the group and the place. Elizabeth was dressed for the hunt, and she already had the only possible prey in her clutches. She was talking earnestly to Kyre, but Jess knew she wasn't making much headway since Kyre's eyes were suddenly hooded, his face aloof and bored to the point of being insulting.

* * *

"Where's the Jonathan in her name?" Jess asked, and Ann said, "For all I know, she might have left him locked in a trunk in their mansion, but rumor has it—oh, I love those rumors—that Jonathan agreed to her coming to rest her poor tattered nerves. All those benefits you know, they are so tiring. I really have no right to bitch. My husband let me come too, but not for the purpose of attacking the first available male. Elizabeth Cooper is too, too rich and much too spoiled. And I am much too jealous."

Dana had overheard and was looking distressed, and so Jess swallowed the question she'd almost asked Ann. She had a feeling that if Ann didn't talk to someone pretty soon, she was going to go off like a rocket.

Rose and Jane were calling for everyone's attention, holding up bright sheets of poster board which listed the first matches to be played. They explained that three of the courts were to be theirs for the entire length of their stay, and that they could use the other two when guests who were not part of Jet Sets or resident members of the Queen's Gate Tennis Club weren't using them.

Dana said, "I don't know about members, but we needn't worry about other guests. I'm sure Mr. Tarkington will be playing with us, and aside from four old ladies who play bridge, two honeymooning couples who keep wandering off in opposite directions holding hands, and that man with the cane, we've taken over the place."

Jess looked instinctively through the crowd toward the back of the pub and caught sight of the empty place where the man had been. She hoped he'd gone for a long slow walk into another parish.

When she finally made her way to the scheduling boards, she saw that Tom had been true to his intentions—Kyre's name had been added to their group, and he had been paired with her for mixed doubles. She had Sally for her ladies' doubles partner. Her first match in singles would be against Millie Cranston which made her feel guilty because, though Millie was still spry, she was, after all, over sixty. She was startled when she heard Millie's voice at her elbow. "Now, Jess, I know just what you're thinking, but never you mind, makes me feel good just to play with you youngsters. And I'm counting on your night life to give me the edge. How about Wednesday morning at eight?" They signed up for a court with Jess warning Millie she planned to go to bed early both nights and Millie countering with a knowing chuckle.

Jess counted and found that aside from the women's ladder, even if she went all the way to all of the finals next Monday, it would still only mean eight formal matches, not much for seven days. The number of games played for top position on the ladder would depend on the enthusiasm of the competitors—you were allowed to challenge anyone up to two spaces above your own name. The names had been drawn and set by chance, and Jess was midway of the nine which read from the top: Jane, Ann, Ellen, Dana, Jess, Sally, Millie, Rose, Sharon. She had known Elsie didn't play, and the lists confirmed that Elizabeth Cooper didn't either. It didn't surprise her. She couldn't imagine Elizabeth perspiring for anything less than the fundamental sport. Definitely nasty-minded, she accused herself, just as Kyre hailed her as partner and asked if she would be willing to play their first doubles match against Sally and Tom the following morning at ten. The other couple was agreeable, and they reserved a court.

When dinner was announced and everyone flowed up the inside stairs to the dining and reception room area, Jess and Kyre sat down with Sally and Tom and were joined by a couple who introduced themselves as David and Ellen Frieberg. The Friebergs were interesting table companions, and the conversation moved at one point to the upcoming presidential election and whether McGovern would make any showing at all.

Jess felt a prickle of guilt, and she wasn't just about to admit she really didn't give a damn about politics anymore and wasn't worried about whether or not she would get back in time to vote. She looked away uneasily, afraid her lack of patriotism must be written plainly on her face, and she caught sight of Ann at the next table. At least Ann's body was at the next table. But all her attention was focused on the discussion at Jess' table. Her face was naked with the yearning to be part of that discussion. Her eyes glittered with a frightening intensity. She was deaf to Dana's voice telling a tale of one of her youngster's pranks, nor was she aware of Jess. Jess shifted her glance quickly, feeling as though she'd seen too much, and her inadvertent survey revealed one positive thing—Caliban had still not come in to dinner. Perhaps he got special service in his room, and she wished he'd stay there for the duration of her trip. The puzzlement and suspicion with which the man regarded her, the piercing gaze which had followed her from the first encounter on the stairs only hours earlier had already affected her tangibly so that the mere thought of him gave her shivers of unease. It was completely irrational that a stranger should have the power to affect her at all, that he should want to in any case. She searched her memory again, but she was still certain he had no place in it.

The only group announcement made during the meal was that the following night's gathering at the pub would be in costume since it would be Halloween. There were good-natured groans about having left the States and the children just to avoid that insane tradition, but most of the faces already wore the abstracted expression of a definite plan forming. Rose finished by saying, "The management has kindly offered to provide old sheets for those who want them, but please, don't do anything drastic to the linen in use in your rooms."

"Drat, there goes my best toga," mourned Kyre. His ready wit made him good company, and Jess found herself relaxing more and more in his presence.

They gathered for coffee in a room made welcoming by lovely old Persian carpets and overstuffed sofas. Kyre kept yawning and apologized, "I can hardly stay awake; it's so warm in here. How about a quick dip in the pool before we turn in? Then maybe tomorrow night if you girls are willing, we can do something more exciting and go dancing somewhere."

It sounded like a good plan, and Kyre left them to go to his room to change. Tom and Sally were still whispering

on the road when Jess went down the stairs to hers and
Sally's room. She was already in her bathing suit by the
time Sally stuck her head in the door and said, "We've
changed our minds. We're going to wander down the road
saying silly things to each other. But don't you chicken out;
Kyre will be expecting you."

Jess' protest died unspoken. She couldn't blame Sally
and Tom for wanting time alone together, and it was
ridiculous to be apprehensive about a swim with Kyre.
Still, she wished it didn't seem as though everyone was
plotting the match. "Fine," she said quietly, "but I don't
plan to stay up too late, so keep it quiet when you come
in, won't you?"

"Why, I'm always quiet as a mouse," Sally insisted as
they walked up the stairs together. Tom met them at the
top, took Sally's hand, and led her away saying, "Good
night, Jess have a good time. Sally, my sweet, let's find a
nice dark place where . . . ."

His voice trailed away, and Jess headed for the pool.

There were no underwater lights, and the area was
only faintly illuminated by lights from the manor house,
but she saw Kyre waiting for her, and he undoubtedly saw
her. As she put her towel down, he gave a low whistle.
"Even better than a tennis dress. Jess, you are a very
beautiful woman."

She wished she could accept the compliment coolly,
but she was no good at that sort of thing, and to her
disgust she heard herself stammering, "Ah, Tom and Sally
decided to . . . to turn in instead. And I . . . I forgot my
bathing cap." She had a curious reluctance to let him know
her room was empty.

His voice was filled with amusement; he knew her
problem, but all he said was, "I don't think you'll get
arrested for that tonight. Come on, let's get in. The
water's warmer than the air."

Protests about getting her hair wet would sound even
more stupid than what she had said already, so she kept
her mouth shut, took the pins out of her hair, heard Kyre's
dive, and followed him.

The salt water of the pool was as warm as Kyre had

claimed, and it felt heavenly to have the buoyancy of sea swimming without the danger. She swam with long strokes, her hair streaming out behind her, and when she stopped for a moment in the shallow end, Kyre was beside her.

"Tom and Sally made a mistake, this is fantastic," he said. "But I'm just as glad they didn't come along." His arms were around her so swiftly, she had no time to pull away, and her gasp of protest was stifled by his mouth coming down on hers. He was very sure, very practiced, and for a moment she was still and dazed in his arms, even feeling her body beginning to respond. Why not? she thought dizzily, he's a gorgeous man, and he likes me. But when his hand wandered with casual expertise beneath the top of her bathing suit, the spell was broken. She wrenched away so suddenly that she took him by surprise, and she had pulled herself out of the pool before he had time to grab her again. She wanted to say something, good night, anything which would return the scene to some kind of normality, but when she heard and saw him begin to follow her out of the water, she panicked. She didn't even stop to slip into her sandals; she grabbed her room key and fled. He was blocking the short way to the road; there was no choice; she took the path which led through the garden and thence around the manor house and other buildings to the road.

She would have stopped; her panic would have subsided had he not followed her. But she could hear him behind her, going more cautiously than she, thinking she might be hiding in the dense foliage, calling to her, "Jess, this is ridiculous! Goddamn it, wait a minute!" The words were those any man might have used in a similar situation; it was the tone of them which frightened her. She had known his power in the first instant of meeting him, and now such a short time later, she had crossed it, and she didn't know how to cope. She just wanted to get away from him.

She rounded the corner and was on the path leading to the road. Her feet were beginning to smart from the abrasion of coral and gravel, her breathing sounded loud in her own ears, and all her senses were concentrated on her pursuer, not on what was ahead.

She ran solidly into the man, nearly knocking him over, but before she could scream, a hand was clamped over her mouth, and she was held in a grip of steel. Her key dropped with a clatter at her feet. She was so terrified, the night began to whirl into a deeper darkness, but a voice hissed urgently, "Don't faint! Stay quiet. He'll go on by."

It was a gesture of desperate trust when the hand was taken from her mouth, and Jess knew it. The man stooped for an instant, handed her the key, and whispered, "This way," and when he pulled on her hand, she followed without resistance. By the time Kyre rounded the corner, she and the man were in the deep shadows behind a thick-trunked tree.

Kyre called to her again and made a desultory search, but he was obviously giving up. She hoped he wouldn't see Tom and Sally and thus learn that she would be alone if she were in her room. That was exactly where she wanted to be. Her brief, damp suit was no protection against the night breeze which was beginning to swirl through the small jungle around them, and she shivered, but it was only from the cold. She felt no fear of her benefactor, and she felt a rising certainty that she knew who he was.

He commanded her to stay where she was for a moment, and she obeyed. When he came back, he said, "You are safe now. He has gone down the road." Docilely she let him lead her to the road, and the dark face she had not been able to see before was faintly visible now in the glow cast by the porch lights.

The young man from the airport said, "We are even now. Today you helped me. Tonight I helped you."

He melted back into the shadows of the garden before Jess could utter a word. She wasted no time looking after him. She couldn't wait to be locked in her room. She darted across the road, ran down the stairs, and sobbed with relief as she opened the door and slipped inside.

4

If of life you keep a care,
Shake off slumber and beware.
Awake, awake!

Jess listened at the door for a few moments, but there were no sounds of anyone outside, and she was too cold to keep her post.

She stripped off her suit and stood under the hot beating pulse of the shower washing the salt water from her hair and body, letting the heat of the water warm her. When she emerged from the shower, she concentrated on the task of drying her hair and combing out the tangles, anything to keep from thinking. But it was no use; over and over she could feel Kyre's mouth on her own, his hands touching her, the panic of her flight. She was bitterly ashamed. She would not have believed herself capable of such childish behavior. She was quite sure that had she simply asked him not to crowd her, he would have complied. Instead, she had run away like a scared thirteen-year-old on a first date. She did not even want to consider what he must be thinking of her now.

She tried to understand where her reaction had come from. In a way, she had asked for his attention, going alone to swim with him in the dark pool, wearing the briefest of bikinis. And his attention had not been unpleasant, just too damn expert. She suspected that was what had given her reservations about him from the first. His power and self-confidence were so evident, every move he made was as sure and graceful as the prowl of a leopard. She remembered how Uncle Arthur had disliked the hulking ineptitude of Larry from his first sight of him, and she realized she had invariably chosen such men since she had first begun dating as a teenager. They had all been men who needed a mother or a psychiatrist more than a girl friend. If indeed Arthur had chosen Kyre Tarkington for her, he had chosen well, a man opposite to her habitual choice which so dismayed him. But she feared Arthur had more confidence in her ability to cope and change than she did. Unconsciously she raised her chin a defiant fraction. It would take some doing to build the image of the carefree sophisticate, and she wouldn't blame Kyre if he couldn't bear the sight of her, but it was worth a try. An island vacation and a spectacular man, what a shame it would be to waste either one.

The words came back. "We are even now. Today you helped me. Tonight I helped you." At the time of their speaking, they had seemed perfectly sane, as had her acceptance of his help once she had realized he was not going to harm her. Now the airport man seemed the maddest part of her insane flight. He had recognized her; he had acted quickly; he had not questioned her actions; and he had risked something to hide her. Even if he had seen her at the pool with Kyre, it didn't make any sense. She couldn't believe that he had been lurking around the Queen's Gate in case she needed assistance. Three times now she had seen him, and twice she had delayed him in his purpose, once to help him in however an inadvertent way to carry on and once to receive his help.

She got her sketching materials and drew the first swift, minimal lines. Even without the details, she had captured him; she would know him anywhere. And though it stemmed from terror, there was something wildly beautiful about the taut lines of the young man's face, the enormous dark eyes, the strong nose with flaring nostrils, the wide cheekbones, the full mouth held in a rigid line. The drawing told her things only her subconscious had picked up. He was terrified, but he was also resolute, committed to some terrible task, a young warrior from an ancient wall painting ready to do battle. She felt as if she had just witnessed a secret ceremony.

She stared at the drawing for a long time. She was incidental to his purpose; only by accident had they had anything to do with each other. In all probability she would never know what the beginning had been or what the end would be. It was an unsatisfactory answer for her new curiosity, but it had to be accepted. She turned the page to block out his image.

The style of Kyre's face changed the style of her drawing. The lines were as heavy as if they had been graven in stone. He stared at her with ruthless power and beauty from the page just as he had since her first sight of him. She stared back at the drawing, a small smile curving her mouth. "Now I know the rules," she whispered, "and given another chance, I think I'll play."

She was still too restless to sleep, and her pencil moved nervously, lining and shading what she had seen as a journalist records in words the events of the day.

She drew the fat woman from the airport, mocking the gluttonous face viciously, a caricature of overindulgence, a woman immediately identifiable as one who owned a Pekinese dog and read romance magazines. An easy drawing to do, all those round, boneless lines.

She was intrigued by doing two sets of drawings on one page—Ann and Dana side by side, and below, Elsie and Elizabeth. She felt the familiar rush of pleasure from knowing something was well done. Dana's normal face appeared vacuous beside the intensity of Ann's, and Elsie's face was what Elizabeth's would become. She felt a twinge of guilt—they were not the sort of drawings she could allow the subjects to see.

She watched with amazement as the next face emerged on the fresh page. Each section seemed strangely unrelated to the rest. And nothing was resolved by the finished product. It was like one of those trick drawings wherein you see at one moment a vase, in the next two profiles of faces, and then neither clearly again. Caliban's face was a mass of contradictions—at first glance coldly polite; then,

briefly, lined with pain, mental or physical, weary and
confused by the pain's intensity; and in the final shift, the
expression was not withdrawn, but grimly intent, a hunter's face devoid of suffering or pity. The twisted one who
haunts every tale of island enchantment. The young man,
was he to be the victim? And what of herself, the man had
reacted so strongly to the mere sight of her.

On impulse she tore the drawing from the pad and
flipped back to the picture of Kyre. She saw it then. In
spite of the physical dissimilarities, the two men were
strangely alike; it showed in the tense strength of the
faces, but most of all, it showed in the brooding watchfulness
of the eyes. So what did that mean, where did that leave
her? She reminded herself that the question need not
even be asked. The men had nothing to do with each
other, and only one had anything to do with her, and that
was doubtful. Still the inevitable thought—power attracts
power, and being trapped between two antagonists such as
these would be dangerous to say the least.

She slammed the sketchbook closed and condemned
herself for late-night fantasies. She had worked herself into
a cold sweat of terror in the middle of paradise. "Have one
of Eden's apples, crazy lady," she hissed to herself and
laughed, but all the same she wished Sally was back in the
room. She turned out the lights and snuggled under a
blanket she didn't need.

She was aware instantly in the darkness of the insistent water sounds, but after a first mute protest, she
listened without fear. The sounds were different here, a
soft symphony of small waves touching land and washing
gently against distant hills. And the pale streaks of light
drifting in through the windows from water reflections
shimmered in time to the music.

She felt her muscles unwinding one by one, felt
herself drifting into sleep with the song.

Footsteps on the walk, then muted by the grass,
something water slapped then scraping, a name she had
never heard before, not a dream, she sat up, every nerve
vibrating as though she had touched an open circuit. The
voice came again, made loud by urgency. "I knew you'd

come, Connor. They know it, too. The boss man's been
prowling like a tomcat for hours. He's back there. You've
got to get out of here now!"

A heavier voice, slow and menacing. "Boy, I'm goin'
break your head one o' these days. You jus' move your
little ol' ass out o' my way. This is my territory."

The first voice was wild with pleading. "It's mine,
too. Connor, I don't want you dead. You're all I've got."

The capitulation was miraculous, all threat gone. "Man,
I must've done somethin' real bad 'fore I was born to have
you dropped on me. Come on, Uncle Tom, I'll take you
home."

The scraping sound again, a splash, the boat in the
water, oars pulling it away. Jess' frozen muscles released
her, and she was at the window, but it was too late; she
could only see the boat when it crossed the streams of
light. The two men were just dark shadows, one moving
with the rhythm of rowing.

She heard someone else coming down the stairs at a
fast thudding pace which checked suddenly. She couldn't
see around the corner of the building to the stairs, but the
sounds carried clearly on the still night air. More people
coming, Sally's "Oh!" of surprise, then her, "Excuse me,
sir, you startled me."

Tom's easy laugh. "I'm Tom White. This is Sally
Carlson." The polite waiting for the other's name. The icy
English voice offering it grudgingly. "Winston St. James."
No explanation of a night walk, no small talk, just the cane
tapping back up the stairs, the cane he hadn't used at all
coming down.

She scrambled back into bed and lay trying to make
her jagged breathing even. It was insane, the whole thing
was insane. She hadn't been in Bermuda for twenty-four
hours, and yet she was being drawn into the vortex of
something sinister—something that included the possibility of becoming dead. She stifled a nervous giggle. "Connor,
I don't want you dead." He had said that.

Sally and Tom stopped outside the door. Sally's key
was in the lock, but the couple wasn't in any hurry to part.
Jess could hear them whispering, Sally laughing softly, the

long kisses. She couldn't involve Sally. It would only distress her. She wouldn't be able to do anything. She hadn't even witnessed any of the pieces of the puzzle unless she had seen the man with the cane wasn't crippled at all, and that was the sort of thing she would mention to Jess if she had seen it. Sally seldom attached motives good or bad to people's behavior, but she was so interested in them that she was a keen observer. Convincing her something dangerous and evil was afoot was another thing entirely, and even if she were convinced, her only possible response would be to tell Jess to get in touch with the authorities. A circle and full stop—not enough to tell the police, whispered conversations and a man who pretended to be lame.

The door opened and Sally came in quietly, moving carefully in the darkness. "Jaybe?" she whispered. Jess lay still, forcing herself to breathe evenly, unable to suppress a sigh of relief when Sally disappeared into the bathroom. In spite of the chaos in her mind, she grinned as she heard the faint burbling humming as Sally washed her face. Sally's efforts at silence always came to naught. When she was happy, which was most of the time, she hummed. Sometimes you could recognize a tune, sometimes there were just joyous squiggles of sound. "Salky is the only person I know who actually hears the music of the spheres and sings along," Sean had claimed.

No, Sean, I won't make Sally afraid, too.

Her breathing was even without force by the time Sally tiptoed out and collapsed into bed and instant sleep. Thoughts of Sean often did that for Jess, often made the world seem more reasonable than it was. She assembled the few pieces she had and tried to regard them critically. The two men, Connor and the nameless one. She knew who he was; she recognized the voice of her airport man.

And Connor was someone he cared about, someone who cared about him—the menace had given away so quickly to rough affection. Both Bermudians, the accent betrayed that, British but island softened. And Connor was black, too—"Uncle Tom" meant the same thing wherever English was spoken. The boss man prowling, who else but Mr. St. James, the lame man who ran so well? She had not noticed him at the airport, but that meant nothing; perhaps there were others involved, others whom the nameless man feared. Yes, the voice had said, "They know it, too." But why any of it was happening was beyond all reasoning, and it was none of her business. "We are even." At least she knew now why he had been at the Queen's Gate tonight.

The weariness of the long day washed over her, making her body feel like a sheet of lead. Her last conscious thought was of the postcard she would like to send: *Dear Uncle Arthur, Bermuda is beautiful, wish you were here. Haven't seen many birds yet but may see murder soon. Love, Jessica.*

She awoke to Sally's clear-voiced rendition of "Green Sleeves" followed by, "Isn't that nicer than an alarm clock? You were so dead to the world, I was tempted to let you sleep through the match. Tom and I aren't proud, we'd take a lazy woman's forfeit, but I don't think Kyre would. Did you have a good swim last night?"

"Yes, it was great," she said smiling vaguely. She wished Sally had chosen some phrase other than "dead to the world." It focused the events of darkness too sharply. She also wished she could convince herself it had all been a nightmare, especially her behavior with Kyre. It was going to be embarrassing to face him. And then she thought of the pounding steps on the stairs. "I slept so soundly, I didn't even hear you come in," she lied. "But I thought I heard someone talking on the steps. Did I miss a party, or did I dream that?"

Jess felt guilty; Sally was so straightforward, she wouldn't even recognize a devious question if the kinks were plotted on a graph. "Nope," she said, "no party I know of, but there were all sorts of people wandering around last night. You would have had to walk a mile to escape our group entirely, something to do with the night air here. You might have heard Tom and me. We met Mr. St. James on the steps, that's his name, your Caliban. What a combination, stairs and a cane." She flashed a sudden, wicked grin. "Ah, ha, I'll bet he was coming to make friends with you, and we surprised him. Next time we'll go the other way so you two can get acquainted."

Jess thought of the two drawings, of Kyre and Caliban focusing on each other, herself in the middle, but she tried to make her voice light. "If you do, I'll scream bloody murder and claim I was abandoned."

But something got through to Sally, and she looked genuinely puzzled. "Why, you really don't like that man. I mean, it's personal and specific, isn't it? Really, I'll bet he isn't that bad, he's probably just super shy."

"There's no hope," groaned Jess as she scrambled out of bed. "You will never be a decently hateful human being!" It worked; Sally's sense of humor took over, and as Jess washed and dressed, she had to listen to a relentless recital.

"I don't like squishy things at all, things like snails and worms, but I can't really say I hate them. And I don't care for rubbery sorts of beasts either, like snakes or brains, although brains aren't creatures, are they? I don't hate either one, but I prefer snakes under glass and brains in the skull where they belong, not on my plate. Then of course, there are loud noises. I don't get along well with them either unless I make them. A whistle for instance is only nice when one is the whistler. But I can't actually blame large things such as planes and St. Bernards for making loud noises, so I can't say I hate them, can I? I've heard there's a hate league being formed; maybe I ought to join. It's awful being so wishy-washy. It's a real handicap, it—"

"All right, quit it, I surrender," gasped Jess. "I could hurt myself trying to brush my teeth and laugh at the same time." When they left the room, she couldn't forbear making an unnecessary comment about the beautiful day and strolling casually, she hoped, to the water's edge. The marks were there, the damaged blades of grass tracing the pattern of the boat.

The Allenbys, Crowls, Cranstons, and Friebergs were already well into the meal, and Jess and Sally received smiling taunts about the slothfulness of the young generation. The four elderly ladies were in the dining room too, regarding their plates as if they were good bridge hands. "I'll bid one egg," Jess whispered to Sally who stifled a giggle and scolded, "You're incorrigible."

They were the first at a table for six. "I like all the empty space for effect. I've done the impossible. I've gotten here before Tom," Sally crowed. And there's no sign of Caliban, the big boss, either, added Jess silently, feeling a sharp stab of resentment at the knowledge that the man was becoming an obsession with her, unwanted and uncontrollable, and above all, disquieting even in his absence.

Tom and Kyre appeared at the entryway within seconds of each other and came to the table, Tom wringing his hands and moaning, "Oh, no, it's happened. Sally got here first, first I tell you! Where is justice? What will I have to complain about if she isn't late?"

"I don't know about your complaints, but Sally must have plenty if you're always this bright in the morning," Jess teased, but her voice was a trifle unsteady and her eyes were on Kyre, waiting to see what his reaction to her would be.

The knot of tension dissolved under his smile, and if there was a gleam of triumph in his eyes as he handed her her sandals wrapped in her towel, she was willing to give him that. She had not considered until now that her flight could have been taken as a tribute to his overwhelming attractiveness rather than as an insult.

"I retrieved these for you. You forgot them last night," he said smiling. And when he had seated himself, he said to Sally, "You and Tom should have gone for a swim with us last night. The water was perfect."

Jess held her breath for a moment and was relieved when Sally answered, "We'll make it the next time," and left it at that, not explaining she had been on a walk with Tom, not asleep in her room.

Tom rattled his coffee cup, and Kyre begged, "Quiet, please. I'm putting my alabaster body back together piece by piece. My kingdom, even my tennis shoes for a silent cup of coffee."

Now that she was feeling comfortable with him, Jess

saw him with new eyes. He looked so much like a sleep-tousled boy, she felt a rush of tenderness and chided herself sternly. Watch it, Jess! Not a small boy at all, no matter how he looks in the morning. The memory of his touch the night before was suddenly vivid, and she blushed. He noticed and gave her a small, intimate smile. She met his eyes squarely. She knew she had just agreed to a whole new set of rules, and she felt good about it.

Sunlight flooded the room, bright on silver, fresh flowers, and tennis whites, and Jess let the light into her mind too, let it vanquish the night shadows.

The four teased each other about which couple would win the morning's match. Tom claimed he and Sally had to be the victors because they had developed techniques never before seen. "We'll use the crossgrain, the twilight zone, and the grapevine," he told Sally, and she answered seriously, "Yes, but if we get into trouble, we may have to show them the golden guinea."

Kyre assured Jess, "They're going to be so confused on their calls, all we have to do is play while they talk." And he made a wager with Tom that the losing team would buy the first round of drinks that evening.

"Hmmm," Jess said, "I have all day to think of something really exotic to order."

They were having their final cups of coffee when Elsie came in. She was wearing a gaily flowered straw hat and had binoculars slung around her neck. She smiled and stopped to talk to Jess.

"I thought of waking you to join me on my early trek, but it seemed too cruel for the first morning. So as a result, I saw all sorts of lovely but nameless birds. I'm beginning to fear I am too old to learn field identification."

"Not a bit of it," Jess assured her. "It just takes practice. And two people make it much easier. I have an early match tomorrow, but so far not a thing before breakfast on Thursday. How about six thirty?"

"Thank you, my dear. I would enjoy that very much," Elsie said and moved onto another table.

"Poor old lady, she seems pretty sad," Kyre said softly. "I'll bet you collect people like that, Jess."

Sally chortled, "Of course she does. Under that grim exterior lies a saintly soul. Other people collect stamps. She collects people who have been thrown away."

Not anymore, Jess thought, Uncle Arthur is changing all that. Aloud she commanded, "Miss Sweetness, shut up," and Sally made a face at her.

On the way back to their room to pick up their rackets, Sally told Jess bits and pieces about some of the tour members—strange romances, sudden tragedies, exotic origins.

"And when I first saw the people on our tour, I judged them all fairly dull members of the quietly rich, assumed they were all pretty much the same," Jess admitted in amazement. Elsie Clinton's story on the plane had begun the change; Sally's information made further changes in the image. She wondered how many more unique tales could be told by members of their tour, and she could not help but wonder also, if truth were the rule, how many would be tales of light, how many of darkness. Uncle Arthur, you have done it, you've opened me up to the world again; I only fear it is flooding in too quickly. If Sally noticed her abstraction, she was too polite to make a point of it, but Jess knew her too well to think her patience would outweigh her concern forever.

By the time they got to the courts, the day was so warm and humid that Jess said to Kyre, "Normally I am very offended by pigging. I allow poaching with finesse, of course, but no pigging. However, in this heat, I might just stand here and let you play."

"Not on your life! I am a liberated man, and I expect you to do your fair share." If his words had a double meaning, only the two of them were aware of it.

"I used to think Tom was liberated, but I've decided lazy is a better word for it," Sally said thoughtfully, and Tom gave her a playful pat on the bottom with his racket. "You are supposed to be rude to our opponents, not to your partner."

Even the warm-up, relaxed as it was, gave a good indication of how fierce the match was going to be. The couples were evenly matched, and the men were both careful not to steal shots from their partners. When they settled down in earnest, no one gave anything away. They had some lovely long rallies, and best of all to Jess' mind, both teams moved well at the net for the fast volleys which were the most exciting part of the game and the best way to win points.

Aside from an occasional, "Well done, partner," or "I've got it!" no one wasted air on talking. At first Jess was conscious of the sound of other players busy on the adjacent courts, but then she moved into the strange realm of total concentration. It was the place she most wanted to be when she was playing, but try as she might, she had never been able to control it. It either happened or it didn't, something she considered the damning mark of an amateur. But now she was blessedly aware of it—an eerie feeling of floating from one shot to the next without effort, as though seconds were expanding and the ball was traveling in slow motion, as though the law of gravity had been suspended and her body had no weight to slow it down.

She and Kyre took the first set six-three, but Sally and Tom were fighting harder for the second. There had been no service breaks, and they were tied five games all when the sound penetrated and shattered the trance, bringing Jess back to earth with a clear miss on an easy shot, a shot which might have given them the first break of the set. Jess heard Kyre's gasp of surprise, but he said nothing, even when Tom took the next two points and won his serve.

The tapping of the cane had stopped. Winston St. James was leaning lazily against the fence, seeming to watch the matches, but not, Jess was sure, interested in tennis at all. She felt his smoky-sea eyes touch her, and she stared back for an instant before turning to Kyre. "I'm sorry, I just lost track of everything for a minute. Nothing like a disciplined mind."

Kyre smiled easily at her. "Don't worry. I know the feeling all too well. We'll take this game. I can feel an ace coming on."

He was as good as his word. His serves sang over the

net with deadly accuracy, and Jess had little work to do before they won the game. It was fortunate her role was minor. She was working so hard to put her mind back in the game that it was a physical effort, and she could feel the sweat running in uncomfortable rivulets down her back. "Damn that man!" she thought savagely, "I will not let him ruin this match!"

Since they were tied at six games all, they decided to play "Sudden Death," a twelve point tie-breaker. Jess fought against her tendency to choke in the swift, shifting service of the tie-breaker; it was her fault they had to play it. Her timing was off, and she hit some shots clumsily, but Kyre was playing so ferociously that they won, reaching seven points before Sally and Tom did.

"Thank you, partner," Jess said as they went to the net to shake hands with the other team.

"I'm getting closer, Tom. At least I've decided on a drink with rum," she teased. "By then I'll need it because I'm off for a shopping spree in Hamilton as soon as I change. Anyone else want to go?"

Sally assented eagerly, but Jess had to laugh at the expression of mutual dismay on the men's faces. The last thing they wanted to do was shop. But then Kyre's face brightened. "How about plan B for us, Tom? Let's let the girls go shopping and have them meet us at the Penthouse for lunch around two o'clock. It's a pretty well-known place right on Front Street, and they have a sandwich place and bar below the main restaurant."

The plan pleased everyone, and Jess asked Kyre if he had ever considered the diplomatic corps.

"What, and bring peace to the world? It would be so dull, nobody could stand it. I offered, but my services were refused," he said mournfully.

Jess kept her eyes resolutely away from Mr. St. James as the group went up the stairs. She was not going to let him spoil her good time, but her impulse was to order him to stay the hell away from her. She could imagine his reaction of mocking disbelief, his denial, but it made no difference; whatever he was up to, he was purposefully trying to make her uncomfortable, and he was succeeding all too well.

She sighed unconsciously, and Sally heard her, but she waited until the men were out of earshot before she commented. "You two really do have something going, don't you? I saw him at the same time you forgot to play tennis."

"I know I'm being silly, but yes, he does bother me. He's like something out of a horror film; I hear that damn tapping and there he is. Let's forget about him now." She knew her analogy was wrong even as she said it. Caliban was a very handsome man; it was his spirit and his reaction to her which seemed twisted. The crippling of his body was a sham.

"Okay," Sally agreed, but her voice was doubtful, her patience wearing thin already, and Jess was even more determined to prevent her from learning of or becoming involved with the night prowlers.

5

Make not too rash a trial of him, for
He's gentle, and not fearful.

Jess and Sally were ready in record time, laughing at
themselves for their greedy raptures over unseen treasures from the British Isles and a host of other countries.
"I'd have to pawn the rest of my trip to buy half of what I
think I want," Sally said ruefully.

The walk to the beginning of the shops on Front
Street took less than half an hour. A narrow paved walk
along the main road skirted the edge of the harbor and led
into Hamilton, and the walk way was not far from the
Queen's Gate. But the change in scenery was startling. No
space could be wasted, and so even around the resort,
there were small patches of cultivated land with borders of
thick greenery, and then suddenly there was the main
road with an unbelievable number of vehicles making use
of it—bicycles, taxis, and motor scooters weaving an intricate traffic pattern.

. "I'm never going to have the courage to scooter
around here, even if they are only going twenty miles an
hour tops," Jess protested, and Sally agreed. "My senti-
ments exactly. Methinks we ought to have the men hire
something we can sit on the back of, then we can all die
cheerfully together. Curse me for being unliberated."

"I consider it truly liberated to know when I need
help to stay alive." Jess wished dead and alive would quit
presenting themselves as equal alternatives in Bermuda.

Front Street was a forever busy place, and there were
more white faces than black since it was the major tourist
shopping area of Hamilton. But here and there, Jess and
Sally received shy, island accented good mornings and
silent tributes to their beauty. The looks seldom lingered
long—a soft comment and then eyes turned furtively
away.

"I wonder how integrated this place really is," Jess
said. "It seems all nice melting pot on the surface, and
since the blacks are the majority, this ought to be one
place where they can enjoy total equality, but I doubt
it."

"I know what you mean. I've seen the sliding eyes,
too, as though something's not right. Human beings are
worse than chickens in their pecking order, aren't they?
Always needing to be one up on someone, and color is
such an easy way to do it, so easy to see." Sally's voice was
sad. "I read some of the material concerning the islands in
my library. Bermuda hasn't had near the trouble in race
relations that most of the Caribbean islands have had,
maybe because she's further north, not really Caribbean,
or maybe because things are a little better here; there's
poverty but not the horrible ghettos some of the islands
have. But there are problems—even with a black majority
of voters, white men hold the key positions, and there is a
group known as the Black Cadre, which is like our Black
Panthers and growing stronger. It's such a lovely place, it's
awful to think of violence and death."

The day was hot, and Jess was stony cold. "Violence
and death," that put it neatly and far closer than Sally
imagined. Jess wondered if the whole thing was in fact
involved in politics involving endless players and endless
victims. She shivered with a sudden intense longing to
flee, to go home, to be in a place where even when the
situation was critical, it was familiar.

Sally's urgent voice came from a long way off. "Jaybe,
what's wrong? Don't tell me it's a bird this time either.
Are you ill or something?"

Jess wrenched herself back to the instant with an
effort. She found she had stopped on the street while

people swirled in eddies around them. "I'm sorry, I can't explain, not even to myself."

Sally nodded slowly in sympathy, and Jess knew what she was going to say before she said it. "I know, I still feel a terrible sadness sometimes when I think of Sean, but he would hate it."

Jess felt a twinge of guilt mixed with her relief until she realized that under the circumstances, Sean would not mind being used as a scapegoat; protecting Sally had been a major part of his life.

Their mood lightened under the seductive influence of the goods offered in the Front Street shops. The pastel colored buildings with white gingerbread trimming gave the street the look of a movie lot, and Jess was reminded of the first view of the island she had shared with Elsie and Ann. Some of the shops still bore the names of the nineteenth-century merchants who had so prospered in Bermuda, the original forty thieves, the forty first families.

She and Sally went into Trimingham's first, and the wealth of goods displayed confirmed their choice. Leather, knits, tweeds, china, perfume, and jewelry turned the place into aisles of rainbow overlaid with some of the most exotic scents in the world. Sally gravitated immediately to a display of cashmere sweaters from Scotland and asked to see what they had in shades of blue. Jess gasped when she saw the variety offered.

"Oh, help!" she cried in mock dismay. "I know you've gotten awfully prompt in most things, but have your shopping habits changed?"

Sally grinned. "No, not one bit. I think I know which color I like best already, but I'll fuss over all of them before I decide. Do you want to go on? We're all meeting at the Penthouse later anyway."

"I'll see you there," Jess said, but Sally's only reply was a vague nod; she was already wearing her glassy-eyed shopper's face. Jess smiled in memory of the days when she not only carried paperbacks in her purse for shopping trips with Sally but had time to read them besides. Her own method was more direct. She either needed something or she didn't, and if she did, there was rarely more than one item which pleased her exactly. And if that item pleased, the remaining question was whether she could afford it or not. Sally called it the Banbridge three-point attack and thought it dull.

Jess stood looking around uncertainly for a moment before her mind slipped back into its normal matter of fact gear. There were lots of things she would like to have, but she couldn't afford them. What she wanted most of all was a good bottle of perfume and an unusual gift for Uncle Arthur, and with careful shopping, she could manage both. But Trimingham's wasn't the place to look for Uncle Arthur's gift since he was in the import-export business and probably handled most of the items the store carried, besides living in the country where most of the goods were manufactured. And though the store had perfume counters, Jess wanted to visit Peniston-Brown, a shop which carried nothing but perfume. She headed for the branch on Queen Street, chuckling over the bobby who was gravely directing Front Street traffic from his position in the "Bird Cage," aptly named since it looked like a cage which had been stretched tall and expanded to house a man instead of a canary.

She was further amused by the shopping guide direction which listed Peniston-Brown's as being "just past the rubber tree," and she found both without difficulty. The woman who presided over the shop held herself in straight-backed reserve as if she were a high priestess waiting for the signal to light the lamps, but her manner thawed when she realized Jess was not going to choose one of the sample size bottles of the overpoweringly flowery scents made in Bermuda. And Jess left the store with a subtly spicy bottle of magic from Paris. Her senses were reeling from everything she had tested, and she expected she smelled like an escapee from a harem.

Her next stop was the post office, and there she found an idea of what to get for Uncle Arthur besides the stamps and postcard she needed to write to him.

The post office was small and wooden grated in the style of years past, and the two employees were from years past too, two little old ladies with gray hair pinned in neat styles Queen Victoria would have approved, bright eyes keeping track of the world through the letters they handled. Jess was admiring the stamps—incredibly vivid patches featuring flowers, birds, and leaping fish—when she noticed the bracelet one of the women wore. It was heavy with charms made from old seals and watch fobs.

"Your bracelet is lovely!" she exclaimed and saw the old face light with pleasure. "Did you find any of the pieces here?"

"My favorite ones came from my father—he had such a fancy for them—but, yes, miss, some of them I've collected locally. There are some fine shops right here in Hamilton which carry them, mostly imported from England, though they do get foreign ones now and again."

The woman mentioned a shop on Church Street as being one of the best places to look, and Jess thanked her warmly, walked up Queen Street, and turned right onto Church. She walked briskly, hoping she could go to the shop and still get to lunch on time.

The further she went, the quieter the area became. The street was well named since the left side of it seemed to have at least a church per block. The street was deeply shaded, and the foot traffic was minimal since many of what shops there were closed for midday. She crossed her fingers and was rewarded to find the jewelry and antique shop open, the proprietor brown bagging his lunch.

He was a round, gnome-like man with brown, myopic eyes enlarged by the thick lenses of his glasses. A jeweler's glass stuck out like an extra appendage from the frame of his spectacles. He was elderly and bald, but his face was unlined. His voice was heavily accented, and Jess guessed he was German or Swiss. But though watches by the look of the shop were his specialty, the seals were his passion. His rather forbidding expression softened as soon as she told him what she wanted and he brought out the velvet tray on which his treasures rested.

He picked up a solid gold seal which bore arms. "This one, it belonged to a great Duke, see his crest. He lost it one day while riding on his parklands, and a gypsy found it and sold it to a small shop in London where it remained for many years until it found its way here in the hands of a rich merchant. And when the merchant died, it came into my hands." His eyes were twinkling fiercely, and Jess' smile matched his. "You are quite marvelous! You ought to be writing tales of adventure."

His laugh rumbled up from his barrel shape. "No, I ought to be minding my major business which is the selling of watches, old and new, but only seldomly does someone come into my shop to share the beauty of these things."

Jess saw it suddenly, as though her eyes had become those of a hawk, telescoping and focusing sharply on one small object of prey. The handle was ornate, pierced at the top to allow it to be put on a chain, the gold shape looking at first like a sinuous intertwining of flowers and tendrils. To be sure, there were flowers, they crowned the hair and decorated the sweetly curved tail of the little mermaid. She was perfect from the finely featured face surrounded by silken waves of hair to the small uptilting breasts and intricately scaled tail. The seal itself was black onyx bearing a deeply carved sailing ship.

"And this one, what is its story?" Jess asked softly.

"But surely you know this is the sorcerer's own, as your ring must be."

Small shocks ran through her. Everything so interwoven, never had she felt the world to be so small. She wanted the seal so badly, it was all she could do to keep from grabbing it, but she knew she could not afford it.

She did not think she had asked the question, but the man answered it. "But surely it is within your means." The price he quoted was absurdly low.

Jess shook her head. "No matter how much I want it, I couldn't take it for that. It would be stealing."

The jeweler's expression was suddenly angry. "If it was a watch you wanted, an Omega or another such name, I would ask a price the same as is asked the world over. This is not the same. This is one of my special treasures, a thing I love, and I care greatly who should have it. I care more about that than I do for its price."

"But I am not even going to keep it," Jess protested. "I have to be honest about that. It is for a special friend."

"But he is like you, is he not—he gave you the ring, did he not?—and he too would love it, more so because you found it for him." The man was uncanny; she had not even mentioned whether the gift was for a man or a woman, yet he knew. Almost she could believe he was seeing Uncle Arthur clearly.

"You win or rather you lose, I can't quite tell which, but I can't resist either. I'll take it, and I promise you, it will be cherished." She paid and thanked him and left feeling that surely the day could hold nothing more special than this encounter.

She wandered on, planning to circle back around to Front Street, hardly conscious of her surroundings, savoring the future pleasure of giving the seal to Uncle Arthur.

The busy life of the street burst on her suddenly. There was a supermarket crowded with shoppers; groups of children ran in and out of the side streets, knots of young men stood talking and laughing. No one made any comment or paid any attention to her, but Jess felt suddenly alien—hers was the only white face in evidence. The last thing she wanted to do was to make herself more conspicuous. She already felt she must appear to be one of those awful tourists who invade every neighborhood in search of the "authentic flavor of the region." But she heard, recognized, and moved toward the voices instinctively.

She saw the two men standing apart from the others. Connor towering over the young airport man. Connor was huge, and the young man was in trouble. His voice carried clearly, pleading, always pleading with Connor. "Please, this has got to end. You're going to get killed. You can't go tonight!"

Time froze, and Jess saw the line distinctly. She had a choice. She could step back, refuse involvement, avoid danger, leave the score even, or she could step across, step into their lives. Uncle Arthur's image flashed into her mind, and she knew the choice was made, had been made when she accepted the first of the sea change, long before the young man had reached out and given her shelter in her fear. Arthur had commanded she think and see and above all feel again—joy and sorrow, pleasure and pain. He had commanded she cease her numb drifting, that she make hard decisions and act upon them. He had commanded she become involved with herself and those around her, and now she obeyed.

Connor's voice, even more menacing than her memory of the night before. "Traylee, I tol' you to keep out of this. I warned you it was none o' your business." His arm went up but before it could descend, Jess was between them, even at her height having to crane her neck to see into Connor's face, hissing at him, "You should be ashamed; you big bully! Leave him alone! Leave . . . Traylee alone!"

The pupils in Connor's eyes narrowed to slits, and for an instant, Jess thought he was going to deal her one blow which would undoubtedly break her neck. She stood frozen, and then watched in amazement as Connor's face changed. The eyes crinkled almost shut, white teeth flashed, and he bellowed with laughter. His words were choked by his mirth. "Oh, sweet, sweet Lord, save me. Traylee done got a white woman for to fight his fight." Connor looked deep into Jess' eyes, shrugged his shoulders in bewilderment, and still fighting laughter, turned on his heels, and in spite of his enormous bulk, lost himself quickly in the crowd.

The faces which had turned in curiosity to the street scene shifted back to personal business, elaborately ignoring the strange sight of the white woman and the young black man caught in mutual and silent staring.

Traylee recovered first. His young face was set in old, austere lines. "Why? We were even. I told you that. What business do you have with me or my brother?"

"I'm not sure," Jess admitted slowly, "but our paths seem to be on a crisscross course, and I know you're in trouble. I'd like to help."

Traylee's voice was as flat and dull as his eyes. "You can't help. You're white."

Jess felt the wall rise between them, the wall of hundreds of years of abuse, hatred, and a complete lack of communication. "I can't help being white any more than you can help being black! I know it can be a frame of mind as much as a skin color, but it doesn't need to be, surely it doesn't need to be when we're facing a common enemy."

"How do you know it's a common enemy? How do you know I'm not involved in bringing down your world?" His voice had life again, vicious with hurt and mistrust. But the fact he was talking to her at all was a measure of how desperately he needed help.

"How in the hell do I know anything? I take it on faith I was born twenty-six years ago. I don't remember, but some papers say it's true. I take it on faith the sun will rise and set every single day. And about you, it's a gut feeling, a deep in the bones feeling—I presume your bones are whitish gray like mine—I know you're committed to something terrible and dangerous and maybe even illegal, but I also know that it's out of love. You love Connor so much you're ready to take on the whole world single-handedly. Well, white as I am, I know how that feels. I had a brother too, and I would have done anything to keep him safe. I lost, my enemy was too strong, but maybe this time I can help, and you can win. That would be something."

His eyes were wide, brown velvet with amber light. He did not ask how Sean had died; he had heard death songs before and recognized the notes in a voice, recognized too that the how was not as important as the injustice of the loss. "You sorrow, I sorrow," he said, and Jess knew she would never have another pledge of trust and friendship so beautifully given. His voice lost none of its gentleness when he asked, "How do you know his name is Connor?"

Jess smiled ruefully, thinking of Uncle Arthur, "The Fates seem intent on involving me in your business." She told him what she had overheard the night before after she had left him. "I think you ought to know too that the man with the cane, Mr. Winston St. James, he came down those stairs right after you left, and he didn't need the cane."

Taylee's eyes gazed blankly into space. "So he was there. Yes, he would be, yes indeed."

He spoke as if to himself, and Jess didn't understand his musing, and she demanded his attention again. "You mentioned the boss man prowling, so of course he was there. Will you please tell me what's going on?"

His eyes searched her face carefully before he answered. "I can't tell you. It's Connor's business, just like he said. I'm just trying to keep him safe. I don't want to have a dead white woman on my hands besides, so you just keep to yourself and know nothing. The running you did last night better keep on," he finished cryptically. His face was weary and old again, and he turned to go.

Jess put a restraining hand on his arm. "Wait, my name is Jess, Jess Banbridge. You know where my room is, but my roommate doesn't know a thing about this, so if you want to get in touch with me, you'll have to be careful of her. I do want to help, please ask me if you think I can."

"My last name's Jameson. You already know my first. You already know too much. You'll be better off if you don't see me again." He paused, and when he spoke his voice was soft and gentle again. "But thank you. I believe you would help." He melted away as easily as his brother had done and was lost in the crowd.

Jess had to remind herself to walk carefully, so blind was she with introspection. She could hardly believe she had interfered in that scene. She glanced at her watch and saw she was going to be late if she didn't pull herself together and pick up her pace.

She turned right again to head back down to Front Street, and, glancing up the other arm of the cross street, she thought she saw a familiar figure going into a building. The height and the flowered hat fit, and the woman was white, but Jess couldn't see her face. She hailed her, but the woman did not even turn around as she went in the door. Jess shrugged and went on her way, knowing that if it had been Elsie, she would have answered the call.

Jess arrived at the restaurant feeling hot and flustered, but she was comforted by the cold drink Kyre ordered for her and by the fact that Sally arrived last of all, loaded down with packages.

"Falling back into old and evil ways, aren't you, young woman," Tom teased.

Sally stuck out her tongue at him and threatened, "You're going to have to be a lot of nice to make up for that or I won't show you the absolutely terrific present I got for you. In fact, I will find someone else to give it to." She turned to Kyre and batted her eyelashes extravagantly. "Now, you're just about the same size, a little leaner and a little more fit, of course, but still..." She yelped in protest as Tom grabbed her and gave her a resounding kiss, much to the amusement of the crowd in the restaurant.

Sally's cheeks were pink, and she gave him her slow, wide smile as she drew away. "That kind of behavior, sir, will get you anywhere. For you, because I love you," she said as she handed him a package.

Before opening his own gift, he reached in his pocket and handed Sally a flat, square box. "I did not forget, my darling, I will never forget," he said softly.

They were so much in love Jess doubted they even remembered where they were or that there were other people in the room. She felt a lump rise in her throat. They were so perfect together and so vulnerable. Sean would be glad, very, very glad.

Her emotion eased when Kyre muttered gruffly, "Makes me feel like a goddamn spy, but it's nice, isn't it?"

Sally and Tom opened their respective gifts, and both began to laugh. Jess couldn't understand it at all since both gifts were so fine—a heavy, cable-knit sweater from Ireland for Tom, a gold compact exquisitely enameled with blue flowers on a yellow ground from France for Sally. Sally saw her expression and explained, "You remember, I'm like you, I love cold weather, but Tom freezes as soon as the temperature drops below seventy, and as for the other, well, you know that one too. I'm forever stopping to powder my nose, in the true sense. Ms. Shiny Face, that's me, and Tom hates those scratched plastic compacts I'm forever producing."

"As a matter of record, I like her shiny face, but she doesn't, so she might as well go unshiny in style," Tom said.

With Sally and Tom in their present mood, the lunch had to be lighthearted. They were sitting at a table on the balcony overlooking Front Street and the harbor, and Jess could not help but be charmed by the bright vista. But she could also not help reliving the scene with Traylee and Connor. The words came back. "You can't go tonight!" Go where? To the Queen's Gate? For what? "You're going to get killed!" Jess came to suddenly to find Sally gazing at her intently. She looked away and pretended to be watching the scene below, and in an instant, she was.

The sidewalk traffic was heavy, but she picked out the three faces without effort, as though she had a third eye for the familiar—Connor at the corner, seeming to lounge, but undoubtedly aware of everything around him; closer to, Elsie Clinton in the same hat Jess had recognized up near Church Street; and closer yet, just within sight before the balcony would have shielded him from view, Caliban leaning heavily on his cane, back toward her. She wanted to look away but could not, and he turned and his eyes found her easily as though he had known all along where she was. Even on the sun-warm balcony, she felt as if he'd touched her, and she saw his small shrug of affirmation. She stared back at him defiantly, and their eyes caught and held for a moment before he turned away to hobble up the street toward the place where Elsie had been. The woman had disappeared, probably stopping in some shop, and Connor was no place to be seen either.

Jess shivered involuntarily; it was as though Caliban was as obsessed with her as she was with him and liked it no better than she did. Suddenly Traylee's words made sense—he must have thought she was running from the boss man, from Caliban—that would explain his advice that she keep running.

Kyre asked, "What's wrong?"

"Goose on my grave," she said, trying to sound carefree, but she avoided his eyes and Sally's.

Sally was announcing more shopping plans, and the men were engaging in an amiable argument about motor scooters when the four left the restaurant.

"Sally, I know this will go against your independent

grain, but would you agree to riding tandem with me? It would do a lot toward preserving my peace of mind," Tom said, and Sally made such a show of her grudging agreement, Jess had to hold her face rigid against a smile. Tom would never suspect the idea suited Sally perfectly.

"Are you willing to follow suit with me, Jess?" Kyre asked, and Jess agreed gladly. It was lovely to savor the growing ease between the two of them, but she tried to suppress the idea that it was also nice to have this big, strong-muscled man on her side. It would not be that way, she knew. It would be Kyre against Caliban, and she and Traylee would be in the middle. God knew where Connor would be. She didn't want to involve Kyre or anyone else. The burden of her pact with Uncle Arthur was her own to carry.

Her three companions were looking at her curiously. "I'm sorry, missed the question," she confessed.

Kyre laughed. "Warm day, one drink, and you're gone. My, oh, my, it's a good thing I'm a gentleman. I'll repeat, 'Would you like to go shopping with Sally or machine hunting with us?'"

"Neither. You may wish to fritter your time away, but I came for tennis," she said with mock severity. "I'm going back to the Queen's Gate and see if there are any other clean-living souls who'd like to play."

A tennis fanatic was something they could all understand, even Sally, and the group broke up quickly. Jess looked up and down the street before she started her walk, but she saw no sign of anyone familiar save for Sally's blond hair gleaming in the sunlight before she turned into the shadows of a shop.

She walked briskly, hoping the steady drum of her footsteps would shut out thought. But she kept hearing the words over and over. And now both Traylee and Connor knew about her, knew where her room was. She had no doubt that Traylee would tell his brother everything. Had she been justified in trusting him? She nearly bumped into another pedestrian and had to mumble an apology. Nor did she notice the sound of a car braking next to her. But then a voice called her name, and she turned to see Elsie in a cab. "Want a lift?" the woman inquired, and Jess got in thankfully; at the rate she was going she was going to mow down someone and be charged with careless walking.

"Ridiculous to take a taxi for such a short distance, but as you see, I have rather too much to carry comfortably," Elsie said, gesturing at numerous parcels. "Looks as if I did your share. However did you resist all the bargains?"

Jess laughed and produced the bottle of perfume and the seal from her purse. "I didn't. I just like things in small packages."

Elsie handled the seal reverently. "It is lovely. And such a fitting companion to your beautiful ring. How will you wear it, as a pendant perhaps?"

"Yes, that's what I have in mind," Jess agreed and felt glad of her lie. She did not want to explain about Uncle Arthur, and the glitter in the woman's eyes as she looked at the seal made Jess uneasy. She had had the same expression when she had first caught sight of the ring. Jess wondered if Elsie was one of those people who, disappointed by human love, becomes fanatically obsessed by precious objects. She had met a few like that—men who felt that acquiring a new company was similar to choosing a new mistress; women whose sensuality was only aroused by the glitter of gold.

Seeking to change the subject, she asked, "Were you up near Church Street this morning? I thought I saw you, but when I called, you didn't answer, so I probably hailed a perfect stranger who has a hat that's twin to yours."

She was appalled by the change in Elsie's face, the blood draining away to leave the skin grayish white with two cheek patches of rouge, the eyes suddenly blank, the face undeniably old. Totally at sea, she searched for something to say, but Elsie recovered first.

"Forgive me for reacting so badly. It has nothing to do with you. Undoubtedly you saw me, but I was so concerned with the past, I was unaware of anything else. You see, Stanley and I used to come here quite often. It was one of our special places, and we became acquainted with many residents. I'm sure you've heard what a horrid man

Stanley was, and it's true he was a gambler and a spend-thrift. But he was also my husband. I loved him very much, and in spite of our difficulties, he brought me great joy. I went to visit one of our mutual friends today, and I was full of memories before I even entered the house."

The taxi stopped in front of the manor, and Elsie would not allow Jess to share the fare. "Your company was payment enough," she insisted.

Jess smiled at her. "Thank you. I hope all your new memories of Bermuda will be happy ones."

"They will be, I assure you they will. I plan to make them so." Her voice carried an oddly grim note, and Jess felt even more sympathetic toward her; she didn't think looking too hard for happiness worked very often.

She went to the pool, hoping to find someone who was up for a tennis match and was rewarded by the sight of the Cranstons and a couple of empty courts in the gardens below. "Mrs. Cranston, would you be willing to play our singles match now? I'm dying for a game."

Mrs. Cranston regarded her with bright eyes. "I know what you're up to, young woman, you're planning to stay out late tonight, and you don't want to get up early tomorrow. I'll be losing my advantage, but I'll go along with it if you'll call me Millie. Anyway, I've been boring myself to death sitting here. George may look like he has that hat over his face for shade, but actually it's to hide the fact that he's sound asleep. Makes for very dull company."

Jess hurried back to her room elated at the chance to play tennis without cane-tapping Caliban watching. She wanted to escape from her mind by pushing her body hard.

6

All three of them are desperate: their
great guilt,
Like poison given to work a great time after,
Now gins to bite the spirits.

By late afternoon, Jess was feeling much more at
peace with herself. Millie Cranston, though not too fast
anymore, was good at placing her shots, and Jess had had
to scramble for her victory. Ellen Frieberg had come along
in time to watch the end of the match and had then
accepted Jess' ladder challenge, and without Caliban
watching, Jess had been able to concentrate fully on the
game, enjoying every minute. Ellen was a fine, active
player whose only fault was that she was having trouble
with her serve. Jess assured her honestly that only that
edge had given her the victory. Ellen was a sporting loser,
but she warned Jess she was going to work on her serve
and demand a rematch when it improved.

Jess was standing under a hot stream of water, feeling
the bliss of tense muscles relaxing when Sally came in.
Even over the water sound, she heard packages hitting the
floor, Sally hitting the bed, and a long drawn out "Whew!"

She got out of the shower and, wrapped in a towel,
went into the bedroom to find Sally sprawled on the bed,
eyes closed, moaning, "Spending money is sooo-o tiring."

"Our timing's perfect. Your turn in the shower. And if
you don't go now, you'll collapse completely and sleep
until morning."

Sally opened one eye. "Hey, that's all right. You look pretty good in a bath towel. Think I'll wear one too, but what shall we say we are? Soap commercials?"

"Get moving or I'll claim both men as my escorts."

Sally shot off the bed. "Not on your life, my one time friend," she called as she disappeared into the shower.

Jess dressed quickly in a long white gown cut in a halter pattern similar to the dress she had worn the night before. The style suited her, and the white set off the deepening copper of her tan, but then she giggled as she put her costume on over it. She waited for Sally's reaction and was not disappointed when her friend emerged and burst out laughing. "If it isn't one of the Trojan Women," she gasped.

There wasn't anything unusual in the borrowed sheet draped and pinned in antique style, but on her head, Jess wore the white plastic cover from her steel racket. With the zipper undone, the cover fit just like a high-ridged helmet curving inward at the neck, the maker's name in bold letters on both sides.

Sally decided to wear the same thing and chortled all the way through her own preparations.

Jess blessed her luck in having such a lighthearted companion. She had worked all afternoon to make her mind numb, and she had been fairly successful, but now she was uncomfortably aware of the dusk coming down outside, the night inevitably to follow. "You can't go tonight!" The words broke over her again in a relentless wave, and she fought desperately to escape the unfriendly sea.

"Sally, I've waited long enough. Tell me about Tom. And tell me why today is special." Her words bumped against each other in their hurry, and a secondary voice whispered, "Child, you can't talk away the dark," but Sally was oblivious to anything else once Tom's name had been mentioned.

"I guess I have felt a little funny about telling you. I mean, I loved Sean so much that if anyone had told me I would fall in love again, I would have been insulted." She saw Jess' expression and answered it. "I know what you're thinking, and you're right. Sean would have been the first to wish me love and joy; he was like that all the way through. But having permission or wishes or whatever doesn't mean it will happen.

"Sean had only been gone for six months when I first met Tom—oh, I had seen him at parties, but we had never exchanged more than distant greetings—and that six months wasn't nearly long enough for me to be seeing men as anything more than animated blots on the landscape. I had begun to accept dates now and then, but only because I was lonely, not because I particularly enjoyed any one man's company. If I'd met Tom in that situation, maybe nothing would have come of it." (Jess smiled to herself at that—the doubt in Sally's voice clearly conveyed the thought that she couldn't really imagine a situation anymore which did not include loving Tom). "As it was, he sort of snuck up on me. His law office isn't too far from the library, and he started coming in after work once or twice a week and then nearly every night. It's an odd library, you know, privately endowed and run by its own crazy code of rules, opening late and closing late to be more accessible to people's hours—very few people outside of students read much besides the newspapers early in the morning, but lots of people like a good book at eight or nine at night. But still, it's very specialized in its collections. We have far more material on ancient law, sailing ships, and the occult than we have current bestsellers. I began to wonder why Tom spent so much time there. I thought perhaps he was researching something, but the books he checked out were too random for that. The puzzle began to fit together because of Mrs. Harkness. Remember her? She's well meaning enough, but she is the biggest gossip I know, and she knows everything that happens for miles around. I swear she has some kind of built-in, supersensitive communications center. She fills in sometimes when there's cataloguing or more than the ordinary paperwork to be done, and one night she saw Tom and undertook to tell me his life history. I'm ashamed to say I didn't try to stop her. The more I heard about his home life, the more his visits to the library made sense.

Some men stop at a bar every night to fortify themselves before going home; Tom needed a book or two to drown his troubles. The more unbearable things were at home, the longer he stayed. He was very polite, very withdrawn, and very careful with the books, but they weren't enough. Oh, Jaybe, I could see him getting thinner day by day, and his eyes had a dreadful bruised look. I couldn't stand it. My mothering instinct went into high gear—at least, that's the instinct I thought it was at the time. I always keep a pot of coffee going, and I started offering him a cup now and then, and then I got into the habit of packing enormous amounts of food for my dinner so I would have plenty to share with him. He was stiff necked and suspicious about it at first, but I convinced him my job was so lonesome I was glad of company. Sometimes he was silent and far away, but other times we'd talk about some book we'd both read or some local happening, or some other mutual interest. He knows so much. He's so much fun to talk to, and all of a sudden I found myself becoming terribly dependent on his visits, disappointed almost to tears when he didn't come. That's when I told myself I'd better get back in my shell while it was still possible. Only catch, I'd waited too long. Everything conspired against me. Even now I swear I was the victim of cosmic forces, crazy as that sounds." (Not to me, thought Jess, not to me, except my cosmic forces don't seem nearly as nice as yours.)

"Things were getting worse and worse for him. He never mentioned any of it, but there was more than enough secondhand information. The housekeeper who was taking care of the children called the library more and more often to ask that he come home because of some crisis. And there were stories constantly about some new escapade of Audry's, his wife. Mrs. Harkness told me a particularly awful tale one day about Mrs. White having been gone for two days with someone else's husband, and as though that wasn't enough, on her return she had spent a drunken half hour in one of the busiest supermarkets, screaming obscenities about her husband until the police came and took her home.

"Tom came in that night, and he looked dreadful. He could hardly hold the books I handed him, his hands were shaking so. His voice sounded like a robot's, and his eyes looked so blind, I couldn't see how he was going to read. He didn't go to his normal place, but disappeared to one of the tables behind the stacks. I waited for about fifteen minutes before I panicked."

Sally's eyes filled, and she took a deep breath before she went on. "It still does this to me, remembering. I heard a strange sound before I saw him. He was slumped over the table, face buried in his arms, shoulders heaving, sobbing his heart out. He was trying not to make any sound, and that made it worse. I like men who can cry as honestly as they laugh, men like Sean, but it wasn't like that for Tom. He had kept all the hurt to himself for so long it was nearly killing him to let it out. I went to him and put my arms around him, and I still remember what I said because it seemed the most natural thing in the world. 'Darling, let it be, there's no one else to hear. It's all right, I love you.' He held on to me, as if he were drowning, and he cried until he was too tired to cry anymore. It was a mutual act of love beyond anything I had experienced with anyone before, even with Sean." Jess nodded her understanding, her own throat too tight for words.

"We were in a whole different world after that. He could have walked out of my life forever because I'd seen him at his most vulnerable time—a lot of men would have—but even having been so long without love did not make him incapable of recognizing it. And he could have gone home with me that night, or any night following. I would have been proud to have been his mistress. He wouldn't do it. He was terrified Audry's malice would touch me, and beyond that, he knew he had to work through his problems before he would have anything to offer another woman. He no longer loved Audry, but he still felt enormous sorrow for her, enormous responsibility. He had offered her every aid—psychiatrists, therapy sessions in the best of rehabilitation centers, his own endurance. But alcoholism was just one symptom of her mental illness, and that illness had started long before Tom married her. He knew she was destroying him; he worried about her effect on the children, but still he would not divorce her. He felt she was even more helpless in face of her condition than her victims were.

"We might have gone on forever seeing each other only in the library, knowing what we meant to each other but saying less than half of it. Audry saved us. Two months after that night, she committed suicide, accidentally or not, no one will ever know. She mixed too many pills with too much liquor. The police found Tom at the library. I didn't see him for a month after that. I never doubted him, but I could see that he might have had to get away from everything connected to his old life, including me, to begin a new one. I said I never doubted him, and I never did, but I doubted I could go on without him. That month was longer than I care to remember. Then, a year ago today, Tom walked in, opened his arms, and I was safely home, in front of Mrs. Broadcasting Harkness, no less. This is the anniversary of our beginning. Maybe we'll get married, maybe not, that's up to him. He has many understandable reservations about it. But I adore him, and I love his children, and I have all three as part of my life. I could not be more content.

"What are you looking at me like that for?" she asked as she finished.

Jess blinked and then laughed. "Sally, I'm so happy for you and Tom. But listening to that story and knowing it is the absolute truth—all of a sudden, I felt as if you were someone completely different from the girl I knew. It couldn't be more dramatic if it included a spiral staircase and several poisonings. Sean would be proud."

"Sean taught me a lot of things, Jaybe. He's more than a little responsible for my joy now. He believed in meeting things head on, in being open, even vulnerable to all sorts of experiences. I can hardly recognize the timid girl I was when I first met him."

There was a knock on the door, and Sally moved to answer it, wondering aloud if it were Tom needing help to pin his toga. The interruption was a godsend for Jess. She

could not understand it, this unmanageable quality of her
sorrow. She loved her memories of Sean; there were so
many good ones, but she had no control over how they
affected her—one minute she was able to talk to Sally
about him, remembering him with no trouble; in the next,
a word, an image, something would set her off and grief
would rise in her until she thought she would strangle on
it or start screaming without being able to stop. The loss of
her parents had left a dull, forever ache, but that she
could handle. It was the sharp agony of Sean gone,
brother, closest friend, so young, that lurked and haunted
and would not be still. She knew again the fear of letting
go, all the unshed tears waiting for a break in her control.

She heard the voice at the door and focused on the
present again. Dana Grant, she realized after a second
glance and felt the heaviness ease. It wasn't that simple
to guess the figure was Dana. Her face was almost
unrecognizable with the two bright circles of cheek rouge
and the exaggerated eye makeup which turned her into
Raggedy Andy. A cleverly folded sailor's cap made of
newspaper and trimmed with ribbon topped her short
hair, and she wore a sailor-style shorts outfit which would
have been acceptable on any golf course but was also
perfect for the character she portrayed.

"I'm so glad you're both in costume! I was beginning
to lose my nerve, and Ann has gone stubborn on me. She
says the whole thing is infantile, and she's just about ready
to uncostume herself. Could I bribe you with a glass of
sherry to come help convince her?"

Sally glanced at her watch. "We've got time. I'm
game."

"Sure," Jess agreed. "Offer me a glass of sherry, and
I'll follow you anywhere."

"The sherry's elegant. We got it in Hamilton today.
The prices are so much lower here than in the States, I
might go home with a drinking problem. But stem crystal
we haven't got, so bring your water glasses."

Jess realized Dana was using lighthearted chatter to
cover her very real concern. She didn't think Dana had
much luck influencing Ann; it was almost as if she feared

her. And she couldn't blame Dana much when she got a
look at Ann's mutinous expression, her tightly held mouth
and angry eyes making the clownish makeup gruesome.
But her look relaxed into a reluctant grin of appreciation at
the sight of Jess and Sally's costumes. "All right, Dana, I
surrender. But you're a sneak to bring in reinforcements."

Dana smiled in relief. "You nearly ruined my evening. Whoever heard of Raggedy Andy without an Ann?"
She poured generous glasses of sherry, and Sally proposed
a toast. "Here's to Dutch courage. It makes it so much
easier to make a fool of yourself."

Ann and Dana's room was larger than Jess and Sally's,
large enough to have a couch and a couple of armchairs
some distance from the beds. Jess teased them about
having connections with the management and then wished
she hadn't. Mention of the management brought the image of Winston St. James to mind instantly. And Jess didn't
believe it; she didn't believe it at all. Caliban, "the boss
man," was no more management or trustee of the Queen's
Gate than she was. She kept the smile on her face and
answered some trivial question from Dana. She was learning to be as devious as the night prowlers.

At the pub, there were crows of recognition and
laughter at the makeshift costumes. Halloween didn't have
much significance in Bermuda, and the American way of
celebrating it had even the normally quiet-faced barman
grinning widely. Most people had done something with
sheets. There were Romans and ghosts in abundance. But
some had been more inventive. One couple peered through
eye holes cut in paper sacks marked "Trick or Treat," and
David and Ellen Frieberg wore tattered garments David
insisted indicated they were castaways, not hobos.

"Shades of the bizarre," Jess whispered to Sally when
she saw Elizabeth Cooper, "if it isn't an albino Cleopatra."
Elizabeth wore a gold lamé gown draped in elaborate folds
from one shoulder. A gold necklace bound her forehead
over extravagantly painted eyes, and the ruby pendant was
blood red against the material of her dress.

They found Kyre and Tom among the white-sheeted
throng near the bar. Sally laughed and told Tom, "You get

an 'F' in draping. You look more like a piece of furniture
under a dust-cover than a Roman."

"I'm too busy plotting to kill Caesar to worry about
my robes. Hasten back to the hearth if you can't keep a
civil tongue." Tom's light-hearted playfulness and his open
adoration of Sally struck Jess as nothing short of miraculous now that she knew the circumstances of their court-
ship. Another miracle she noticed with less complacence
was how Kyre looked in his costume. Far from appearing
ill at ease, he looked magnificent. The white set off the
deep bronze of his skin, and the casual drape of the
material somehow contrived to lend added grace to his
long-limbed body. The perfect emperor. Jess' pulse
quickened, and she knew she'd been staring. She wished
she were wearing something as exotic as Elizabeth's dress
until Kyre smiled lazily at her and said, "Even under that
helmet, you're beautiful. The four of us, we are enough to
start a brave new world. What do you say, Tom?"

Tom leered at Sally. "I'm for it! And you, my sweet?"

"Mind your tongue, or I'll fall in love with that paper
bag over there," Sally warned.

Jess could barely follow the drift. Her mind had
stopped on Kyre's words. They were Miranda's. She had
repeated them with joy, loving Miranda's openhearted
enthusiasm and wonder. *"How beauteous mankind is. O
brave new world, That has such people in it!"* The Tempest,
the plot—island innocent girl and the prince who claimed
her—Uncle Arthur's ring, Uncle Arthur's words. The ring
had sudden weight on her finger. She looked searchingly
at Kyre, thankful he was turned half away, talking to Tom.
He had mentioned the ring when he first saw it; had he
now made the reference on purpose? If so, why did he not
tell her he knew Uncle Arthur, knew the plan? It was on
her tongue to ask, but she swallowed the words. If he
knew and did tell her so, it was for his own reasons, for his
own plan, and she would have to be content. But she was
more sure than ever now that he was the sea change
Arthur had conjured. She tore her eyes away, and her
body flinched, then tensed at what she saw.

Caliban, his street clothes looking strangely foreign

among the costumes, stood talking to Elizabeth Cooper in the back wing of the L, and beyond him stood a tall ghost, a ghost whose sheet had swung away long enough for Jess to catch sight of black hands. He was too big to be Traylee, had to be Connor. "You can't go tonight!" But he had, and violence, perhaps death would follow him.

Jess hadn't any clear idea of what she was going to do, all she could think of was getting to Connor before someone else discovered him. She mumbled an excuse to her party and started to make her way through the crowd. She was almost to Caliban when the lights went out.

The darkness was complete in the low ceilinged room, and the short, stunned silence was followed by a babble of protest and the sound of furniture being bumped, chairs being overturned. Jess tried desperately to keep on course in the dark and nearly sobbed with relief when her foot caught what had to be Caliban's cane since a very British voice asked what in bloody hell was going on. Jess thought she saw a pale glimmer of white sheeting, but she couldn't be sure it was Connor. She could only see one course, and she took it, ramming herself against the Englishman with all her strength, hearing his gasp of surprise as he fell.

"Get out, run!" she hissed, and the white mist swirled and disappeared toward the back of the pub. She was sure it was Traylee's voice which said, "This way, I've got the boat!"

She turned to get back into the crowd before the lights went on, but Caliban was too swift for her. He was back on his feet. His hands shot out, grabbing her in the darkness. She stifled a scream of horror and then of pain as he gripped her arms with merciless power. She was disoriented by the lack of light, but she kicked out as hard as she could and caught the hard bone of his shin. He grunted in pain and relaxed his grip momentarily. It was enough. Jess twisted desperately and was free, blundering through the dark, startling several people on the way. Her heart was pounding so loudly she could hardly hear anything else, and she prayed her sense of direction was not totally lost. She nearly sobbed aloud with relief when she heard Kyre's voice saying, "Jess, where are you?" close beside her. She realized everything had happened in a much shorter time than it seemed, but still it had been too long for her to pretend she had been close by all the while.

"I'm right here now. I was going to ask Rose Allenby something when the lights went out. I hate dark, closed places, and I just panicked for a moment." Her voice sounded false and high to her own ears, the excuse lame, but Kyre seemed to accept it. His touch was warm and gentle as his hand found her shoulders and drew her close. "That's okay. I know lots of people who have claustrophobia. No problem."

She relaxed against him, trying not to wince when his hand pressed against the bruise on one of her arms.

The lights went on as suddenly as they had gone out, and she made no attempt to move out of Kyre's protective hold. Please, let Caliban believe she had been here through all of the darkness. But it was no use. She felt his eyes and could not prevent herself from turning her head to look at him. She saw why Elizabeth had not been part of the exchange, plastered as she was against the wall, still white-faced with fear. She must have backed up to find solid support as soon as the lights had gone out. Jess also saw the look on Winston St. James' face. Pain was there, raw, harsh, and anything but physical. She could not understand that at all, but she could understand the swift rage which followed, filling his eyes and drowning the pain. He knew who had pushed him over, he knew beyond any doubt.

Jess shivered, and Kyre hugged her close. "What you need, my dear, is a medicinal potion and more of my comforting presence," he said, and Jess managed to laugh, thinking even in the aftershock of terror that handing the role of protector to a man certain improved a relationship. You are a cynic, Jess Banbridge, she accused herself.

She concentrated on Kyre and absently sipped the drink he handed her. The noise level in the pub was soaring as things returned to normal and people recounted exactly how they had felt in the dark. Jess' heart began to return to its regular rhythm. She was sure Traylee and

Connor had gotten away, and Caliban had not followed them, so that was something. The bruises on her arms were something, too. Her costume covered one arm, but the other was bare and the purpling blotch was beginning to show plainly. Sally looked at it in horror. "My heavens, how did you get that?"

"You know how easily I bruise. Everything was so confused, I either ran into some piece of furniture or it might have happened when I nearly knocked someone down. My fault for being so clumsy."

"Whoever it was has a grip like a bear," said Kyre, and he leaned down to plant a gentle kiss on the bruise. Jess felt the blood flaming in her face and muttered to Sally, "You and Tom are decidedly a bad influence."

Sally grinned at her. "No, decidedly a good one, I think."

Jess thought it was a good thing she was growing content to be paired with Kyre since the match seemed to have universal approval.

When they went into dinner, she noticed that Elsie had just come in and was not in costume. She looked pale and old, and Jess went to her in concern. "Are you all right? You look as though you're not feeling well."

Elsie smiled at her. "Don't worry, I just overdid it a bit this afternoon. I forget sometimes that I'm getting to be an old woman."

"Pooh to that," Jess said. "But if you need anything do let me know. I've played my match already, so I'm free for birding tomorrow morning. Would you care to go?"

Elsie agreed and thanked her, and Jess turned to find that Elizabeth Cooper and Winston St. James were seated at the table with her three friends. She felt a rush of anger she struggled to control as she was helped into her seat by Kyre. Tom introduced everyone to the Englishman.

Jess made her expression sweet and her voice dripped honey. "Mr. St. James, how nice it is of you to dine with us! Having one of the owners for company is like sitting at the captain's table. Do you spend much time here?"

She noted with satisfaction that he was taken aback by her direct attack. For once his eyes slid away from hers, but his voice was calm. "No, this is my first visit. I've only recently bought into the venture."

"How interesting. What do you normally do?"

She watched his growing anger with malicious amusement. He knew she was calling him a fake. "I normally do very little, Miss Banbridge. I am one of the unfortunate members of the idle class."

Jess heard Sally's small gasp of surprise at the man's rudeness, and Elizabeth's comment: "My, it doesn't seem that you two have hit it off at all," but she didn't care; her one clear thought was that Mr. St. James, Caliban, was a liar and not a very good one at that. She was quite sure he had known her name long before Tom's introduction, and she knew the hands which had caused such bruises belonged to anyone but an idle man. "I can hardly imagine your life. Do you ride to the hounds, that sort of thing?" she asked deliberately.

His eyes found the bruise on her arm and remained there. "Not very often, but when I do, I prefer a spirited mare above all other horseflesh."

There was a deathly silence before their table burst into half-finished sentences of attempted small talk. Neither St. James nor Jess had said anything which should merit interest, but no one at the table had missed the fact of double meanings aimed at insulting. Jess only felt guilt about making Sally look so troubled. She felt no guilt at all about the Englishman, only relief that whatever its cause, the tension between them was now openly acknowledged.

The conversation swirled around Jess and the Englishman, neither of whom made any attempt to participate. Even Elizabeth gave up trying to charm the man and turned her attention to Kyre who suddenly did not seem that unwilling, Jess noted grimly. Her anger was dissipating, leaving an ache in her throat. Winston St. James was destroying the joy of her trip with no effort at all, and she had the feeling of clutching futilely to bits of happiness.

She heard the voice at first far away and then quite close. "Jaybe, Jaybe, this isn't like you! Since when have you become a gutless wonder?"

"Since you died, Sean."

"You make my death more complete that way, Jaybe."

"No, never that. I'll quit feeling sorry for myself, promise I will."

Jess looked up suddenly, fearful she might have spoken aloud, but no one was paying her any attention, no one but Caliban. His look gave her a peculiar sensation, for it was different from anything she had seen on his face before. The lines were still there, the expression grave, but the blue-green eyes were curiously lightened and gentle. His whole look was gentle, concerned, as though he had heard every word of her mental conversation with Sean and sympathized. The shutter came down swiftly, so swiftly Jess wondered if she had imagined the softness. She did not believe she had. Never would she have guessed that Caliban could look like that—welcoming, sheltering. She could not erase the image from her mind.

She was relieved when the dinner was over, and she and Sally were instructed that they had fifteen minutes and no more to shed their costumes and be ready for the Kyre-Jess victory celebration. Back in their room, Jess forestalled Sally's comments by saying, "Look, I'm sorry about that rude little interchange at dinner, but I don't want to talk about it. It's just one of those things. There's no explanation for it, but sometimes two people dislike each other on sight." She realized with an inward start that dislike was a totally inappropriate word for whatever was happening between herself and Winston St. James. What she wouldn't give to see that particular sweetness of expression again, the thought rose unbidden. But she was ever more conscious now that her judgment from the drawings, her sense of the power generated by the two men was correct, and she did not want to play the battleground for them. Kyre had staked first claim. Let it be.

"Okay, subject closed. Really, I do sort of understand. There's something frightening about Mr. St. James. Even I can feel it."

Frightening, dangerous, and a whole lot of other things, Jess added silently, but she found it odd that Sally

didn't sense the same in Kyre. At least she partially
understood without having to be involved.

The men had a taxi waiting, and they headed for the
new Southampton Princess Hotel. It was two parishes and
a goodly drive away on a stone-walled road overhung with
greenery which traced glistening black patterns on the
wall, and because the drive seemed to be taking them
further into the heart of the countryside, the first view of
the hotel was a shock. It was enormous and ablaze with
light. "Very impressive," Jess admitted, "but I can't help
feeling it looks more than a little like a medical center."

"Antique freak," Sally snickered. "Would you prefer
more Victorian gingerbread?"

But even she admitted that the feeling of larger than
human space prevailed in the interior. The lobby was so
high-ceilinged, the chairs so far apart, people sitting there
would be forced to use megaphones if they wished to talk.
And the whole place smelled of wet stucco, as though the
architect's dream hadn't had time to set. Jess breathed a
sigh of relief that the Jet Sets' planners had chosen a small,
homey place for their stay, even while she conceded it was
nice to step out in elegance for an evening.

They went down a wide staircase and found the
discotheque on the lower level. It was designed much
more in keeping with the needs of human intimacy, softly
lighted, low-ceilinged, full of cozy chair and table group-
ings. And though the music was taped rather than live, it
had been chosen to keep the dance floor crowded. And
the dance floor itself was spectacular, a bright floral pattern of mock stained glass lighted from underneath. They
found a good table close by, and as Kyre led her out, Jess
laughed and said, "I feel as though I'm walking on a wall
or a ceiling, anything but a floor."

They danced to a fast beat, and Jess loved every
moment of it, especially since Kyre turned out to be as
good at that as he was at everything else. He had none of
the embarrassed stiffness of so many men, nor did he
imitate the extravagantly stylized gestures of the young.
He simply moved easily to the music, half smiling, eyes
paying tribute to his partner. And when the music switched

to a slow tune, Jess let him take her in his arms and heard him whisper, "That's better." There was satisfaction in his voice, and for some reason it rankled, but she did not protest. It was impossible not to respond to the magnetism of the man.

Back at the table Tom announced importantly that it was time for the victory drink. Jess ordered promptly, "Rum, ice, and the nectar of exotic fruits in any combination the house is famous for."

"I'll have a ditto, please," Sally said, and Tom gave her a severe look which failed in a grin. "You'll probably have a headache, but all right. Kyre?"

"Plain scotch and water; the company is exotic enough."

"Just listen to the man! Tom, you'd better practice your flattery a bit more," chided Sally.

When the drinks arrived, Jess took one look at the huge glass giving off rum fumes from the Planter's Punch and gasped, "If anyone wants a coherent answer from me about anything, now's the time to ask. Later will be much, much too late. But what a way to go!" They laughed and proposed silly toasts, enjoying each other's company.

Jess heard the tapping behind her even above the music and before Tom waved a welcome to Elizabeth Cooper and Winston St. James. Tom caught the look on Jess' face and whispered quickly, "I'm sorry, they seemed lonesome, and Mrs. Cooper asked where we were going. I didn't exactly invite them, but I did tell them to join us if they cared to."

"They cared to," Jess said flatly and saw that Kyre looked no more pleased than she.

When Caliban asked if he could have the seat next to hers, Jess nearly said no but thought better of it and gave him a stiff nod of permission instead; no use causing a scene. She half turned away from him, and she clung to what she hoped was a look of bored indifference, the last thing she was feeling. What was it about this man, she wondered, that moved her to so many swift and conflicting emotions.

She smiled graciously when Kyre asked Elizabeth to dance, his wink asking Jess to understand it was only because Elizabeth had just announced so pointedly how much she wanted to. She even managed to keep her air of sophisticated calm when Sally and Tom left the table, leaving her alone with the Englishman. But all her pretenses fled, and she turned to stare at him astonished by his words.

"I would like to offer my apologies, Miss Banbridge. We have gotten off on the wrong foot altogether. Would you consider beginning all over again?" His eyes shone with light again as they had at dinner. They were still wary and had a weariness about them that did not come from lack of sleep, but they were not threatening. Now she knew she had not been mistaken. The gentleness in his expression touched her, enveloped her, and revealed his sudden vulnerability. She had an intense longing to see his mouth really smiling, his eyes with all the guarding of emotions vanished.

There seemed no time gap between the asking of his question and her answer, for he was regarding her with the same intensity, as though truly seeing her for the first time.

"What do you suggest?" she asked quietly.

"For a start, my name is Win."

"All right. Mine is Jess. What's next?"

"Why are you here?"

"To play tennis, to get a suntan, to see the sights, to go dancing." Her anger was making the words come out in staccato bursts. The friendly interlude was over. His last question had been spoken as an insult, telling her he knew she was up to something, telling her she lied. She reminded herself this was the man Traylee had told her to run from, but it did not ease the pain.

"More to the point, Mr. St. James, Win, what are you doing here besides pretending you need that cane when you run very well without it? Can one hire you to kill someone, or do you do it for pleasure?" Rage was making her foolhardy, but she couldn't help it. It hurt doubly that his act of offering a new footing had been so welcome, that with so little effort, he had been so attractive.

"I'll trade you that information for the names of your

friends who were in the pub tonight. I presume you would rank yourself an amateur, but that was quite, quite good," he said, and his voice was so deadly, Jess shivered and felt hysterical laughter threatening. Amateur, professional, she didn't even know the game, let alone the ranks or the rules. Strangely, his reaction matched hers, as though he were speaking from similar hurt.

She saw Kyre's return to the table and his request for the next dance as a lifeline, and she took it so gratefully, he exclaimed, "Whoa there! I should be flattered, but I suspect you're jumping into my arms to escape our friend. Your heart's making awfully funny noises. Was he being offensive again?"

"No," she murmured. "We just have so little in common, so little to talk about, it was nerve-racking to be alone with him." It seemed inevitable that these two men should be on opposite sides, dominant males of most species usually were, but she hated the idea of being the female in the middle. And she knew she had made it worse by turning to Kyre with such obvious relief. His words confirmed it.

"I will take on the pleasant duty of making sure you are not alone with him again. Alone with me is another matter," he whispered.

The words should have been gratifying to her, but they were not. They carried an unmistakable threat, and she saw Caliban's brief betrayal of vulnerability as clearly as though she were still gazing at his face. The urge to escape rose in her again, the urge to escape both of these men, but this time she was ready for it, and she stayed where she was, in Kyre's arms. It will be all right, she told herself. I seem to have made a choice, and I will be safe as long as I have Kyre to protect me. She thought of telling him everything but resisted the impulse. It would only make things worse. He was not a bystander type.

When they went back to their table, only Tom and Sally were there.

They finally decided to call it a night though Tom looked at his watch and pointed out it was far more properly morning. Sally started it, and they sang all the way back to the Queen's Gate, and even their taxi driver couldn't resist their high spirits and sang along when the song was familiar.

Tom and Sally stopped at the top of the stairs on the walk back to the girls' room, and Kyre laughed softly as he guided Jess on. "That, my dear, is savoir faire."

She checked for an instant, and the arm around her shoulder tightened. The words she wanted to say were left unspoken as she continued on with him. She was not going to make a fool of herself as she had the night before. She knew it was basic and unreasonable stubbornness which made her want to resist his sure command of every situation.

They stopped in the dim glow cast by the porch light, and Kyre drew Jess into his arms. She closed her eyes and tried to give herself up to the sensation of his kiss. She felt every long, hard muscle of his body against her own. A sea change indeed, Uncle Arthur. But something wasn't right. She opened her eyes suddenly, answering the pressure. Kyre's eyes were closed, his mouth against her neck, teasing. Traylee's face gleamed for a moment in the farthest reach of light, eyes wide with shock and anger, nostrils flaring in disgust. Then he was gone, only a faint rustle telling of his passage, no boat gliding into water. He could be anywhere, in the foliage by the water's edge, around the corner of the building, somewhere in darkness.

Jess shuddered. Kyre blinked in surprise, and his arms let her go as he stepped back. "Jess?" The speaking of her name carried puzzlement, but his eyes were hard. She didn't blame him; again she had been unspeakably rude. She searched wildly for a plausible excuse and then stammered something close to the truth. "Kyre, I'm so sorry, I really am! I don't know what's wrong, but I think I'm out of my depth with you. Can't we just be friends?" She hadn't said those words since she was a gawky teenager, and they sounded worse now, but they placated Kyre.

His face relaxed, and he gave her nothing more than a friendly peck on the cheek before he said, "You have a strange innocence; it's one of the many beautiful things about you, but I find it difficult to remember when I'm

close to you. My fault for rushing my fences. I must learn
to school myself to patience. But I have no intention of
giving up. Good night, Jess, sleep well."

He left her, making no attempt to touch her again.

Her throat ached and tears made the lights on the
water swim in iridescent pools. She should have been
reassured by his words, but she wasn't. She knew he
meant it when he said he would not give up, and it made
her feel trapped and angry with herself for feeling that
way. He was the most attractive man she had ever met,
and yet every time he got too close, she stepped back in
fear. Maybe she was even more of a mess emotionally than
Uncle Arthur suspected.

And Traylee, what of his reaction? He must have been
waiting to talk to her, but his face had registered more
than annoyance that she was not alone.

She wiped at her eyes angrily and retreated into the
room. She washed her face and got ready for bed in a
rush, not wanting to talk to Sally. She was in bed by the
time her roommate came in, and Sally was so preoccupied
with Tom that she accepted Jess' sleepy murmurs—yes, it
had been a nice evening, yes, Kyre was special—and let
the conversation go at that.

Jess was too tired to brood anymore, and gratefully
she let sleep take her. Surely things would be clearer in
the daylight. She did not hear Sally humming along with
the water sound as she washed and got ready for bed, nor
did she hear the tapping on the walk outside.

7

My master through his art foresees the danger
That you, his friend, are in, and sends me forth
(For else his project dies) to keep them living.

Jess awakened just in time to turn off the alarm before
it rang. The last thing Sally would want would be to get up
for bird watching. She dressed quickly and found the
world in full sunlight already, but the morning still smelled
sharp and seawashed. She took a deep breath and her
spirits lifted.

Elsie was waiting for her on the road, and they set off
in the opposite direction from that which would have
taken them into Hamilton. The road was bordered by the
inevitable tangle of greenery over a stone wall on one side,
salt water on the other.

Jess' first clear sighting was a pair of kiskadees, and as
she pointed them out, she laughed. "I think they're
following me. They're probably the same pair who watch
the tennis matches with such interest."

"They're beautiful. Are they in the parrot family?"

Jess glanced at her in surprise. The woman hadn't
been kidding when she claimed she knew very little about
birds. "No, they're flycatchers." She told Elsie the story of
their importation and added some tips on how the shape of
their bodies and their bills, coupled with the sudden darts
of flight, helped indicate the family. She was fearful Elsie
would be insulted by what amounted to a lecture for a

rank beginner, but the older woman assured her she wanted very much to learn.

They saw house sparrows and starlings which Jess noted with disgust. "I swear, they're the plague of the bird world. They go everywhere and drive the more attractive birds away. Of course, in actual species count, Bermuda isn't really among the great birding spots of the world, so even starlings fill in some of the bare spots. I think there are something under ten species of song birds here, though there are other categories."

She stopped suddenly and pointed out a tiny, very active bird. "It's a Bermuda white-eyed vireo. Locally they call it chick-of-the-village. Hear its call, that's what it sounds as if it is saying."

Elsie looked totally lost and had a terrible time getting her binoculars focused on the bird. Jess suppressed a wave of annoyance—poor old woman, she couldn't help her beginner's status, but she certainly wasn't much help in the field. She kept turning her binoculars to gaze out to sea which meant she missed the birds close at hand. Finally Jess said, "You'll be disappointed. Seabirds are really scarce here. There isn't sufficient food in the waters to attract great numbers of them."

"But I thought we might see a Bermuda petrel. I've heard about them. Of course, you'd have to identify it for me."

"A cahow? Not a chance! They were thought extinct until 1951, and they are still so few, the only place you could see one would be at the reserve, and they don't even allow visitors yet."

Elsie laughed at her own ignorance, but still her glasses strayed forever back to the sea. "I think I'm better at boat watching," she admitted. "Do you like to sail?"

"No, not much," Jess snapped and was ashamed of her brusqueness.

"How tactless of me to forget. Rose Allenby told me the story, but I just didn't think," Elsie murmured in distress.

"I've got to get over being so touchy about it. Honestly,

I'd hate to think of people tiptoeing, having to be careful of everything they say around me," Jess assured her.

They turned back, and Jess added a catbird and a cedar waxwing to her list. Elsie pointed out an eastern bluebird and seemed pleased to have spotted something on her own at last.

Back at the Queen's Gate, they parted to go to their respective rooms, and Jess found Sally had already left for breakfast. The thought of the meal made her mouth water, and she went back up the steps two at a time and almost collided with Winston St. James at the top.

"Looking for me?" she asked. The bastard, she thought, he wants me to be conscious of him every minute, he expects me to be.

"You keep strange hours, Miss Banbridge, late to bed, early to rise, unhealthy." His voice was grating and weary. His hours, she knew, were much the same.

"I don't want to miss anything. What's your excuse? No, never mind. I don't give a damn about what you're doing as long as you leave me alone. I have a nickname for you. Ever heard of Caliban? It fits rather well, I think. There's plenty of room on these islands for you to do all the mischief you please, but leave me out of it." If defiance disconcerted him, she was willing to try any amount of it.

She watched in fascination as his face changed. Suspicion and anger vanished as he searched her face intently as though trying to see into the furthest reaches of her mind. She felt as curiously naked as she had the night before when it had seemed as if he heard all of her mental conversation with Sean. An eerie wave of warmth touched her, flooded through her. She saw his vulnerability again; whatever the tension between them stemmed from, it was not from fear on her part. His power might be similar to Kyre's, but his effect on her was not.

Devilry glinted suddenly in the sea eyes, and he quoted softly, "Thou didst prevent me; I had peopled else This isle with Calibans."

Jess was helpless against the blush rising in her cheeks, and his deep laugh made it worse. She had to grant it was clever to use the old lines for a bawdy suggestion for the present, but she was too furious to give him credit, especially since she had asked for it by calling him Caliban. "Enough! Just leave me alone," she snapped as she brushed past him. His words floated after her. "You would do well to watch the company you keep." The laughter was gone.

She was still scowling so thunderously when she met the group for breakfast that Sally said, "Hello, Miss Smiling Face, I can see early mornings still agree with you."

Jess managed a smile, but she was uncomfortably aware of Kyre watching her, beginning his pursuit all over again. It was another disquieting difference—even when Caliban's eyes were as icy and impenetrable as the frozen surface of a lake, they regarded her as an equal antagonist, while Kyre's made her feel uncomfortably like a rabbit caught under the eyes of a hawk.

She forced herself to ignore the image. She was safe with Tom and Sally, and she might as well take advantage of having a handsome escort such as Kyre.

Her tension eased, and she joined in the discussion of the day's plans. Though Jess had nothing scheduled until two o'clock, Tom, Sally, and Kyre all had matches beginning shortly after noon. They discussed various possibilities and decided they had time to go to the beach for a couple of hours. "If Sally can get ready pronto," Tom amended.

"For the beach, my friend, I hurry," Sally said and was off like a shot. Jess followed and within ten minutes they were arranging themselves on the backs of the men's motor scooters. Jess put her arms around Kyre, holding on firmly, making no fuss about it, feeling his heart beat and the ripple of his muscles with detachment. She was beginning to be able to cope with him, and she didn't even mind when he acknowledge the difference for the wrong reason. "Getting used to the idea, aren't you?" he said, and she didn't contradict him.

She missed some of the sights on the way because she couldn't prevent herself from closing her eyes when the traffic was heavy. Even twenty miles an hour seemed fast on the bike, but Kyre was a good driver, and Jess was breathing easier by the time they arrived at Horseshoe Bay. She wondered if there was anything Kyre did not do well.

"It really is pink!" Sally exclaimed, shaking her head in wonder at the tinted sand. "I don't care if it is crushed coral, it's magic."

The water was just brisk enough to be refreshing, and they swam and lay in the sun, relaxed and peaceful, making little effort to talk. Jess was nearly asleep when she was struck by the full import of what had happened with Winston St. James. She kept her eyes shut and hoped she still looked relaxed, but her pulse was beating fiercely. He had answered the part easily, knowing her reference. It wasn't really so strange; most people had to read *The Tempest* at some time or other if they took English, and lots of people had amateur experience in playing the parts. Or perhaps the man simply enjoyed Shakespeare and had a wide knowledge of it.

Then again, perhaps that was precisely why Uncle Arthur had used the play for his scheme. Winston St. James had nothing in common with Arthur save his English accent, common in this part of the world, and his rude manner was completely opposite from the old man's courtly charm. She knew she was making excuses, not wanting Winston St. James to be part of Arthur's plan, or if a part, Caliban. And she did not want to consider the current which flowed between them without her volition. "Watch the company you keep." Sally, Tom, Elsie? No, of course not. Traylee and Connor, yes, very probably them. And Kyre. Everyone at the Queen's Gate knew she was paired with him. The cold washed over her, and she shivered. Caught in the middle of the two.

Beside her, Kyre opened his eyes and exclaimed, "Well, young woman, that's enough sun for you. You've got goose bumps. If you get a chill in this heat, you must be sun sensitive. Why didn't you tell me? We could've gone back earlier. Time to go now anyhow, no excuses. And take care to protect yourself when you play your match, wear a hat or something." He started to gather their things with no further delay.

Jess caught Sally's look and ignored it—Sally's face was saying plainly, "What is this? The sun never bothers you." It was getting to be more and more nerve-racking to be around Sally. Jess remembered how attuned to each other's moods they had been in the old days, but it was eerie to find it had not changed at all. "Sally, keep out of this," she implored silently.

When they arrived back at the Queen's Gate, Jess felt jumpy and at loose ends with time before her match, so she took her sketching materials outside and sat on the grass by the water's edge.

Drawing usually had an almost hypnotically calming effect on her, as though she were watching the tracery of lines flowing from the pen of an invisible companion. She closed her eyes for a moment, willing the peaceful feeling to come. At first she drew aimlessly. Leaves and flowers grew to border the page; birds peered through the foliage. Strange beasts joined the birds, claws and fur and wild eyes staring from cover. Her pen began to move faster.

The figures stood in a clearing by the sea. Five. One, an old man in long flowing robes decorated with cabalistic signs. He was giving the girl something. She looked small and lonesome, standing by herself, for the other three figures obviously belonged to the old man. A prince stood on one side of him, a prince by the royal circlet on his head. A hunch-backed, twisted figure crouched fearfully on his other side. And peering over the old man's shoulder was a tiny, pointed face, fine-etched and unearthly.

Her pen stopped. Jess stared at the drawing in horror. It was very, very good, one of the best she had ever done of the type, an intricately perfect drawing for a fairy tale. It had none of the insipid roundness of the drawings done for Larry Foreman's play books; it was something straight out of the attenuated and horrific beauty of the plates which had fascinated her young eyes in the books of her childhood.

But it was all wrong. Uncle Arthur was the sorcerer, Prospero, the father, giving the ring to Miranda, to his

daughter, to herself, casting the spell. That she had known
for a long time. But Caliban, the monster, the slave, and
Ferdinand, the prince, shared the same face, distorted
and dangerous on one hand, youthful and innocent on the
other, both of them versions of Winston St. James' face,
neither of them bearing the slightest resemblance to Kyre.
And the spirit, hovering, watching—Ariel ready to do the
sorcerer's bidding—neither old nor young, not quite human, but still a version of Sean's face.

So much in the drawing was different from what she
wished, from what she'd thought she'd seen. It was too
hard to cope with the images of good and evil, different
faces of the same man. She preferred to think of him as
completely Caliban because then the bond would be
easier to break, the bond which kept her searching for him
in every crowd, kept her listening for the tap of the cane,
made her flinch inwardly when pain touched his face.

"I don't want it to be that way!" she moaned aloud.
Her hand moved to tear the page, then stopped. In some
way she could not understand, destroying it would be just
one more way of confirming its validity. She closed the
book and took it back to her room. Then with great care,
she took off the ring.

"Uncle Arthur, enough. The ring has been seen. Your
spell is moving, but now I doubt its goodness. I doubt
your power to help me, and I do not believe Sean is part
of it."

She dropped the ring into her bureau drawer, making
no attempt to secure it in a safe place as she had the seal
which was locked in her suitcase in the back of the closet.
Let someone steal the ring. Let someone else bear its
burden now, evil burden.

"Sea change," she said viciously. "Your sea change has
made me half mad, old man." She wanted desperately to
get back to the space where the familiar Jess had been,
the space of a rational, even if dull, existence where spells
did not move and beasts did not go bump in the night.

She jumped and barely checked a scream when someone knocked, but then she took a deep, steadying breath

and answered Ann by opening the door. "I'll be ready in a minute. I had so much time I lost track of it."

Ann nodded wearily. "That's okay. I've got nothing but time right now. It was supposed to be time to think, but that's the last thing I want to do."

Jess came out of her own problems with a start. "Do you want to talk about it?" she asked gently.

Ann gave her a long, level look before she spoke. "It shows, doesn't it? The woman of discontent." Jess started to protest, but Ann forestalled her. "No, I can feel them myself, what my children would call bad vibrations. I do want to talk to someone, but not now. Not until I'm sure I won't break into a thousand pieces. But I thank you for the offer, I really do, and if I can get it together, I might take you up on it."

Jess was struck anew by the strange combination in Ann—the middle-aged housewife with the strangely young and troubled spirit. And she understood only too well the fear of coming apart emotionally. Uncle Arthur, Kyre, and Winston St. James were managing to shred her into small pieces.

They played their match with a fierceness which had nothing to do with any antagonism between them, both of them wanting to work off their separate troubles. There was no sign of Caliban to break her concentration, and Jess felt an overwhelming sense of thankfulness as the game took her completely. She played better than she had in months, moving easily, angling shots precisely, serving with force and accuracy, finding that her opponent countered with such skill that it was a shock when the match was over and she had won. Ann smiled and congratulated her. "I think we both won, don't you? I haven't felt that free in a long time." Jess shook her hand and knew a bond had been formed between them, each aware that the other was troubled.

She clung to her fragile feeling of peace. While they were dressing for dinner, she even managed to say quite calmly, "Oh, it was getting too cumbersome to wear," when Sally asked about the absence of the ring. She knew Sally wondered where the ring had come from but was too polite to ask. She felt sorry for not telling her, but not enough. She had no intention of trying to explain Uncle Arthur.

They met as usual in the pub before dinner. Matches were being discussed and planned, and Rose Allenby teased Jess about heading for a quiet sweep since she was now in the singles finals, the mixed doubles semifinals, and near the top of the women's ladder. Jess knew she should feel doubly happy since Caliban was nowhere in sight, but she could not; she had become strangely dependent on the sight of him, even when he was being unpleasant. And everytime she looked at Kyre, she thought of the drawing which excluded him.

Outside the dark was coming down again. Stupid, stupid child, she accused herself, to fear the dark as though you were a five-year-old. But it didn't help matters any when Tom and Sally began discussing their plans for club-hopping after dinner, and Kyre demurred. "You'll have to count me out tonight. I'm just too tired. Sorry, Jess, we'll make it some other night."

His voice was easy, but his eyes did not meet hers, and he did look tired. She would have been safe if the two of them had gone with Sally and Tom; she might even have had a good time. She might have managed to forget Caliban and the drawing. But now Sally and Tom were going off in one direction, and heaven only knew what Kyre was up to. She did not believe he was going to his room to bed when he excused himself right after dinner while the rest of them were having coffee in one of the side rooms. Even Sally and Tom exchanged glances at his abruptness.

A new possibility occurred to Jess when she saw Elizabeth Cooper following in Kyre's wake a scant two minutes later, leaving a full cup of coffee to grow cold. Elizabeth Cooper, false to her husband in every sense? Probably. Even the ruby looked fake to Jess' jaundiced eyes. She knew she ought to be relieved that Kyre's attentions might be wandering in another direction, that her confusion about him might be ended for her, but she wasn't. It didn't fit. She had seen his look of distaste when encountering Elizabeth. Perhaps Elizabeth was acting on her own initiative, stepping up her own pursuit. Perhaps Kyre really had gone innocently back to his room. And perhaps he had excused himself so that he and Jess would not be in the company of the other couple. Perhaps he was planning to wait for her by her room. If this was a new part of the game, she wasn't going to play.

Tom and Sally were being so sweet Jess wanted to scream. They kept urging her to come with them—the three of them would have a lovely time. Tom couldn't remember when he had had the chance of taking not one, but two beauties out on the town. Three, what an ugly number, Jess thought, but she managed to be as sweetly insistent that they go by themselves. "I'm tired too, and I want to do Sally proud tomorrow in our doubles match, especially since she will probably fall asleep on the court due to your bad influence, Tom."

Her impulse was to flee to the shelter of her room as soon as they were out of sight, but she made herself stay where she was. If her guess about Kyre was correct, she wondered how long he would wait.

Quite a few of the group were still in the room having coffee and after-dinner drinks, talking and laughing. Jane and Will Crowl, David and Ellen Frieberg, Ann and Dana, and the Allenbys all offered the possibility of good conversation, and there seemed to be no exclusive grouping. As it turned out, Jess didn't have to make the effort to approach anyone. Rose Allenby, with her unerring sense of when things needed organization, had everyone grouped within speaking distance of each other within a short time and with little obvious effort.

Jess winked at her and whispered, "Good work."

"It's easy. We all have a natural herd instinct," Rose responded.

The talk turned naturally toward affairs at home, particularly the upcoming election. But that ground proved rather dangerous, with some tempers quick to rise from passionate and partisan beliefs. Jane and Will, who from the little Jess knew of them seemed as reserved and disciplined mentally as they were in their neat, ivy-league clothing, startled her with the vehemence of their political theories. And Ellen Frieberg, who was very liberal in outlook, smiled good-naturedly and reassured her husband. "All right, honey, I won't spoil your evening. I don't think I could convert many people here anyway."

Recent best-sellers and award-winning films provided safer ground, and the talk flowed smoothly and enjoyably since most of the group were well-read and cosmopolitan. Dana was the only one who had little to say and who confessed cheerfully to her ignorance. "I am on the way to becoming a complete ignoramus. I just never seem to have a spare minute. I keep thinking that as the kids get older there will be more time, but it seems to work the opposite way." She did not seem at all distressed by this, but Jess saw the look of disgust Ann sent her friend.

The conversation drifted to the subject of mutual acquaintances. Rose Allenby said innocently, "I saw Lori Smith last week. Poor dear, she's running herself ragged getting ready to move. Her husband's been transferred, you know, clear out to Los Angeles. And, of course, Lori's having to quit her job which is sad, she loves it so."

Jess wasn't paying much attention since she had only known the woman by name when she lived in Marblehead, but she became fully alert when Ann started to talk.

"Lori Smith is a very talented woman. I know she does more than half of the designing for the textile firm she works for. Why is it everyone accepts as a matter of course that she will drop everything and move three thousand miles away because her husband's company says so? Why is her job so much less important than his? Why is it always that way?" If Ann had been shouting, it would have been easier to listen, but her voice was deathly quiet and filled with despair, her restraint finally broken, hurt sounding in every word. Everyone looked stunned, and Dana gulped and began nervously, "Ann..." and got no further.

"Shut up!" Ann snapped. "Shut up unless you have some reasonable answer to give."

Jess broke the uneasy silence which followed, saying firmly, "Come on, Ann, let's go for a walk." Ann rose meekly, and Dana looked grateful. As Jess and Ann went out, they heard the voices rising behind them, nervous with relief.

Jess had no intention of wandering too far in the dark, and there was no need. There were chairs by the pool, and the place was deserted.

Ann's face was illuminated briefly as she lit a cigarette. "I'm sorry, I guess, for causing the upset in there, but I'm not even sure of that. I mean, most people just accept the status quo and are glad to do it no matter how unjust it is. Sometimes I am so angry I want other people to be angry, too."

"I know what you mean," Jess agreed thoughtfully. "Sometimes I am so outraged by the attitude—endlessly reinforced by myths and the media and by some of my best friends—that because I am a woman, I am necessarily less worthwhile as a human being, that I find it impossible to contain my anger, to use it productively. I haven't really got much of an answer yet, but I am beginning to understand that fear of various kinds but mostly fear of change is what makes people so unreceptive to new ideas about women. And the fear of a couple of those women we just left is more specific, I think. It's the fear they made the wrong decision way back when, wasted dreams and talent, and have no way to change it now.".

Ann's voice was soft but carried an unmistakable note of strength. "That's my problem. I won't believe it's too late, not for me. But I'm afraid of telling you about it, afraid you won't be able to understand my discontent. How's that for a courageous and new woman?"

"Ann, communication is hard enough without adding silence to the burden. Try me."

"All right." The cigarette glowed brightly for a moment, and she exhaled jaggedly. "I married Peter right after college, and all I wanted was him, a house full of children, and a chance to make their lives pleasant. I thought that would in turn make my life full. I've had it all for a long time. I still love my husband. I always will. I love my children, too. But my family is not enough. I've done work with some ghetto projects in Boston for years

now, and Peter thinks that's grand, as long as it is classified
as volunteer, Lady Bountiful, that sort of thing. But now I
have a chance for a full-time job, which would include
getting my master's in sociology in the process. And I
would be paid a good salary! And Jess, I'm good at the job,
I really am. I care about the people, they care about me,
and we have so much to learn together. I'm not the
answer, but I can help. And in helping, I can feel whole
again, something I haven't felt for such a long, long time."

"Why, why not then? I believe you. Why do you
hesitate?" Jess asked quietly.

"Because Peter has forbidden it. Volunteer work is
fine, the job is not. It would mean leaving early, not
returning from Boston until fairly late. He says the children need me, he needs me. He says there isn't room in
our marriage for me ar 1 my job. What he really means is
that there isn't room for two whole human beings, only for
one and a half." The dead, despairing voice again.

Jess spoke hesitantly, awed by the responsibility of
Ann's confidence. "I'm not married nor do I have children,
so I'm not in any position to advise you on that score. But
I am a woman, and I do have a career and very strong
ideas about my right to have it. Your children are not in
the toddler stage anymore, the youngest is in her teens,
isn't she?" She paused an instant for Ann's confirmation.
"Well then, it seems to me you have the same right to
grow as the children have, and that your marriage must
have room for that, or you haven't any marriage at all."
She stopped, appalled at what she'd said. She'd virtually
told Ann to give Peter a shove if he didn't let her take the
job.

Ann moved suddenly and surely in the dark to stand
near Jess for a moment. "Don't worry, you haven't said
anything I didn't know. I was just too scared. I needed to
hear someone else say it. I've got to go my own way and
hope Peter and I will still have a place to come together. I
think we will. We've loved each other for a very long time.
And I've got to ease up on Dana. She's happy in her job at
home. It's her choice, and she does it well."

Jess sat by herself for a long time after Ann had gone.

She heard noises from the road, people moving, talking softly, and once a strangely harsh series of sounds followed by what must have been the thud of running feet. She didn't care. She was absolutely drained. She could not believe she had had the temerity to advise Ann when she herself could make nothing but a muddle of her own life. She wondered where Kyre was. "To hell with that, too!" she swore as she hauled herself up. If she didn't get to bed soon, she was going to fall asleep right here. She was sure not even Kyre would have waited this long.

The road was empty when she crossed it, and she was glad. She didn't want to talk to anyone else tonight. She felt as though she were the last person on earth, and in her present mood, that suited her perfectly.

8

Do not infest your mind with beating on
The strangeness of this business: at picked leisure
Which shall be shortly, single I'll resolve you
(Which to you shall seem probable) of every
These happened accidents.

Jess fitted her key into the lock and opened the door into the blind darkness of the room. Her foot caught something which was probably Sally's racket, left on the floor in her normal rush to get ready for the next activity. She heard the alien and separate click just as she switched the light on.

The scream which should have followed her gasp of shock never came.

"If you make the slightest sound, I shall be forced to shoot you." Winston St. James' voice was calm and emotionless. He lay on the far bed, her bed, propped up with her pillows and seeming at ease save for the hand which held a short-barreled gun and the glitter of his eyes watching her through lids half-closed against the light. She noticed with curious detachment that it was his unneeded cane she had touched with her foot. She noticed quite a lot now that she had passed from tiredness into pure adrenalin-pumping terror. The curtains were closed; she and Sally had left them open. She wished she'd noticed that before she had come into the room. She also noticed that the hand holding the gun was perfectly steady, very professional-looking, as if it were announcing it knew well how to use the weapon and would be quite willing to do so.

She wondered if fainting carried the death penalty and decided not to risk it—fear had her nerves jumping so erratically that a faked faint would undoubtedly look more like an epileptic seizure. And not so long ago, she had been hungry for the sight of this man. She choked on the beginnings of hysterical laughter.

The man on the bed looked suddenly apprehensive. Shooting someone for laughing was probably a bit much even for him. The gun wavered for an instant, and Jess moved her hand swiftly. One chance to switch off the light and drop to the floor.

"Don't try it!" the voice snarled, and she dropped her hand. The gun was aimed steadily at her again. "Drop your handbag, then walk slowly around and sit on that bed, facing me."

Jess did as she was told, moving like a robot, eyes riveted on the gun. But once she was seated, she began to notice things again. Caliban's face was gray, the lines deeper than ever, sweat beaded his skin, and what might have been dirt on one cheekbone was more likely the beginning of a bruise. His clothes were dirty and stained. And he hadn't gotten up from the bed, not once. Surely even with a gun, he would want the added superiority of standing over his victim?

She decided. He was hurt and fairly badly too or else he would have gotten up. She didn't know where his injury was, but it didn't matter; any violent impact was going to hurt him enough so that he would be off guard, and she could make him drop the gun. Either that or she was going to be dead. She blanked that out of her mind and tensed her muscles, waiting.

Win's efforts at controlling her since she had entered the room had tired him. His eyes closed for an involuntary instant. It was enough. Jess launched her body with one swift motion and landed on him with a jarring impact.

His scream filled the air with tearing agony for a second before it stopped abruptly as Jess felt his body go limp. She scrambled off and stood looking down at him, shaking uncontrollably. She took the gun out of his nerveless fingers and placed it with elaborate care on the bedside table.

It had happened in such an incredibly short time, but she knew it was true. The winter sea eyes had opened in time to see what she was doing, they had understood. He had used the split second not to protect himself, but to fling his arm back, to get the gun out of the way, to keep it from going off. His finger hadn't even been on the trigger when she took the gun out of his hand; that precaution too had been taken lest the gun fire with reflex action.

His face had been gray before, now it was waxen blue as though the sun had never touched it, as graven and still as a death mask. Jess wondered if she'd killed him, but then his harsh breathing registered. He groaned softly with each breath, and his chest rose and fell unevenly. Suddenly she understood the strange noises she had heard early from the road.

She was fairly certain of what she would find even before she unbuttoned his shirt, but when she saw it, her stomach heaved. His whole left side was bruised purple black with beads of dried blood decorating it in grotesque patterns. Jess didn't believe anything less than repeated kicking or beating with a heavy weapon could have inflicted such damage. She froze into stillness for an instant, listening tensely, struck by the thought that whoever had done this might still be outside somewhere. She crossed the room and switched off the light before she opened the door. No form lurked in the dim light at the end of the porch, and the only sound was the gentle lapping of water. She had no idea what she would have done had someone been there.

She closed the door, locked it, and heard the stillness matching her own as she turned the light on again. His eyes watched her across the small space, and she could see rather than hear his carefully controlled breathing, his attempts to keep movement from his ribs. Even though he was in severe pain, she was sure he could reach the gun if he wanted to, but he did not try. Instead he made the effort to talk.

"You were...very foolish, could...have killed...you."

Without thought Jess was beside the bed, smoothing back his hair, crooning to him as though he were a small boy. "Quiet now, don't try to talk." It seemed the most natural thing in the world to be touching him, trying to ease his pain, even as it seemed natural that he had come to her, to no one else, when he was hurt.

She got a glass of water and held his head while he sipped it, and she sponged his face off gently with a cool cloth. He submitted gratefully with closed eyes, and she thought he was drifting back into unconsciousness, but he learned otherwise when she reached for the phone.

"No!" he rasped, and she hesitated, protesting, "But you're badly hurt, more so because of me. I don't care what you've done or who you're running from. I've got to help. I don't want you to die." She almost added "here," thinking of all the trouble he had caused her, but she refrained.

He heard the unspoken word anyway because a faint smile lightened his face before it settled back into the grim lines of painful explaining. "No one must...know...here. Be all right...in a bit. Trust...won't hurt you." His face was twisted in agony, his breathing was reduced to sharp gasps. Jess stared at him in amazement. "Nothing can be worse than dying, you fool! You can't even breathe!"

"Strap."

Jess went blank for a moment until comprehension dawned. Strapping, of course, that's about all one could do for broken ribs unless something vital had been punctured and needed repairing. But you had to have the tape, and you had to know what you were doing.

She shook her head. "You must be crazy. I haven't the slightest idea of how to do it, even if I had the equipment. And I am not at all resourceful," she added firmly.

The smile ghosted across his face once more. "Too bloody...resourceful." His eyes closed again.

Jess felt as though her mind were staging a full-blown stampede, and it was a physical effort to slow it down enough to sort the thoughts out one by one. The man was dangerous and involved with dangerous people and undoubtedly illegal dealings—drugs, the white slave trade, gun-running, all sorts of possibilities presented themselves. Traylee and Connor were involved too and had probably been the ones who had beaten him up. Win, the boss man? She remembered Traylee's words overheard on the first night so why hadn't the others, "they," protected their top man?

The sensible thing to do was to get in touch with the authorities immediately. But could the authorities protect her, would they believe she was not involved in spite of the fact the man had sought shelter in her room, in spite of the words she would have to confess to having overheard and left unreported? She was angry at having been drawn into the whole mess. She tried to sustain it to make her decision easier, but she could not deny that she was feeling something even stronger than her desire to protect herself. The man had come to her for help, and he was badly in need of it, criminal or not. And she wanted to help, felt compelled to help. He looked so vulnerable lying there, but his power over her was still as great as if he were spinning a great web around her. She told herself any kind of commitment was better than none, but she knew the plan which had flashed into her mind would probably make her an accessory to a crime if not worse. She wondered if Uncle Arthur had the power to get her out of a Bermuda jail. She wondered if he would if he could.

She made her voice harsh and firm. "Mr. St. James, Win, whoever you are, I'm going to get Dr. Cranston. He's part of our group." He started to protest, and she snapped, "Shut up! It's the best I can do. I'll get him here with some story, and you'll just have to trust his professional oath to keep your nasty secrets. And if you're gone when I get back, I'll blow the whistle and report I saw you, that you were hurt, and then you can explain your way out of that by yourself."

She heard him whisper "Resourceful," as she switched the light off and slipped out, locking the door behind her. It couldn't be midnight yet, and she prayed Sally and Tom would stay out for hours. If Sally checked in now, it was all over. But there was no alternative and no use in fretting about it.

She stood in the shadows by the door for a moment before she crossed beneath the porch light and into darkness again, but the sea made the only sound besides her footsteps.

She thanked God she knew which room was the Cranstons'; breaking and entering the office in the manor house to find the listing of the rooms would have been too much.

The Cranstons were staying in a room two buildings down the road, not far to go, Jess assured herself. But once on the road, she checked in terror. Though the manor looked bleak and deserted with only one faint light glowing in the lobby, there were scurryings and rustlings in the bushes all around her, and she thought she could hear the crunch of careful footsteps on the gravel. She felt a thousand pairs of eyes watching her, and her knees went weak so suddenly that she nearly pitched forward on the road. "Jess, walk, one foot at a time, no choice," she commanded herself. Her movements were jerky and puppetlike, but at least she was moving again.

She passed the first building and was crossing the dark space in between when there was a slight sound behind her. The hiss of her name, a hand covered her mouth before she could scream, and her blood roared in her ears, delaying her recognition of the insistent, supplicating voice. "Please, if I take my hand away you will be quiet? It's Traylee. I won't harm you."

His grip on her eased, and she nodded slightly. He took his hand away from her mouth, and she turned to face him. Now that her senses were beginning to function again, she could smell it, the scent of fear from both of them. She felt the same rush of protectiveness she had from the first sight of Traylee, Traylee forever resolute in the face of his terror.

She could barely see him in the shadows, but she could hear the swift race of his breathing. "This is getting to be a habit. Why?" she whispered.

He answered with a question of his own. "You have the man?"

She knew she might be endangering Win even further, but she could not relinquish her trust in Traylee. "Yes. Did Connor do it to him or did you?"

His voice was sharp and impatient. "No, not his style, or mine either, no matter what the man is, to go hitting him from behind and beating on him while he's down. Head on, fair fight is Connor's way, my way. The man, what are you going to do about him, is he going to be all right?"

She explained her errand briefly, and Traylee was silent for a moment. Then he said, "It's got to be. You're safe for now. You go along. I'll watch for you."

Nothing made any sense. Traylee didn't like Win, but he was relieved he would be all right, and he had seen the incident, but neither he nor Connor had done it. She opened her mouth to ask for an explanation, but he sensed it before she spoke. "No, nothing to tell. Hurry up now. Don't waste time." Young as he was, younger than she, his voice carried authority, and she obeyed, looking back only once and seeing nothing but darkness behind her.

Though a porch light illuminated the door, the lights were out in the Cranstons' room, and Jess hated herself for being willing to involve the doctor, but she knocked softly anyway, hoping no one in the rest of the building would hear. She heard movement, and then the doctor's muted voice asking who was there. He was obviously trying not to wake Millie, and Jess kept her own voice down, "Please, it's Jess Banbridge. I need your help."

The door opened immediately, revealing the doctor in his robe, his expression already fully alert from long years of night calls.

Jess tried her lie. "Sally, my roommate, slipped on the stairs and I think her ankle is badly sprained and needs taping. I'm sorry to bother you, but could you come look at it?"

The young eyes in the old face regarded her intently, and Jess knew he didn't believe one word of what she said. She swallowed hard and knew panic was showing in her own eyes. The doctor touched her gently on the shoulder. "Just a moment, I'll get my bag. Don't worry about Millie. She won't wake up. She's exhausted from trying to keep up with you youngsters."

He found his black bag unerringly in the dark and was back in an instant. Jess blessed him silently for a true healer, for knowing that while she lied, her need for him was genuine.

They walked in silence, and Jess was comforted by the knowledge that Traylee stood guard, though by no sign did he betray his presence.

When they were inside her room, and Jess switched on the light, all Dr. Cranston said was, "Sally has changed a good deal since I saw her at dinner."

Win lay as Jess had left him, and it seemed an effort for him even to open his eyes, but the gun was nowhere in sight. Dr. Cranston's levity was quickly replaced by grave kindness as he got a better look at his patient. Jess told him that besides the ribs, Win had gotten a crack on the head and God only knew what else. Win's eyes widened and regarded her intently when she said that, but she ignored his look; she'd be damned before she'd tell him the information about his head injury had come from Traylee.

Dr. Cranston's preliminary examination was brief and efficient; he listened to Win's heart, took his pulse, and checked his eye reflexes. "I'll know more later, but your pupils are responding normally to light, so you haven't injured the optic nerve. Can you hear clearly, noises not too loud, too soft, or full of buzzes?"

"I can . . . hear perfectly. It's . . . these . . . hellish ribs."

Jess winced at the labored speech, and Dr. Cranston nodded. "You know you should be in a hospital for proper treatment, but I presume that it is my care or none, or else Jess wouldn't have come for me. You aren't bleeding from the mouth which is a good sign, but only X rays can tell for sure whether or not you've got internal injuries. I'm no doubt every kind of fool, but I can't leave you like this, goes against my grain, so I'll do the taping job. I've got the equipment for that—sprains and strains are com-

mon on these tennis trips—but I don't carry any narcotics
when I travel, too easy to have them stolen, so I can't help
you there."

Win nodded once, and then closed his eyes as the
doctor's hands began to explore his injured side. Jess saw
his jaw clench, and sweat gleamed suddenly on his contorted face. She reached out instinctively to stroke his
cheek, to comfort him.

Her own breath rattled out in unison with Win's
when Dr. Cranston quit probing. The doctor's voice was
sharp with unconcealed anger. "They did a good job on
you all right. There are at least three ribs fractured and
probably more." He was too angry to pretend that anything other than human maliciousness could have caused
what he had just discovered. After seeing Win in so much
pain, Jess shared the doctor's disgust. No matter what Win
had done, there were laws to deal with every crime, and
there was no justice in beating a man bloody.

The next half hour of assisting Dr. Cranston convinced Jess that she had been correct in rejecting the idea
of a career in medicine at an early age. She was so
appalled at Win's suffering, only sheer will power enabled
her to follow the doctor's instructions instead of fleeing the
room. Worst of all was getting the patient from a prone to
a sitting position so that the tape could be run about his
rib cage. Win's one sharp cry and a mumbled "Sorry"
during the process left Jess so blind with tears that the
doctor said, "One patient is all I can handle," but his tone
was compassionate.

Once the surface wounds had been bathed and treated
and the ribs were firmly bound, however, the transformation was amazing. Though still pale, Win's face was no
longer pulled and rigid, and though he spoke carefully, his
voice and breathing were close to normal again. He breathed
a small sigh of relief. "I am indeed deeply grateful, doctor.
I promise you won't suffer for having helped me."

Jess felt a rush of jealousy and was ashamed of it, but
it was as though the two men had exchanged some kind of
bond which excluded her even after all of the trouble
she'd gone to for the Englishman. And it got worse after

Dr. Cranston had inspected the lump on the back of Win's head and pronounced it a tender nuisance but not likely to be lethal.

The doctor then turned to Jess and said in a brisk, professional manner, "I would appreciate it if you would be a good girl and give me a few minutes alone with my patient. I want to check for injury in other vital areas."

It was a reasonable request on the surface, but Jess suspected angrily that other than a brief examination, the time would be spent by Win taking Dr. Cranston into his confidence, or more likely into his confidence game. And she wasn't going to be told anything at all. She started for the door with her back ramrod-straight to register the insult, but Win stopped her. "Not outside," he ordered, "go into the loo, close the door, and keep the water running."

She whirled around, prepared to tell him exactly what she thought of him—he wasn't even bothering to pretend, demanding running water so she wouldn't hear a single word—but a strangely urgent look in his eyes took some of the sting out of his words. And she admitted privately that she didn't really want to be outside, even just outside the door. Her terrifying walk had been enough for one night. She shrugged and with as much dignity as she could muster, obeyed his command.

Once in the bathroom she wished they had sent her outside after all where she wouldn't have had to see her reflection. The mirror showed her a smudged face framed by long tendrils of hair which had escaped from the smoothly pinned wrap of early evening. "I am definitely not cut out for this sort of work," Jess told her image and proceeded to do more than follow orders. She scrubbed her face hard and let her hair down, brushing it until it fell in a smooth black curtain. The water sound prevented so much as a murmur from filtering in from the bedroom.

She was considering a shower to pass the time if they didn't let her out soon when Dr. Cranston knocked and told her the coast was clear. Both men stared so intently at her that Jess blushed.

"You look like an eight-year-old scrubbed and ready

for bed," the doctor teased. But then his face sobered as he picked up his bag and headed for the door. "Though I think all things considered, my patient will do well enough, I would prefer that someone stay with him tonight. It is always the wisest course in cases of head injuries and possible internal bleeding. However, Mr. St. James has refused my services. Perhaps you will have better luck. You would be quite safe with him," he added with a twinkle in his eye, "if he got fresh, all you would have to do is thump him in the ribs."

"I think I could do that," Jess said and heard Win snort.

Jess followed the doctor to the door, and before he left, he spoke so softly to her that Win could not hear. "I'm torn between concern for my patient and care for you. I hesitated to ask you to care for him any further. He is a dangerous man pursuing a dangerous course. It would be best to disentangle yourself as soon as possible."

"Thank you for everything, Dr. Cranston, and I'll take your advice, you can be sure." The doctor's words only confirmed her own thoughts, but she found she was dismayed when she turned to see Win standing, obviously ready to depart.

"No. You'll stay here until sunrise." It was rather nice to be giving him orders.

"Just how are you going to manage that? I believe you have another girl staying with you." He was wickedly pleased with her dilemma.

"Wipe that insufferably satisfied expression off your face!" she snapped. "I'll think of something, and I won't let you leave. I'll scream the place down if you try." She thought of going to his room with him but discarded the idea quickly. She did not want to go outside again, and if his attackers were waiting anywhere, his room or nearby it would seem most likely.

Win swayed slightly, and his face was still very pale.

"Do sit down," Jess said, and he did. She guessed he was feeling too shaky to argue much more. "I've got a plan," she announced. She marched into the closet, thankful it was a walk-in, which provided some privacy. When she came out, she was wearing her long, filmy blue nightgown made barely decent by its matching robe.

Win looked dazed. "Is that part of the plan?"

"Yes. When Sally comes, I'm going to commit moral suicide," Jess said pleasantly. The whole night had been so crazy that one more mad act seemed perfectly in order.

Win's voice was suddenly soft and hesitant, completely changed from the one which barked one command after the other. "Miss Banbridge . . . I—"

"Jess, for heaven's sake, we're sharing a bedroom."

"All right, Jess then, Jess again. I am grateful beyond words for all of your help, and I apologize for involving you, but I am at a loss to understand why you are willing to go to such extremes to protect me, especially after our . . . uh, unfortunate encounters."

Another time, another place. She recognized the feeling which had been growing all night, perhaps even longer than that, perhaps a hidden seed planted even at the moment of her first meeting with this man. It was twin to the one she had felt for Sean through much of their childhood, a fierce protectiveness which had made her stronger and more resolute than she was otherwise. Though Sean had been two years older than she, he had been small and frail until his thirteenth year had started a remarkable period of growth which left him tall and well-built by sixteen. She, on the other hand, had been taller and stronger than most of the other children all the way through grammar school, and in spite of constant admonitions that ladies never used their hands for violence, she had done so repeatedly in Sean's defense. She could not bear for anyone to pick on him, an easy target because of his smallness, and few tried it once they found Sean's sister would and could give them a black eye or a bloody nose without hesitation. Sean had claimed he had finally triggered his own growth on purpose because it was embarrassing to be defended by his sister. Oh, Sean, your sister needs you now. She saw the spirit's face, Ariel's face of the drawing, Sean's face, and she was not comforted.

She had been so far away, she had not even seen Win get up, and she jumped when he touched her. His hands rested lightly on her shoulders as he stood looking down at her, and his voice was husky with concern. "You look so sad. I'm dreadfully sorry for whatever I said to cause it. Can I help?"

Jess swallowed hard and backed away from him. His hands dropped from her shoulders instantly, and she spoke quickly to cover her rudeness, and more, she knew, because she did not want to see the ice return.

"Honestly, I'm fine now. Everybody has them, I think, old, long ago ghosts that come back to haunt sometimes."

"Yes, everybody has them," he agreed, and she saw he really did understand. She wondered about his ghosts. She wondered a thousand things about him, things she would never have wondered about Kyre.

"Please, would you lie down? I'd feel so much better if you were resting."

"So would I," he said with a weary grin.

He lay down on her bed, and his eyes closed instantly. She herself was beginning to feel lightheaded with fatigue; she could hardly imagine how he felt. She slanted the bedside light so it would not shine on him, turned off the overhead light, and settled down on the other bed to wait for Sally. She checked the time. It was one-thirty, and Sally and Tom would probably be home within the next half hour or so. She set the alarm for five-thirty, deciding that would be early enough to get Win up and out before anyone saw him.

The minutes ticked by slowly, and Jess strained to hear footsteps on the walk. She heard the constant lap of water and the occasional soft moans from Win when he moved too abruptly in his sleep. She was too confused to think clearly about anything save what she would say to Sally. She kept rehearsing various lines silently, realizing that any way she said it, it was going to shock her friend.

She heard them approaching finally. She switched off the light and stood at the door, heart pounding so loudly, it was difficult to hear the slow steps, the muted whispers. But it was easier once they were right outside enjoying their usual long pause. Jess wasn't even ashamed to be eavesdropping; all she could think about was her hope that Tom would follow his customary procedure and leave Sally at the door in deference to her roommate.

She heard the final good-night, the last kiss, Tom's footsteps departing, Sally's key in the lock. She didn't want to scare her to death, so she called her name softly but distinctly before she opened the door from her side.

They couldn't see each other clearly in the shadows, but she heard Sally's puzzled asking of her name, "Jaybe?" and she answered with a rush. "I'll explain when I can, I promise. I know it's awful to ask, but just for tonight, could you find somewhere else to sleep, maybe with Dana and Ann? They've got that couch in their room."

Dark as it was, Sally could see enough. "Jaybe, are you crazy, standing there in your nightgown, asking me to sleep somewhere else? What's going on?"

Jess took a deep breath and blurted out the words. "I've got a man staying with me. Please, could I have the room just for tonight?"

After one incredulous gasp, Sally said nothing for a moment, and when she did speak, her voice carried no censure, just exquisite care not to say the wrong thing in spite of being stunned. "I guess I could go stay with the girls, though I don't know what I'll tell them. I could go be a fallen woman and stay with Tom, or you could give me Kyre's key and I'll go stay in his room since he's here." Sweet Sally, trying to be matter of fact about it. Woman of the world she will never be, Sean.

Jess said gently, "No, that wouldn't work. I presume Kyre is sleeping peacefully in his room. He isn't here. If you don't want to bother Tom, go next door. Ann and Dana are grown women; just tell them the truth." The truth as it seems, not as it is, she added grimly to herself.

Sally lost her composure completely at the news and stammered, "Not, not Kyre? Oh, Jaybe, are you all right, do you know what you're doing?"

She sounded as if she were going to burst into tears, and Jess made her own voice brusque. "I know exactly what I'm doing. I won't get hurt. This old girl has just decided to take a real vacation. The room will be clear again a little after six, okay?"

Sally made a poor attempt to match Jess' coolness. "Sure, that'll be fine. I'll see you then. Well . . . good night."

Jess shut the door and locked it because she could not bear to face Sally for another second. Even without the light, she had a clear picture of her standing there looking forlorn and worried. She choked back a sob convulsively; hurting Sally was the worst thing she could think of.

Win's voice touched her. "Oh, my poor dear." She heard the bed creak, and she found her way to him in the darkness, not wanting him to see her face, saying in a strangled voice, "Don't get up again. You've got so little time to rest before morning."

She didn't know whether she had gone of her own accord or if he had pulled her down, but she found herself half kneeling, half on the bed, impossibly comfortable for so awkward a position, with her head nestled against his shoulder, his arm around her. His other hand ruffled her hair.

"Good friends forgive anything, and I'll explain as soon as I can so she will have nothing to forgive." His lips found her mouth and kissed her gently. She felt warm and content, and. . . . She sprang up suddenly, out of his reach, eyes wide and blind. What was she doing? Only the night before she had been kissing Kyre. Whatever Sally thought about her was justified.

"Your ribs," she croaked and hated herself for making an excuse.

His voice was lazy, intimate. "They were doing quite nicely, thank you."

She wanted to break the spell between them; she wanted distance, and she could handle him better when he was on the defensive. "You explained why and how all this happened to Dr. Cranston, I know you did. So why not me?"

She succeeded all too well. His words were frozen, clipped into precise English. "Because he is a physician and bound by oath to respect the confidences of his patients. You, on the other hand, are a woman, and there is no oath on earth I know of to keep you quiet."

"Why, you arrogant bastard! You don't mind fondling one now and then, but you don't really like women at all, do you?" Jess was so angry she was trembling, but a small voice in the back of her mind was telling her the fault was nonexistent, that Win had not really done anything save to offer comfort.

"No. I do not like women very much, Miss Banbridge." His voice was weary and hurt. Jess knew she had heard that; she would have liked to pretend it was something else, but she could not.

"Why?" she asked softly, and his hesitation told her she had caught him off guard.

"My wife. Reason enough. Margaret has red hair and slanting green eyes. She has white skin and a small perfectly made body. It should hardly seem significant that she has no heart. She does not even love herself. She uses herself mercilessly to acquire men and possessions, though I doubt she enjoys either. The worst of it is, she is not so different from other women. And now, good night."

"Good night." Jess' response was barely audible. She suddenly knew a great deal. She knew he had meant to be cutting, to warn her away because he was as drawn to her as she to him and felt as powerless against it. And she knew his lapse into gentleness had been just that, a lapse he regretted. *Wife* was a raw, savage word in his mouth, a four-letter obscenity. She doubted very much that Winston St. James knew how much more anguish than anger he had expressed in his description of Margaret. Jess hated the woman with a force which left her breathless.

Uncle Arthur, she said in her mind, *this much I know, a married man and a woman hater besides is no part of your plan for me and no part of my plan.* She shut the drawing from her mind. She felt as if she had gotten tangled with an octopus, one tentacle after another pulling her toward a dark, consuming maw. She shivered though the room was warm. The more she thought about Winston St. James, the more dangerous she realized he was. She was sure he had not been attacked in the room since nothing was out of place, and his whole reason for coming had been to seek aid after he had been hurt. Yet, even in his battered condition, he had remembered to bring along the cane, the prop needed to sustain the lie in case someone saw him. And he had either obtained a passkey or he was adept at picking locks, for her door had been locked when she had used her key. And he had known she would return first, had known Sally was out with Tom and would be late—she was sure he had known. And he had a gun which he knew how to use. How had he kept that in the scuffle? His attention to details was awesome and ominous, the mark of a cold-blooded man long used to subterfuge. The warmth of his kiss flooded through her as though his mouth were still on hers, and her mind spun with the contradictions—sun and ice, good and evil, promise and threat, two faces in the drawing, one man in the flesh. She could not wait for the alarm to go off, to get him out of her room and her life.

She didn't think she would get any sleep at all, yet when the shrill bell sounded, she surfaced with a start from fathoms under. Win's eyes were already wide awake and alert when she turned the light on. He drew his body stiffly to a sitting position and started to get up, but Jess forestalled him. "Wait a minute, we've got time. I must be crazy, just like Sally said, I want to see this thing safely through. But not in this outfit. It'll only take me a minute to dress."

He shook his head in bewilderment, but it was no greater than her own. She couldn't for the life of her understand why she thought she still had to protect him when the best thing for her would be to have him gone. She put it down to her basic stubbornness which made her see a job through, even a bad one, like Larry's books— what a lifetime ago. She did not want to consider the hunger rising in her, making her ache for Win's touch, his kiss of the night before.

"I doubt very much there will be any more trouble. If they had wanted to kill me, they could have done so. They didn't even take my revolver. It was a warning, nothing more." One harsh warning, thought Jess, and for what, but she kept silent.

"But in the odd event something did happen on the way to my room, what could you possibly do about it?" he asked.

"Scream, kick, be a vocal witness, learn instant karate, the options are endless," Jess said on her way to the closet. A moment later she heard the door shut and raced after him, still buttoning her shirt.

"Would have served you right if I'd run after you stark naked," she scolded when she caught up with him on the stairs.

"It would have given me great pleasure," he corrected dryly. "You are a most persistent person."

He was using the cane again, in case anyone was watching, and Jess glanced around fearfully but saw no one. The world was caught in the eerie blue gray light of dawn beginning, faint rose streaks crossing the sky. The air was a cool blend of sea and growing things, and birds chirped sleepily in the lush undergrowth. It was impossible for Jess to reconcile the image of this peaceful paradise with purple black bruises, broken bones, and a gun.

Win's quarters in the manor had an outside staircase leading up to the balcony—even shareholders in the business needed privacy. Shareholder, indeed, Jess thought. She stopped at the foot of the stairs and watched him walk up slowly, cane tapping a steady lie, but body in truth tired and sore. He stopped midway and looked down at her, his face unreadable. She expected him to thank her again, an unnecessary exercise, but instead he said slowly and so softly she wasn't sure she'd caught the words correctly, "It just might be true."

She watched him out of sight and still she waited, and he returned to the top of the stairs. "I'm safe. There is no reception waiting." A rueful smile paid her tribute, and his disquieting eyes saw everything about her and were still warmer than the first sun breaking. He turned and disappeared.

Jess was so tired and so confused, she closed her eyes and wondered how she could ever get through a day which included tennis matches, not to mention just staying awake.

No sound warned her, but she knew she was being watched. She whirled around and nearly cried aloud in dismay. There, standing on the path which led from the back of the manor to the road, was Sally, face white, eyes wide in disbelief.

Sally made the first move. She came toward Jess and when she was close, she stopped. "Oh, God, Jaybe, Caliban? I thought you couldn't stand him."

"It's not what you think, I swear it's not, but I can't explain now."

Sally moved suddenly and hugged Jess, saying fiercely, "I don't care what you do as long as you're happy! I don't make moral judgments about people as long as they're not hurting anyone. I don't have any right to judge, no one has, but I think you're getting into a terrible mess and hurting yourself besides. That's what I can't bear!"

Jess' words were choked. "No wonder Sean loved you so! But don't worry, please don't. I'm not in trouble, and I won't be."

She stepped back and looked at Sally closely. "Where did you sleep, by the way? You look as if you chose a vegetable patch and not a very comfortable one."

The color rose in Sally's fair skin. "I just couldn't go bearing tales to Ann and Dana, I couldn't. So I slept by the pool, on one of those fold-up things."

Jess hugged her tightly again. "Sally, I can't comprehend your kind of gentleness, but I love you for it. Thank you a thousand times. And a great pair of players we're going to be on the courts today," she added, her gaiety forced but more than welcome to both of them. Sally did not even ask why Jess and Win had not used Win's room.

9

You have often
Begun to tell me what I am; but stopped
And left me to bootless inquisition,
Concluding, "Stay: not yet."

In spite of a cold shower and prebreakfast coffee begged from the kitchen, Jess could not shake her numb feeling of exhaustion. She knew it was as much emotional fatigue as physical, but knowing didn't help. She felt once removed from everything around her, as though she were operating on a separate plane, observing everyone else under glass. She kept missing the point of the chatter at the table, but when Kyre joined them, her attention sharpened. She had to know; she couldn't wait any longer. She wished she'd asked the question long ago. She was wondering how to broach the subject when Sally did it for her, describing how she and Tom had ended up at the same table at the discotheque the night before with people they knew from home. "Small world, trite but true," Sally finished.

Jess kept her voice very even. "I think that's happened at least once on every trip I've taken, started right out with it on this one, seeing Sally again. It just occurred to me, Kyre, that we might have a mutual acquaintance. Do you happen to know Arthur Barton? He's in the same business you are."

He thought a moment before he answered, and when he did, Jess knew he was telling the truth. "No, can't say I

125

do. But then, we're not overly friendly in my business; a good buy is best kept a secret."

"Of course," Jess murmured and wondered if everyone could hear the pounding of her heart. It was too random. Uncle Arthur had nothing to do with this man; the drawing had been accurate in that. Was it also accurate in making Winston St. James both hero and villain?

Oh, Sean, what have I gotten myself into? She dropped her eyes, not wanting anyone to see her sudden panic. She fiddled with her silverware and let the conversation pass over her. And then her eyes focused with chilling clarity on Kyre's hand as he picked up his coffee cup. The knuckles were bruised, the skin broken here and there.

"Kyre, what ever did you do to your hand?" she asked and was amazed by her steady voice.

Something gleamed in his eyes and was gone in an instant, but Jess knew she had seen it—a tiny vicious flicker like the flame in a snake's eyes before he strikes. Nothing like the clean power of a hunting hawk. The excuses she had made for her unease about him, how thin they had been. She knew now that Arthur would never have had anything to do with this man, and Sean would have loathed him.

Kyre looked at his hand in seeming surprise and shrugged. "Clumsy of me. I barked it on the wall when I was going back to my room last night, but I didn't know I'd hit it so hard."

Jess hoped her smiled looked sympathetic. Her body was so cold and rigid that she couldn't even be sure she was smiling at all. "Poor hand, I hope it can still hold a tennis racket," she murmured and saw in his relieved expression that he thought she believed him. But her mind was ticking furiously now. Kyre had no idea she had seen Win's injuries, surely he had no idea or he would know she did not believe his explanation. But she was absolutely sure the hand had been injured while it was slamming into Win's body. Her stomach lurched at the memory of the purple and broken flesh, the bruise on Win's face.

There was no protection for her now. Both of the men were involved; they were enemies to each other, and she was in the dreaded middle place. A tidal wave of anger rose and swept over her. She was tired of being threatened; she was tired of being drawn ever deeper into something she knew nothing about; she was tired of being a victim, especially such an ignorant one. There had to be a way to find out what was going on—clues left somewhere, a chance she might pry some information out of Traylee if she could just find him again. The stakes must be very high to provoke so much violence, and that meant there had to be a tangible, precious substance hidden somewhere. She wondered if she had chanced on the middle of a gang war. She had heard of such things, one group of criminals battling to take over another's territory. It happened quite frequently in Boston. There were so many people working against each other here, it was a possibility. And Win had said his injuries came from trespassing.

Arthur's plan—it had happened before, a sorcerer who planned a dream and conjured a nightmare. More often, the sorcerer's first intention was nightmare, and dreams were never mentioned. She came to with a start. Sally was saying, "She's often like this before a match. It's a good thing; it means she'll play like the devil as my partner this morning." Sally chattering brightly, covering what she thought were Jess' brooding regrets for a night spent with Caliban.

"Well, I'd sure prefer her to be on my side and not my opponent's when she's wearing that grim expression," Kyre teased, but there was nothing humorous about his watchful expression. *Careful, careful, Jess,* she cautioned herself, *everything is changed now, and that he must not know.* She wished she possessed the pure innocence of Miranda discovering one wonder after another to please her eye. She hoped she could play the part as well for Kyre as she had for the college audience. She managed to say, "I've been running through the whole match in my head, and if the other three players will just do as I wish, Sally included, we'll win."

She was relieved of the pressure of Kyre's regard by the advent of Ann and Dana who stopped to say good morning. "Those will be our last friendly words until the match is over," Ann warned, and Jess returned her smile. Ann looked so much more relaxed, so much happier, Jess felt there at least she had accomplished something positive. Behind them she saw Elizabeth Cooper come through the door, looking cool and elegant in a white linen sheath dress with a gold pendant hanging between her breasts, and she thought with a new, cold cynicism that if Kyre had had time to be with the woman, it must have been a short time with all the other things he had been up to in the night.

Elizabeth felt her gaze and nodded briefly, and Jess turned away. But the image of the gold pendant remained, and she was puzzled, wondering why it seemed so significant. Then she knew. It reminded her of the ruby which, even disliking its owner as she did, she coveted. She was startled by the feeling—how awful to want something so extravagant, so beyond her means. But she hadn't wanted it last night; it had looked cheap and flashy. Because it was, her mind said distinctly. She was sure. It had not been her confusion regarding Kyre's motives which had made the stone look different. Her eye for color, line, and light was too highly trained to be so deceived. The stone had looked different because it was not the genuine blood and fire flashing ruby she had first seen. A precious substance indeed. Her mind reeled. The night prowlers, the violence, all for that ruby? No, for the ruby and other like gems. And well-plotted stealing it was too, to have a stone to substitute in the setting. When, how had it been done?

Her reverie was broken by Sally nudging her and saying in exasperation, "Honestly, you have gone too far into your victory-think. That page is for you. One of your admirers is calling long distance. Get going!"

Jess heard her name distinctly this time, and she saw Kyre's speculative look as she left the table. Overseas call, of course, anywhere from here would be overseas, but which way? It had to be one of two people—Uncle Arthur from England, or perish the thought, Larry Foreman from home.

The telephone system at the Queen's Gate was antiquated and minimal; there was no privacy beyond the desk clerk's polite withdrawal into the back business office, a move which tickled Jess since the phone itself rested on the ledge with the guest register, and she had to stand in the lobby to use it. She was thankful the room was empty. If the caller was Larry, she might embarrass eavesdroppers.

Her fears were groundless. As soon as she heard the operator and identified herself, Uncle Arthur's words reached her with great clarity. "Jessica, my dear, are you all right?" His voice was more urgent than she had ever heard it, as though he fully expected her not to be all right. She shivered; perhaps he truly was a sorcerer, perhaps he had seen everything of last night's encounter with Win. Win, not "Caliban" or the "Englishman." Just Win, gentle hands, gentle mouth, warm eyes. Just Win.

She was so confused that her voice crackled angrily over the wire. "Of course I'm all right! Why shouldn't I be, I'm in Paradise, aren't I? Tennis, sun, and lotus-eating, what could be wrong with that? You'll get a postcard soon confirming it officially."

He hesitated, and when he did speak, he did not sound convinced. "What are the people like whom you've met? Are they all Americans? Have you met people outside of your group?"

You are doing this very badly, Uncle Arthur, circling around what you know to be the truth with ponderous footsteps. She took a perverse pleasure in pretending not to understand. "Uncle Arthur, really, I'm a big girl. I can take care of myself." Except with people who prowl at night, beating each other up, using guns, and stealing things. She went on, hoping the quaver in her voice would sound like suppressed laughter. "I've only met a couple of people besides the members of our tour. We're good traveling companions, and we don't need much help from outsiders to have fun."

She was sorry for her flippancy as soon as she heard

Arthur's response. He sounded old, tired, worried. "Jessica, I can tell by your voice you are not telling me everything. I am at this moment condemning myself for being a meddling old man who had an exaggerated idea of his power. When I arranged for your trip to Bermuda, I was quite sure I was giving you nothing more than the possibility of good changes in your life. I find, however, there is a small, but to me frightening, chance that I may have put you in some danger. I am not at liberty to explain my reasons, but I beg of you to take care, to cease wearing the ring, and to leave the tour and fly home immediately if you feel anything is amiss, if you feel in any way threatened."

Jess blinked back tears. He did meddle, but the sound of his voice made her believe again that it was only for her benefit, save things had gotten out of his control. Nightmare, not dream. She had the chance now to tell him that, whether he still wanted it or not, his spell was moving to completion. Instead she said, "Don't worry, please don't. I will follow your instructions, I promise, but I am so surrounded by members of the group. I can't be anything but safe." Why not add another lie for his benefit? He had not seen the drawing: he knew nothing of the strange working of her mind. "Perhaps I'll meet the Prince here if I keep looking. Princes are, after all, difficult but not impossible to find."

He was not amused. "The play is over. I set it in the wrong place at the wrong time. Keep yourself to yourself and go home unharmed." There was another pause, and then he asked, as though fearful of the answer, "In this tell me the truth. You have not met and you are not involved with an Englishman?"

"No. Why in the world are you asking that?" The final lie, and the final confirmation.

He did not explain. His voice held a strange note she could not interpret, though relief seemed uppermost. "Then I will trust all is well. Good-bye, my dear Jessica. I will see you soon in America."

"Good-bye and thank you, Uncle Arthur." The connection was broken, leaving Jess gripping the phone and feeling a wave of lonesomeness for the old man, for the time of trust and truth between them, the time before. But her sadness changed swiftly to frustration. There hadn't really ever been full trust or truth between them. Arthur had never told her his plan. And his call had been as cryptic as everything else. He had not told her what he knew; he had asked the questions, answered none. He had no way of knowing her knowledge was for once ahead of his. And something else had changed, too; he had not been Uncle Arthur doing things his way; he had been more like Arthur bound and gagged, unable to give his reasons because they were no longer his own. A spell gone wrong.

"I feel as though the whole world is involved, and no one will let me in on the secret. I am becoming a complete paranoid," she said grimly as she hung up the phone.

"Do you often talk to yourself?" His voice was solicitous, but his eyes were not when she swung around to face him. The carpet had muffled the tap on his cane. His eyes were narrowed, speculative, searching her face, glancing once in warning toward the desk clerk who had reemerged, silencing the angry words Jess would have spoken.

Instead, she spoke with the same deceptive kindness he had used. "I always talk to myself when I need some agreeable conversation, Wi . . . Mr. St. James. But usually not with an audience. It puts people off. I didn't hear you come in. You ought to have a bell on your cane for when you cross carpets," she added sweetly, malice getting the best of her. She heard the clerk's outraged gasp, but Win's chuckle of amusement was genuine. "Touché," he said. "Would you do me the honor of going for a walk in the garden?"

The stilted, archaic language of politeness to cover a command. Jess looked at him sharply. He was impeccably dressed, but she could picture him without his shirt, his side battered under the careful taping job Dr. Cranston had done. Leaning with seeming negligence on his cane, he was giving as good an impression of a carefree man out for a little flirtation as his dour face would allow. But his

eyes betrayed him; beyond the intentness of the hunter,
the strain showed—weariness and pain underscored by
dark circles and by the bruise on his cheekbone. He had
covered it with something, but because Jess knew it was
there, she could see it like a faint birthmark. Her refusal
died unuttered. "A walk would be lovely, though I've got a
match to play soon," she said loudly enough for the clerk
to hear and then added very softly, "You need a better
makeup man."

"You're just jealous because I am a natural beauty," he
whispered back as they left the lobby. Jess glanced at him
quickly and away again. His moments of amusement,
those brief intervals when his face lost its tenseness and
relaxed, unnerved her, the change was so complete, the
years dropped away so suddenly, and her urge to protect
him rose to the bait. But even criminals must relax
sometimes, she reminded herself.

He led the way to a shaded bench and surveyed the
area carefully before he said anything. They were out of
sight of the downstairs pub entrance, and Jess knew this
was on purpose, like everything else he did.

Very quietly, Jess asked her morning's question for
the second time. "Do you know Arthur Barton?"

Just as quietly Winston St. James answered, "Yes, I
know him. I know him all too well. I believe I heard you
call him 'Uncle Arthur' on the telephone. He is in fact my
uncle, and I know you and I are not first cousins."

Jess stared at him incredulously, trying to find some
likeness. Perhaps stripped down by ages, his face would
have the same aristocratic arrogance of bone which Arthur's
had, but it certainly wasn't evident yet, and there was a
basic difference in the faces aside from features. Arthur's
face was so peaceful, so happy and at ease, while Win's
was bitter with only brief, partial flashes of joy. Then she
remembered thinking Win's face had seemed hauntingly
familiar, and now she knew why. But no matter how
cryptically, Arthur had warned her against this man just
minutes ago. None of it made sense, and she felt as
though she were drowning in confusion. She clutched at
one straw. "The ring! That's why you looked so shocked

when you first saw me. You knew who I was all along, didn't you? Why didn't you tell me who you were and have done?"

"Because of a wager."

He saw the look on her face and said, "Yes, that's a damnable word, isn't it? And it's not quite what I mean, but it is close." He ran a hand through his hair distractedly, leaving the ends tousled. Jess had an urge to reach up and smooth it back in place, and a strange tenderness welled through her, making her as blind to everything save his need as she had been the night before when he was hurt.

She came out of her trance to his silence. His face was completely vulnerable as he looked at her, and then he shifted his eyes away, and his voice shifted too, into flat control. "Arthur and my mother, Lady Elspeth St. James, are brother and sister. We're not a very prolific family. Arthur and his wife, Lady Juliana, had no children, and my parents have only me, bad luck for them. Arthur and Juliana went half shares on raising me, and I will be forever grateful to them. They made many things possible which would not otherwise have been so. It happens in many families—one branch may be very wealthy, another impoverished. My branch belongs to the latter. I love my father. He is very much the countryman, Winston Senior is. He considers it a catastrophe to spend even one day in London. I don't know how my mother felt about it at the start of their marriage, but she has certainly followed suit for years. She hates to leave her gardens at Michelfield Hall. Her passion is roses, and though she can't afford a gardener, she won't give up a single bush. Her dowry was long ago poured into the estate, and I don't think she's ever regretted it. It's just one of those facts of life—death duties and less and less money generation to generation, and all the while buildings and land need care.

"Arthur has a place in the country too, but the similarity ends there. He is very wealthy indeed, and he has the knack of making his wealth grow. He and Juliana were both very cosmopolitan and addicted to travel, to excitement, to a wide range of friends. As I expect you know, Uncle Arthur is still like that, even though Aunt Juliana is gone."

Jess nodded, saying nothing, fascinated by the picture of his background, a picture peopled by lords and ladies and countryseats. Uncle Arthur was a lord no less, not Mr. Barton at all. And the more she learned about Winston St. James, the less sense anything made.

Win's face and voice hardened; his eyes brooded on a place miles and time away. "It was a mark of my own lack of wisdom that I could have been so surrounded by wise and happy people and still have made such a botch of my life. Arthur warned me as strongly as he dared; my mother and father looked as though they were planning a funeral for weeks before the wedding, but I knew better than all of them. I would marry Margaret, and I did. Arthur detested her from the very first. The ring was to go to my wife on our wedding day. When Arthur met Margaret he changed his plan."

Win paused and looked at Jess. Then he said very deliberately, "He bet that he could find a better woman for me. I didn't know who you were; I still don't, but I knew you came with Arthur's approval."

"My God, ringed, signed, sealed, and flown to you air mail!" Jess gasped, and Win did not contradict her. He looked as miserable as she felt. She tried to generate anger against the old man and could not. She had been a fool. Not once had she considered the possibility that Uncle Arthur loved someone more than he loved her. She had gone along with everything sure that her good was uppermost in his mind. She deserved what she had gotten. In a strange way, she could even see that Arthur might have thought a few days with this man would be a gift to her, so great was his love for his nephew. Love can be very blind. It had made Win blind enough to marry his Margaret, blind enough to go on with it in spite of the disaster it apparently was. Then why had Arthur warned her?

She felt Win looking at her and kept her own eyes turned away. Eyes told too much. Two doubles matches were going on on the far courts amid good-natured shouts of dismay when an opponent hit a particularly good shot. "Does your uncle know what you do?" she asked and the words sounded strangled.

She heard his sharp intake of breath, but his voice was expressionless when he answered, "Yes, he knows I have an interest in the Queen's Gate. He helped me purchase it."

The anger which would not come before flooded through Jess. "That's a damn lie! Since you've let Arthur help you before, why don't you let him help you now. I know he suspects something. It will break his heart if he finds out you're involved in . . . in whatever it is."

"Exactly. You do not know, and you will stop meddling. My relationship with my uncle is my own affair. He made a terrible, if ignorant, mistake in sending you out here. I do appreciate what you did for me, but someone saw what happened last night and told you about it. I want to know who he is." His voice touched her like cold steel.

A pair of small gray birds waddled in and out beneath a bush nearby. They were as perfectly formed as glass birds with no feathers out of place, bright bead eyes cocky. Jess turned her head away, watching them. "They're ground doves," she said and added softly, "I haven't anything to tell you."

His hands clamped painfully on her already bruised upper arms as he jerked her around to face him. He no longer made any pretense of even temper. His eyes blazed in his grim face. "I don't know whether or not you know what you're doing, but either way, you are a bloody fool!"

"I'll repeat, I have nothing to tell you, and if you don't take your hands off me, I'll have the whole place here in two seconds," she hissed at him and resisted the impulse to rub her aching arms when his hands dropped away. "The most foolish thing I've done was to help you last night. I should have called the police or dumped you in the sea. Among other things, you're an ungrateful wretch. Arthur was wrong, wrong about everything, and I was wrong to trust him. You've done your best to spoil my vacation ever since I got here, following me around, glaring, lying. Everything about you is a lie, and I'm sure the truth is even nastier. Uncle Arthur can't help being related to you. Go lurk after someone else. Whatever anyone else planned, I didn't come here to find a pet vulture!" She brushed the tears away, damning her reaction, worse because this man had so much power to hurt her.

She heard him ask, "Is this what you came to find?" but her vision was blurred, and she did not see his intention soon enough. Her outraged "No!" was muffled by his kiss. His hand held her head rigid; his mouth was savage, trying to force hers open, devoid of any feeling beyond the will to master. She had enough freedom of movement in her arms to give him a good jab in the ribs, but she had a split second of knowing even the pain would give him gratifying proof of some response. And response there was in spite of the insult. She could feel the warm tide rising in her as it had done the night before when he kissed her. Not Kyre, surely not Larry, no one had ever had this trigger quick effect on her, and she was furious at her body's betrayal of her mind. .

She did not struggle. She made her body go limp, let her mind float above it. Even her mouth went slack. She thought it must be very much like kissing a corpse, and Win's look of defeat and disgust confirmed it as he drew away.

"Pardon me. I thought you might have gotten bad news with that phone call. I've been looking all over for you. I thought you might need a friend. I see you have one." Chillingly polite, Kyre's voice.

Jess looked up at him. "I do need a friend. What you saw was none of my doing, just a bad breach of British manners."

Kyre took a menacing step forward, clearly intending to do some damage to Win, and Jess shuddered inwardly at his cruelty. He knew Win was already injured. She went instinctively to Win's defense, forestalling Kyre by putting her arms around him and leaning her head hard against his chest. "No, no need. I never ask anyone to fight old ladies or cripples on my behalf."

The tension eased in his body, and his laugh sounded

nearly normal. "Okay. I'm out of practice for defending the honor of fair maidens anyway, even if the opponent is less than a dragon." He ruffled her hair, and her skin crawled—it reminded her of Win doing the same thing the night before, and now she was between the two who hated each other and people who interfered.

Ignoring Win completely, Kyre took her arm and led her away. Win's silence and his gaze followed her, but she did not allow herself to look back. And she went wobbly with relief when Sally caught sight of her and yelped, "Come on! We're supposed to be playing in ten minutes. Let's go get our stuff."

Jess mumbled a thank-you and fled with her friend, vowing she would never be trapped alone again with either man. Their course was set, and they would run down anyone in their path.

Her impulse when she and Sally reached the room was to hide there pleading a cold or some other nebulous ailment, but then she glanced at her bed. No one had done the room yet, and the imprint of Win's body was clear to her knowing eyes. She answered her roommate's question about the call by saying it was purely business, drawings to be done when she got home, and she gathered up her tennis equipment with manic speed and vacated the room, Sally panting at her heels, telling her she hadn't meant that much of a hurry.

On the way to the court, she searched the spot where she had left Win, but he was gone. She wished she felt better about that, but all she could think about was the possibility that Kyre had him somewhere and was hurting him.

She nearly voiced her self-disgust aloud. She could not afford to have one kind thought about either of those men, those thieves, those killers—that was the thought to keep in mind. It must not make any difference that Win was beloved by Arthur as a son. Fathers without number had suffered the death of pride through their sons.

She played well in the doubles match, hitting with controlled savagery, making her stormy emotions work for her as they had the day before. When she and Sally, the victors, shook hands with their opponents at the finish, Ann said, "See what my new peace of mind has done. It's ruined my game. I'm sorry I couldn't have offered you the same, Jess."

They headed back to their rooms to shower, and Sally's silence was ominous, but Jess' attention was elsewhere. Elsie and Elizabeth were getting into a taxi, and Elsie called to Jess, "We're going into Hamilton for some more shopping. We'll wait if you want to go with us."

"No, thanks. You'd have to wait too long, but maybe I'll see you there later." *That'll cover me if I do, I hope,* she thought. The plan forming in her mind was worth the risk; one piece of solid evidence would be a beginning at least.

"All right, what's going on? And since when did you decide to shut me out?" The hurt in Sally's voice made Jess wince.

She started to protest, but Sally stopped her. "Don't tell me it's nothing. You're either jumpy as a cat or else you go off somewhere so far away your face looks like a stone effigy with glass eyes. You started out with Kyre, and now you're keeping company, to put it nicely, with a man you profess to hate." She checked abruptly, and then buried her face in her hands, muffling her voice. "Oh, Jaybe, I'm sorry I said that! It's none of my business. I'm so miserable, I guess I wanted you to be miserable too. I'm jealous, that's what it is. I feel as though you've decided our friendship is inadequate or something and you can't share things with me anymore."

"God, no, that isn't true! Please, please trust me. I'll tell you all about it when I can. Ann doesn't know anything except that I'm upset." Jess fought against the impulse to tell all now, to force her friend into the lonesome place where she herself was.

The softness flooded back into Sally's face. "I know what you're doing. How stupid of me to doubt you. It's Sean all over again. Sean protecting poor Sally from anything harsh. But I'm a grown woman now. I don't need protection."

Traylee rose in Jess' mind. "But some other people do," she said gently.

Sally sighed. "Okay, though I can hardly believe Mr. St. James needs a champion. He appears to be a very self-sufficient man in spite of his handicap. I'll wait like a good little girl until you're ready to tell me."

Jess answered her smile, but her mind was spinning, seeing again the image of Win's pain. She tried to shut it off. He's a criminal; he's dangerous; he's married and hates women besides, and I don't give a damn about any of it, none of my lectures have done me the slightest bit of good, she realized in wonder, in fear. She had to swallow hard before she could answer Sally's question about lunch. "No, I'm not hungry. I might take a walk or something," she said vaguely. Don't let Sally ask where. Don't let her want to go along.

"Well, I've got to run. Tom will be waiting for me, and I have another match in less than two hours," Sally explained on her way out.

Jess moved slowly to the mirror and stood looking at herself. It seemed an age before that she had seen the first of the sea changes that night in Lexington. Now she could scarcely recognize herself. Her heart was pounding with terror at what she was about to do, but the sure rush of power which came from being committed to a course of action, no longer a victim but an instigator, was stronger. She understood Traylee more fully now. And stronger than anything else was the heady feeling about Win. Sally was undoubtedly right—she was going to get hurt, but that changed nothing. She was drawn powerless to the man, and even when he kissed her in anger, she responded. And being on his side made her an enemy of Kyre; being on either side made her an accessory to crime. The thought was like an icy shower, sobering her, warning her. She looked at her watch. It was past noon, and she had a match to play with Kyre as her partner at four. Her stomach contracted at the idea of doing anything at all with him, but from now on she would have to be very cautious. He was already suspicious, of what she was sure. She had very little time.

Uncle Arthur, you began it without knowing beyond his misery; you can claim a certain innocence, I can claim none. I am continuing with full knowledge.

10

I shall no more to sea, to sea;
Here shall I die ashore.

When Jess left her room a short time later, she was
relieved to see there were few people about. Most of the
guests would still be eating lunch, and there were only a
couple of maintenance men working languorously in the
heat. She could hear voices coming from the pool area,
but no one from her group was in evidence.

Walk naturally, she admonished herself, *no one has
the slightest idea what you are planning.* But she could
not control the quickening of her pulse as she reached
Elsie and Elizabeth's room. She knocked to be absolutely
sure, and there was no response. The door was locked,
but the locks at the Queen's Gate were as antiquated as
everything else. She took out her nail file, suppressing
nervous laughter at the image of Jess Banbridge, female
burglar. But it worked within seconds, the lock slipping
open with a satisfying click, and she was in the room. No
wonder Win had been able to get into her room; she
suspected he'd had so much practice in lockpicking anyway, the locks at the Queen's Gate must be boring for him.

She discovered without effort which drawers were
filled with Elizabeth's belongings. The clothes were exquisite, expensive, and all chosen with an eye for pleasing a
man. She hoped her reading of Elizabeth's character
continued to be valid, trusting it had to be for the ruby to
have been taken at all.

140

Her hands found the heavy weight of the jewel case under a pile of dainty lingerie. The case was soft brocade, closed by a zipper, the kind of case most women use to carry their costume jewelry. It fitted with Jess' image of Elizabeth as a woman who was so wealthy she did not even fret about the possibility of loss. No, it was more than that. It was as though she used the wealth as a front but cared little for it beyond that. For the first time, Jess wondered what went on in Elizabeth's head, but she shrugged the thought aside, having no time for it.

The ruby pendant lay tangled with the other necklaces. No, the once ruby pendant, Jess corrected herself as she drew it out. She found the earrings in a side pocket. Their small stones were the same as they had originally been, deep and true, making the pendant look even more false to her eyes. But she wanted confirmation, and with no guilt, she put the pendant in her handbag. She left the room cautiously, but there was no one to see her. If Elizabeth arrived back before she did, perhaps she would not discover the pendant was gone if there were no signs that anything had been disturbed. But Jess didn't even want to consider how she would return the pendant in that case.

Back on the road, her luck held. Two of the bridge brigade ladies were just paying off their taxi when Jess claimed it. The driver chatted merrily all the way to Hamilton and did not seem at all offended by Jess' lack of attention. She tipped him generously, glad of one friendly, uninvolved soul.

Only as she walked into the shop did her heart misgive her. The jeweler was waiting on someone, but he smiled in recognition when he saw her before answering his customer's question. Her mind went blank—how was she going to explain her request? She was still searching wildly for a plausible lie when the customer left and the gnome fixed his full attention on her. She fumbled in her purse, and her words were as clumsy as her hands. "I . . . well, that is, I have a question."

"Surely it cannot be so bad that you must be in this distress." His voice was so gentle and kind, Jess took heart and lost the impulse to lie.

"If what I think is true, then it is bad, but I need your knowledge to confirm it." She drew the pendant out and handed it to him. "Could you tell me please, what you think about this?"

He flipped the jeweler's glass down over the lens of his spectacles and examined the necklace carefully. Puzzlement was replaced by anger on his face. "But this is a sacrilege! It is an old piece. The gold is good, the workmanship fine, but the stone, it is a falsehood, a piece of glass, nothing more. And it has been recently done; the marks of the crime are fresh on the gold, not worn by time. You must tell the police immediately."

"No," she said, shaking her head slowly, "that is exactly what I must not do, and I beg you do not do so either. Perhaps the woman who owns it has reasons of her own for exchanging the stone, perhaps she needed the money." But I doubt it very much, she added silently.

"It is not yours then. Why do you have it?" The voice was not so gentle now, and the magnified eyes watched her closely.

"Though I would prefer to say I borrowed it since I will return it immediately, the fact is I stole it. I had to know if my guess was correct. But I cannot explain to you why I had to know."

They stared at each other in silence for a moment before the man spoke. "I am most assuredly a foolish old one, but I trust you. You do not have the eyes of a thief, cold, hard, not telling. Your eyes tell very much. You have fear, but you also have courage." He handed the necklace back to her. "I will keep silence for you. It is not, after all, my affair. But I will also worry for you. If it was a ruby which was there and of that size, and if it was of the same quality as the gold work, then it had great value, and such value makes greed. And from greed comes danger. You will take care?"

She smiled at him gratefully and put out her hand. "I will take care. My name is Jess, little enough to offer in return for such a favor, but I thank you deeply."

"I am Otto, and the favor will be repaid if you will tell

me when all is well." His hand was warm and comforting, sealing the secret between them.

Once back on the street, she stood irresolute for a minute and then shrugged. There wasn't much of a chance she would find Traylee in the same place where he had stood arguing with Connor, but she had so little to go on, anything would be worth a try.

She recognized some of the faces from the time before, and she knew some of the people recognized her—talk died here and there, eyes saw her and then did not. There was no sign of Traylee, and her courage was beginning to waver. She tried to hold on to the last of it as she approached one of the young men who had seen the encounter of two days before. She saw his look of apprehension swiftly followed by a cultivated blankness which indicated clearly he did not want to be involved with any crazy white woman. She didn't blame him; she didn't want to be involved either.

"Please," she asked softly, "do you know Traylee Jameson?"

She saw the truth in his eyes even as he denied it and began to edge away. She could not control the frantic note in her voice. "I don't want to cause trouble for him, I promise! But I've got to see him. Maybe you know someone else who might know him. Traylee knows where I'm staying. If he'd only come tonight, after midnight, I'll wait for him near my room. Please get the message to him if you can."

The man's look softened at the pleading note in her voice, but all he said was, "You're in deep waters. Sure do hope you can swim." This time his steps were purposeful as he walked away from her, but Jess was sure he would tell Traylee.

She went swiftly to the cross street, looking for a taxi along the way, hoping she would not have to go clear down to Front Street to find one. She had to get back as soon as possible, before Elizabeth and Elsie returned to their room.

She sighed with relief when she hailed a cab at the corner, and it stopped for her. As they pulled away from the curb, she glanced back up the street, remembering that was where Elsie had gone visiting. Her body froze. She shook her head in disbelief and rubbed her eyes. Not Elsie, but a man was going into the house. Connor Jameson, she was sure of it. Fear prickled all over her body, and her mind was caught in a whirlpool, whipping around in crazy circles. Coincidence was not an applicable word. Connor had gone to that house for something specific, as Elsie had. Elsie, part of the whole mess? It seemed incredible, that frail, worried old woman. The same old woman who had access to Elizabeth's jewel case; the same whose eyes had grown so bright when she noticed Jess' ring and later when she had seen the golden seal for Arthur; the same who went birding early in the morning, knew nothing about birds, and looked continually out to sea. Elsie, Kyre, Connor, Traylee, and Win, what an unlikely group.

She was so intent on the puzzle, she nearly missed it, but she was running so scared now that when the taxi turned onto Front Street, she glanced instinctively up the street, feeling as though the whole world was crawling with enemies. She was not far wrong. She saw Elsie and Elizabeth getting into a cab.

"Driver, can you hurry? I'm late for a tennis match!" Her words sounded strangled because fear was closing her throat.

The man turned to smile briefly at her but said firmly, "They are very strict here, no more than fifteen miles in the city, only twenty outside."

"Yes, of course," Jess said and prayed the other taxi's driver was as law abiding as hers.

The drive seemed interminable, and her hands were shaking so that she could hardly get the fare ready. She kept looking out the rear window, but she could not see the other cab. A little time at least. She was clutching the nail file by the time the cab stopped, and she wrenched the door open before the driver could even get out, handed him the money, and ran, hoping no one would see and question, having no choice anyway.

Her hands were so clammy by the time she got to the

room, she cursed in desperation as she worked clumsily at the lock and nearly fainted in relief when the bolt slid open. She found the jewel case and jammed the pendant back in. Her hands left damp marks on the brocade, but there was nothing to do for it save to trust Elizabeth wouldn't notice.

She was out of the room and had just gotten the door relocked when she heard their voices as they came around the corner. "God, let them believe me," she muttered and then took the offensive as the two women caught sight of her. "Elsie, I wondered whether you were back or not. I've just heard rumors of a superb Audubon film to be shown somewhere in Hamilton tomorrow. If I can find the time and place, would you like to go?"

It worked. Elizabeth made no attempt to hide her amused contempt, and Elsie was little better. "Well, thank you, my dear, for asking, but I think I'll skip it. I'm sure it would be way over my head."

Jess tried to look disappointed, but she did not protest; she was so relieved the pretense did not have to be carried any further, and Elsie's attitude simply confirmed Jess' suspicions of her.

She told the two women she had a match to play and had better get ready for it, and she made herself walk when all she wanted to do was run.

She knew she was being watched, and she knew who was watching even before she lifted her eyes to the balcony of his room. And she knew defeat because she had no weapons left against him. She could not glare back in anger anymore. She knew how suspicious her actions had been—undoubtedly he had seen her run from the taxi. He saw everything. She felt a great aching sadness. She wanted him to comfort her, not to hate her. She had not felt this lonely since the day she had lost her family.

His voice cut the air between them and made her flinch. "You are much too busy for your own good. Rushing around in this heat is very unhealthy. Even Arthur would tell you that."

Her shoulders drooped and tears blurred her vision as she raised her head to look at him. She blinked the tears away and saw that his face mirrored the weary sadness of her own. "I. . . ." She could find nothing to say. She shrugged and walked on, knowing he watched her out of sight.

She got ready for the tennis match, moving like an automaton, mind far away from body. She had one solid piece of evidence now. She was sure Elizabeth was not in on the theft. The woman had too much money to have cause to steal the family jewels. But it was so complicated. How could she prove who had done the actual stealing when she herself did not know? Kyre and Elsie were the prime suspects, but perhaps Win or Connor had accomplished it. Or Traylee? Traylee, she was sure that if he got the message, he would come tonight. She would wait. She had to give him the chance to explain. And she admitted that she was not ready to face the possibility of Traylee being arrested, or Win.

She was not surprised when she checked for Arthur's ring before she left the room and found it gone since morning. She had done everything save asking aloud for it to be stolen. She could even see a certain grim humor in the fact that someone had paralleled her accomplishment in the field of burglary. But there would be no return of the ring with a false stone substituted; the carved emerald would be hard to duplicate. She would never be able to explain to Uncle Arthur why she had not put the ring in a secure place. At least Arthur's seal was still safely locked away. She hated the thought of someone handling her things, looking through her possessions to find the ring. And because of the few, hard-earned pieces of the puzzle she had, she hated most of all the knowledge that whoever it was had trusted that when the theft was discovered some innocent maid or maintenance man would be blamed. She could not believe that of Traylee. She wondered if Win had taken back what was in fact his.

As soon as she met Kyre for their match, she knew it was going to be a disaster. She had chosen sides now, and she could no longer control her fear of him. Her knees were shaking and sweat was springing out on her skin before they even began to play.

"Are you all right? You look as though you feel ill," he said, the kindness of his voice belied by the gleaming watchfulness of his eyes.

"I think I might have a touch of the traveler's flu or something, but I'll be fine," she protested weakly.

But she was not fine. She played as though the game were totally alien to her, and her terror grew as Kyre lost patience. "God damn it, Jess, hit the ball!" he snarled at one point, and she could feel his will to win as though it touched her physically. Victory in everything no matter how ruthless the game, the only rule he played by.

They lost dismally because he could not win alone, not for all his skill and trying, and Joe and Sharon Kadas, their opponents, had found the weak spot quickly, hitting everything they could at Jess. They were a little embarrassed about it, but Jess assured them it had been her fault, she could have called the match if she did not feel up to playing.

The Kadases invited them for a drink afterwards, and Jess accepted out of good sportsmanship, though it was the last thing she wanted. Kyre accepted also, though he was having a hard time struggling with his disgust at their loss, his fury that she had played so badly. The feeling between them as they sat in the pub was so tense, Jess had to struggle with the hysterical laughter of fear—the lion and the lamb together for anything but peaceful reasons, the lion very hungry. She realized Sharon was watching them with a secret smile, judging from her own happy viewpoint that they were having a lovers' tiff which had caused Jess to play badly, judging things would come right in the end. Jess felt a wave of nausea at the idea of Kyre touching her, a wave of revulsion that he had, and she knew she was going to bolt, knew she could not prevent it.

"I'm sorry, I really don't feel well. I think a shower would help. Thank you for the drink. If you'll excuse me." Her words were quick with panic as she rose from the table. Sharon asked if she could help, her concern genuine, but Jess managed to dissuade her, Kyre's explanation of too much sun ringing in her ears.

She made it back to her room and was promptly sick. The only thing she could find to be thankful for was that Sally was not there. She dumped herself into the shower and stood under the sharp, beating streams of water for a long time, willing herself clean of fear, knowing it was impossible. Afterwards, wrapped in a warm towel and still shivering, she sat on her bed and faced the fact that had she said it aloud, she could not have told Kyre more clearly what she suspected, what she thought of him. The whimper died in her throat as she heard the voice, "You're not alone, Jaybe, you're not. Where's all the fine, fierce courage? There's my sister, there." Sean in my mind, only in my mind now, she acknowledged, but anywhere is enough. The frantic beating of her heart slowed. Nothing could ever be so bad again as that day had been, and she had survived. This too she would survive.

By the time Sally returned to get ready for dinner, Jess was dressed in a deceptively simple black dress which was high-necked and full length but left her arms and most of her back bare. The drape of the jersey managed to look soft while revealing every curve. Her skin looked pale, her deep blue eyes more enormous and darker than usual because of the emotional turmoil of the day, but the black dress contrived to make the whole effect seem like a fashion plate. She felt that way too, as though she wore a cloak of calm boredom over her dress. She knew it was a false calm, an emotional numbness which would not last, but she was no less thankful for it.

Sally whistled and exclaimed, "Excuse me! I think I must be in the wrong room, Countess Whosis. Loaded for bear hardly covers it. What are you up to?"

"I'm not really sure," Jess admitted. "Maybe I just did it for that forever female high of knowing you look ready for a party." Or for a man who hates women but might be persuaded otherwise, she added with silent honesty, and she knew she would be desperately disappointed if Win did not see her tonight. She was dressing for the hunt as Elizabeth Cooper had the first night.

Sally sang and skipped through her dressing process, drawing a laugh from Jess when she declared she would wear jeans as a contrast to the black finery of her room-mate, though in fact she looked lovely in the skirt and blouse she had worn once before.

The pub was full to overflowing by the time they arrived, and Jess took a deep breath as they went in. Her quick survey of the room revealed that Win was not there, but she had little time to brood about it. Kyre saw her instantly, and a shudder ran through her as she saw his eyed widen and then narrow in appreciation. She had been only too successful in her tempting, but with the wrong man. He knew she was the enemy, and that only made the challenge more exciting. He would take her, even kicking and screaming. It would make no difference to him at all. His polite veneer of sophisticated flirtation had dropped long enough for her to see his wanting, his eternal will to have what he wanted.

Rose Allenby spoke at her elbow, saying how sad she was that Jess' winning streak had been broken, and Jess mumbled a reply about the fun of playing, aside from winning, and hoped she sounded gracious. She saw Dr. Cranston approaching, and she knew her finery fooled him not one bit. His eyes were so concerned that when he took her hand, she would not have been surprised had he found and counted her pulse.

"It won't do, young woman, stress is a terrible disease, and you are far too young. Our mutual friend can take care of himself." Though he knew nothing of the real circumstances, she realized he was right. She knew she was in danger, and the thought was never far from her mind, but Win's danger was greater, and her compulsion to find out what was happening, what his part was, to protect him was strongest of all. She was becoming ever more like Traylee.

She moved toward Sally, Tom, and Kyre because there was no way to avoid it without making a scene. Sharon Kadas stopped her to tell her how pleased she was that Jess was looking more fit than she had this afternoon. Jess thanked her for her concern and moved on until she stood within reach of Kyre. She met his eyes bravely, and he gave her a tight little smile which held no humor at all.

She wondered how she could ever have thought him handsome, he so repelled her now. But of course, he is a fine-looking man when he is getting his own way, she reminded herself.

The talk between the four of them had lost all of its ease, but only Tom was puzzled. Sally, like Dr. Cranston, judged everything changed by the night Win had spent with Jess and for the wrong reasons, she too was right.

She heard the tapping before Kyre sneered softly, for her ears alone, "I think you called him Caliban once. I'd give a great deal to know what you call him now."

Her knuckles turned white from the pressure of her hand on the glass. It was all she could do to keep from throwing her drink at him. Instead she turned her back on him and saw Win at the same time he caught sight of her.

The dress was worth it; the fear was worth it; everything was worth the look on his face. His hunger for her was in essence the same as Kyre's, but in all other aspects it was different. Where Kyre would take by force and destroy, Win would cherish. Jess knew it instinctively. Win's face was so open, so full of wanting, and so hopeless, Jess could have wept. He looked in that instant, vulnerable again and much younger than before. And she knew he was not just answering the siren call of her black dress, her night of elegance; he was losing a battle he had fought for a long time, and he was not sure whether he felt joy or sorrow for losing. And he was seeing pleading as great as his own on her face, a face no less naked than his. Something had caught fire between them at their first sight of each other, and the flames had been burning hotter, brighter, more voraciously every minute onward. Their separate efforts to extinguish the blaze had been utterly futile. Nothing was as it had appeared to be in the beginning, yet everything was as it should be. Uncle Arthur had succeeded far too well.

How did this happen, Jess wondered. I hardly know the man, and yet I know him totally, want him totally. He has a wife, and all I feel for her is pity because I will have him. And I know that's wrong. I have never done such a thing before, vowed I never would. I am far worse than

Elizabeth Cooper. I think she is only playing. I am in earnest. He even looks completely familiar now, as though I have known him for years instead of a few days. What joy to bring such light into his eyes.

She watched him shutter his face, saw the eyes growing cold, the grooves cutting deeper, the mouth thinning as though each was a separate and difficult physical process, and when he turned deliberately away, she felt no defeat, only triumph mixed with compassion. It would be more and more difficult for him to accomplish the shutting down; she would see to it until it was impossible.

It seemed as though time must have stopped, freezing everyone as they had moved without moving to meet each other, and she was surprised to find it was not so. People talked and swirled around her as though nothing extraordinary had happened, all save Kyre. He had no capacity for love, but she recognized him as a good hater, very good indeed. She glared at him defiantly, saying without words, "Hands off. You lose."

But her defiance dissolved in a cold wave of terror at his answer, spoken quietly, maliciously. "I have a feeling Mr. St. James is accident-prone. I have a feeling he will be even more so in the future."

"If you harm him again, I'll see you dead, even if I have to do it with my own bare hands," Jess hissed and saw Kyre's eyes widen in shock at her revelation that she knew of the previous encounter. At least she had the satisfaction of knowing he was not pleased about that, did not like the idea she and Win might have been together long before the scene in the garden. She had the sense Kyre feared Win had told her something he himself wanted to know and had been unable to discover. It was so frustrating! She knew so little, and now her danger was double for false reasons.

"Don't tell me you two are giving each other a hard time about this afternoon's match! Whatever the outcome, no hard feelings afterward, that's the only way to enjoy the game." Sally's voice, Sally's smile, Sally to the rescue and completely oblivious to the true situation. Sally was safe in her ignorance, an ignorance Kyre could see without effort.

I was right to protect her from knowledge, Sean, I was right, and now she is protecting me without even knowing it, Jess thought.

"You're absolutely right. No way to play it over. Now you'll have to entertain both men because I have to ask Rose a couple of things." Jess made the smile stay on her mouth as she slipped away. Kyre did not follow her; such a move would be far too obvious for him.

She drifted through the crowd, talking to people here and there, and she did stop to talk to Rose but only to say how well her planning had paid off in fun—after all, it wasn't the organizers' fault they were unwitting accomplices to crimes past and those yet to be. But her main object was to find Win, to warn him she had made matters worse for him. There was no sign of him in the pub, and she had still not found him when dinner was announced. He was not in the dining room either, and Jess had no choice but to sit with Tom, Sally, the Friebergs, and Kyre who enjoyed the mock politeness of holding her chair for her, his eyes glittering in amusement at her discomfiture. She watched him closely in return. She knew where Elsie was sitting, and she wondered if Kyre would betray his knowledge of the old woman, confirming her belief that they worked together, but his eyes never glanced in that direction. He had trained himself as well for this game as for all the others he played.

She picked at her food, making an effort to swallow though she had no appetite at all. What had Sally called her, a stone effigy with glass eyes. She knew she looked like that now, but behind her still face, her mind was doing a rabbit run, zigzagging in panic from one horrible image to the next, all images of Win in danger, Win in pain, Kyre attacking him in various brutal ways.

She made herself stop. In her urge to protect him she was losing sight of the fact that he was no weak victim though he had come off the worse for that one encounter. He was no less dangerous than he had been simply because she loved him. Loved him . . . the words had a strange sound in her head. Uncle Arthur, you began it but you did not know it would come to this. You warned me, but you did not know it was too late. Intention does not change the fact—nightmare or dream.

When they went for coffee in the sitting room after dinner, Jess' pulse quickened as though she'd run a mile rather than walking a few steps. She had to find Win, and she had to stay out of Kyre's reach. She managed to mumble to Sally, "Please, don't count me in on your evening's plans, okay? I really don't want to go anywhere, and I don't want to argue about it." Sally looked unhappy, but she agreed, saying she guessed Jess had lots of things to think over—Win again, and how true.

She accepted a cup of coffee, but the cup rattled so loudly against the saucer, betraying her nervous hands, that she abandoned it quickly and sat with her hands clenched tightly in her lap, wondering how she was going to get out of the room, away from Kyre.

When she saw her chance, she jumped at it. Ann and Dana were talking to the Kadases, saying they'd only be a minute, just long enough to get their wraps and then they'd be ready to go out on the town. Jess went to them and asked, "Going my way?" Her voice was overloud and anxious, but she couldn't help it. Ann looked at her oddly but nodded and, once outside, said, "Do you want to come with us? You'd be very welcome."

"No, thanks. I don't even want to go back to my room. I just wanted to get out of there." She had seen Kyre's frown when she left, his indecision about following her right away or waiting a moment. She didn't have much time.

Dana was frowning in complete puzzlement, but Ann could understand Jess' feeling even though she didn't know the cause of it, and she took her sister's hand saying, "Come on, let's not keep Joe and Sharon waiting."

Jess was wrenching off her evening slippers before the two women were out of sight, and then she was running, hardly feeling the scrape of the rough road against her feet. She glanced back toward the main entrance, but there was no sign of Kyre yet, and she prayed she had time. She took the stairs up to Win's balcony two at a time, and when she gained the top, she fumbled in her handbag until she found a handkerchief, and protecting her hand with it, she reached up and unscrewed the bare bulb of the porch light. If Win were there, he would probably notice the light going out, but in any case, she would not be illuminated for Kyre's benefit. She hoped he wouldn't notice the absence of light.

She saw him then emerging from the manor, striding purposefully toward the stairs which led down to her room, and as he disappeared, she realized what a fool she'd been. This was the next place he would look. Kyre was more used to the idea of her involvement with Win than she was. She tapped on the door and called in a frantic whisper, "Win, please, are you there? Let me in!" But there was no answer, and she could not stay where she was.

She sped down the stairs and had reached the bottom when she saw Kyre stepping onto the road again. She had no time to think, her flight was instinctive, but by the time Kyre had reached the foot of the balcony stairs, she was well concealed in the dense foliage beside the manor.

She knelt, keeping her face down, hoping no light would catch the flesh of her arms. She had another cause to be thankful for the black dress, but her major thought was that the whole thing was insane. There were people all around, yet here she was crouching in terror in the bushes. She would have given anything to have Traylee protecting her now as he had the first night. She stifled a scream as something large dropped onto her arm, scuttled down it and landed with a soft plop beside her. One of her guidebooks had mentioned the enormous spiders of Bermuda, and Mark Twain had claimed one of the creatures had stolen a pair of boots from him one day. Hysterical laughter began to rise in her, and she put her hand over her mouth to stifle the sound. This was ridiculous; she would just get up and give Kyre hell, bluff her way out.

He had come back down the stairs, and something in the quality of his voice stopped her. She could feel his eyes as he peered into the darkness, calling softly, "Jess, come on, baby, I won't hurt you. I just want to talk to you." Her skin crawled. Not even when he needed to do so, could he keep the threat out of his voice.

He was suddenly still, waiting to see if she would betray herself by some sound, waiting to see if she was as close as he guessed her to be. She held her breath, and her lungs began to pump painfully. She couldn't help it; she took a breath of air with a small gasp, but her lapse was covered by Elizabeth Cooper's voice calling petulantly, "Kyre, where are you?"

She could feel Kyre hesitate as he debated whether or not to reveal his presence to the woman, but finally he spoke. "Over here, Elizabeth. I was just getting a breath of night air."

"Your back to nature trip has taken quite long enough. If we don't leave soon, the night will be over and all the clubs will be closed. I've called a taxi. Everyone else has already gone, but maybe we can catch up with some of them."

Jess thought she had never heard so sweet a sound as Elizabeth's complaining voice. As the lights of the cab illuminated the road, she could see the blonde take Kyre's arm possessively and lead him toward it. She took a deep, sobbing breath and sat back on her heels. "Bless you, bless you, Elizabeth Cooper, for having no moral sense whatsoever and a predatory instinct to rival Kyre's."

She did not come out of hiding until the taxi had gone, and then she made a dash for her room as though she were still being pursued. She wished Win had broken into her room again; it would simplify matters greatly, but the room was empty. Bits of vegetation clung to her gown, her face was smudged, her hands filthy, and her feet scraped. She took her time getting cleaned up. She had far too much time. Though it seemed as though it had been hours of hiding from Kyre, it was only nine thirty, a long way from her meeting with Traylee. She had to believe he would come.

She changed into slacks and a sweater and forced herself to wait for patient half-hour intervals between calls through the switchboard operator to Win's room, but there was never any answer, and she cringed in embarrassment at the operator's growing sympathy. "Perhaps you ought to wait and try in the morning, dear, the gentleman doesn't seem to be coming in tonight," the woman said finally, and Jess murmured her agreement, fear for Win's safety vying with unreasonable anger at his absence when she needed him.

She took out her sketchbook and stared for a long time at the fairy-tale drawing before she began to draw angry, abstract shapes, letting no faces form.

11

Now does my project gather to a head.
My charms crack not, my spirits obey, and time
Goes upright with his carriage.

Jess left the room when the clock still lacked ten
minutes to midnight. She was so relieved to be done with
waiting, to be moving into purposeful action, that her fear
receded until it was no more than a dull ache.

She moved out of the light and stood listening intently
before she crept quietly up the stairs. She could hear
distant voices, but there was no one on the road and Win's
balcony remained dark. She went back down to the green
in front of the rooms and called Traylee's name softly but
received no response. She settled down in the shelter of a
bush near the water's edge. A gentle breeze stirred the
leaves now and then and sent ripples of water across the
streaks of light. She watched the water, sure that would be
the way Traylee would come, sure he would come.

She saw the shadow cross light before she heard the
faint splash of oars, and she waited until the boat touched
the bank before she whispered, "Traylee, I'm here. Thank
you for coming."

He pulled the boat up and then over until it was in
the shelter of the bush before he spoke. "I came because I
was afraid not to. I want to know what you're up to,
stopping my friends on the street, telling me where to
be." His voice was belligerent but she had come too far to
be afraid of him.

"I know what Connor's into, and I know some of the other people who are involved. Do you want to talk about it, or shall I just go to the police." Don't let him call me. Don't let him ask why I haven't gone already, she prayed.

"I want to talk about it," he answered softly.

"We can stand out here and risk being discovered or we can go in my room. What's your choice?"

Traylee made an explosive sound but managed to keep his voice low. "Your room! Do you know what would happen if I got caught there, a black man in a white woman's room? Where in the hell are you from?"

"Obviously not from the same place as you are. My roommate has already given up hope for me. It wouldn't be any problem at all to get rid of her if she comes in early, which I doubt she will anyway. I don't care what kind of screwed up ideas this place has, you're not going to get into any trouble unless I made it, and I have no intention of doing so. Trust me?"

"Lord, I guess so. But I can't figure you out at all, and I think you're more than half crazy. If you know anything, you know this isn't a game. No problem at all to get hurt."

"Or dead. Yes, I know. Are you coming with me?"

The silent tension stretched between them, and Jess knew hers was the stronger pull. Traylee could not afford to refuse her unless he could get rid of her at the same time, and that ruthlessness was not part of his character.

"All right," he said finally, as though he were accepting a prison sentence, and followed when she led the way.

She switched on the light for a brief moment only, and they looked hard at each other, brown black eyes meeting the deep blue ones. "There, we've seen each other. We know who we are. Neither of us seems to have a weapon. We'll just have to trust in how the voices sound to know if someone's lying because I don't want to leave the light on advertising we're here. Okay?"

Traylee nodded, and she switched off the light. There was an eerie intimacy in sharing the darkness, unable to see each other's eyes or facial expressions, but Jess told herself firmly that somewhere along the line she had to trust someone, and instinct told her to trust Traylee. He was part of the nightmare, but no less a victim than she was. She would go on believing that.

She took a deep breath and began to speak slowly, making each word distinct. "I'll tell you what I know first, then I want to hear what you can tell me. I know the ruby has been stolen and my emerald ring has, too." She heard Traylee's gasp of surprise at the detail of her knowledge, but he said nothing, and she continued. "I know Kyre Tarkington and the old woman, Elsie Clinton, are both involved and Connor with them. I've even seen Connor go to the same meeting place, the house near Church Street, where Elsie went. And I know the old woman knows nothing about birds but is very interested in boats and goes nearly every morning to watch the harbor from the road. I know Kyre and the Englishman, Winston St. James, hate each other. I know Kyre beat him up though I suspect he had considerable help. What I don't know is why they hate each other, why they're working against each other. And whom does Connor want to kill, who wants to hurt him—which of the two men? And what is everyone waiting for? I can feel them waiting—Elsie, Kyre, Win, Connor, you—what in the hell for?"

"You feel and you guess, but you can't prove anything, can you?" Traylee asked sullenly, but his doubt sounded clearly.

"Do you want to take a chance on that?" she asked.

Silence again and then a dry sob and his control breaking as his grief spilled into words. "God, I've tried so hard, but there's no way out for Connor. Whatever happens now, he's going to be caught in the middle. It's the old story, and it's going to go on forever. You won't believe this, you can't, but he's a good man, and almost everything he's done, he's done for me. There're only the two of us, have been ever since I was small, and he's spent all these years trying to raise me right." Jess heard Traylee's voice from the first night, "You're all I've got," and pity rose in her, but she didn't interrupt him. "You can hear it in the way we talk. I sound like a book; he sounds like the street. And he's proud of the difference. He's worked his whole life to make it happen, to give me the best education money could buy, to give me a chance to make it in an educated, white world. He doesn't even want me to stay here, says a place that looks so black and thinks so white rots a man's soul. I don't know where he expects me to go. He's like a child sometimes. He's never been off the islands, but he's got this faith that somewhere things are different, somewhere things would be perfect for me. Not for him. This is the only world he knows, and he wouldn't leave even if someone handed him a ticket."

The wild, keening note in his voice was suddenly gone, leaving it toneless with despair. "He probably couldn't get the passport to leave anyway. He's got a record for theft. He started early. My education cost a lot of money, private tutors sometimes and then three years in England. I hated it there, dark and cold, but I learned, oh, yes, I did. I'll quote Shakespeare, ma'am, or if you prefer, Tennyson or Yeats, while I paint your fence. Those books, those times, they cost Connor, but he never complained about not having the money. He just went out and got it."

"By stealing things such as Elizabeth Cooper's ruby and my ring?" Jess asked softly.

"Not at first, but now, yes, now he's in the big time. The boss man, he's one clever dude. Everybody he hires is poor and has been in trouble with the police. Makes people keep secrets real well. I think that bastard must get a copy of police records as soon as they're printed. And he pays well, knows the value of owning a man's soul."

"The boss man, which of the two is he?" Jess couldn't wait any longer. She had to know.

"Your friend, of course. Does he kiss as well as he steals?" Traylee asked viciously, and Jess' mind went into blind panic for a moment until she realized Traylee was talking about Kyre because he had seen the good-night kiss on the porch.

"No matter what you saw, he is not my friend. He is, as a matter of fact, my sworn enemy now. I will count myself lucky if I can stay out of his reach." Even without being able to see him, she could feel Traylee's complete puzzlement at being told things were not as they seemed, and she pressed her advantage. "I would have guessed Elsie or Kyre took the ruby, was it Connor instead?"

"No, Connor didn't take it or your ring. I don't know—I didn't even know they'd stolen anything yet—but your first guess might be right. The woman probably took it, gave it to the boss long enough for him to make the switch, and then replaced it." He drew a deep breath, and Jess knew suddenly that she'd won. He trusted her, and he was relieved to have someone to talk to. His next words confirmed it. "You can't be all bad if you've got the same enemy. Like I said, he's clever. He covers all the angles. If he knows of the stone ahead of time, he can plan a switch, and it might be years before it's discovered certainly long enough so he doesn't get caught. I think the old woman helps in this, knowing which stones are worth stealing and where they're going to be. She's got a lot of old society connections, and she can get close to women and the jewelry easier than Tarkington can. But they don't always work that way. They don't usually come together; usually one steals, then someone like Connor keeps the stones hidden until the pick up time is arranged and the other comes for the stones and carries them out after there's been time for them to cool off just in case someone is looking for them. Works somewhat the same way for outright stealing, when none of the stones are replaced. Though sometimes the boss steals the stones, most times one of his men does it at his direction, and again the stones are kept until it's considered safe to move them. If you're the one stealing the stones, your pay is more because people can get caught when something's missing and there's nothing to replace it," Traylee added grimly.

"But how can Kyre trust the men once they have the gems? Why don't they just sell them themselves?" Jess asked.

"You are an innocent!" Traylee snorted. "I told you, all the men have records. They're not in any position to get good money for stolen articles. Oh, they might get something but it wouldn't be any more than the boss pays them, and the minute they try to sell something like that, they get nailed. The boss, now, he's different. He's got connections, and he's got money and mobility. He knows what to steal, and he knows where to sell it. I expect he sells as much of the loot in Europe as he does in your country. And he's got something else too, he's got the power to make men afraid. A couple of men who were working for him have turned up missing, and no one ever did find out where they went."

Jess shivered in spite of the fact that the news did not surprise her at all. "So much violence and death, it's hard to believe it's all worth it, hard to believe there is enough here for him."

"There isn't. You understand, Connor doesn't talk much, and it's taken me a long time to learn what I know. Most of the information has come from other men, men who assumed I knew most of it because I'm Connor's brother. But I've heard rumors that there are similar operations set up further south, in the Caribbean, always in places where the rich visit or live. Maybe they work the racket in the States too, besides selling there. If you know how, you can hire poor and desperate men anywhere. But all that, even that, it isn't enough," he whispered very softly, and Jess' skin prickled.

"What else, what are they waiting for?" she asked.

"He wants to get into the drug traffic. From things I've heard, he is into it." Traylee's voice was so hopeless, Jess wanted to reach out to him, to comfort him, but she had nothing to offer save her silence as he talked. "I feel like I'm running blind, but some things I do know. I told you Connor is a good man. He steals, he breaks the law, but only with things which don't destroy lives. That woman, she won't live or die just because she's minus one ruby now. Connor didn't take it, but he would have if he'd been given the job. But drugs are different, and Connor won't touch them. And he's furious because he thinks the boss planned this all along and has tricked everyone into a position where they have to go with him. Some others feel as Connor does. I think even the old woman feels that way though I expect it's only because she knows how dangerous the traffic is and doesn't want to take the risk. She's not into violence, a very civilized old witch, she is. That's why Connor was at the pub that night. He has a friend who works here as a maid, and she told him about the crazy Americans going in costumes. Connor was trying to get to talk to the old woman, but he wouldn't have minded roughing up the boss if he had to. I pulled the fuses, but your yell was what made him split. The house where he went, well, the man who owns it is a merchant, and he's not above a little shady dealing now and then. I think the old woman knew him way back when and for a price he lets her use his house for meetings. It's a good cover, a respectable front. Connor went there hoping to talk to her, but she wasn't there."

"I know," Jess interposed, "she was down on Front Street with Mrs. Cooper, the woman who owns the ruby."

"You do get around," Traylee said with grudging respect. "The problem is that some of the men are all for the deal. They know how much money is involved, far more than you can make stealing jewels. There is a war going on, but nobody knows for sure where the lines are drawn; nobody will know for sure whether it's happening until the shipment arrives."

"Heroin?" Jess' throat was so dry, the word was a croak.

"No, at least I don't think so. Running blind again, but from what I've heard sounds more like coke and a lot of it from South America. Do you know what that is?"

"Traylee, I'm not a complete baby. Yes, I know what cocaine is. Charlie, snow, girl, white lady—whatever you call it, very expensive, share some with your friends as a mark of esteem. The pimp's drug, reward for a lady who knows her job well." She'd been to a couple of pretty weird parties where the hosts had offered it in lieu of after-dinner drinks. She had declined because of an innate conservatism about drugs and because the idea of snorting something, breathing it in until your nose stung with the abuse did not appeal at all, no matter how high the high. But it puzzled her that a man like Connor would refuse. "I don't understand. Coke is a rich man's drug, and I've never heard that it's physically addictive, though I guess some people get pretty hung up on it psychologically, and it's hard on your body. I'm surprised Connor feels so strongly about it."

She knew how woefully patronizing she sounded as soon as the words were out of her mouth, and Traylee's reply was furious. "You just don't understand, do you? Connor steals, so Connor would do anything, maybe not push heroin, but anything else. Big, black, bad Connor, right? Wrong, whitey, wrong. Connor doesn't want anyone, rich or poor, black or white, hung up or hurt on drugs. Oh, I'll grant you he isn't going to go insane about a little grass, but once you're into the chemicals, uppers, downers, and the powders and crystals, opium, heroin, coke, God help you if Connor finds out. He's known on the street for being a crazy man about it." His voice was so full of pride that tears stung Jess' eyes.

"I am sorry for what I said, more sorry than I can say, but you've got to understand, too, Traylee. My whole world has been turned upside down in the past few days, and I don't know where I am or what's happening. It all seems totally unreal. And I didn't mean to slight Connor. I hardly know him, but I did know quite a few people in college, mostly white, mind you, who were willing to deal in any drug they could get their hands on, usually with the exception of heroin. The others were all the same to them as long as they got paid."

"Okay, lady, okay. I believe you." For the first time this night, Traylee's voice held the gentle note she had heard once before, and she breathed easier.

"Do you think the cocaine is coming in by boat then? Is that why Elsie keeps looking out to sea? No, wait, that doesn't make sense unless there is a good market for it here. Hell, the more I think about it, the less sense it makes."

Jess couldn't make the connections until Traylee explained patiently, "The coke will eventually come in by boat, but first that boat will come in clean so that customs could search all day and find nothing. I'd give a lot to know the name of the boat. Then at some particular time in some particular spot on the open sea, a low flying aircraft will make the drop, and the boat will be there to pick it up. That stuff is coming all the way from South America. If it came all the way by boat, it would take a long, risky time. Once the boat picks it up it will be smuggled into Bermuda to cool off, just like the jewels, and then it will be shipped to the States or to Canada and then into the States. It isn't destined for here at all. This is just a stop along the way. Cocaine is big money and needs a big market. And I haven't proof that any of this is going to happen and neither does Connor," he said miserably. "It's just what we've pieced together. The boss is suspicious of Connor and maybe a little afraid of him too—he's not telling him much anymore, but some of the others are still learning things, and some of them, not enough, but some trust Connor more than they trust Tarkington."

"I'm sure you're right. Elsie is looking for a boat, and she's not happy, not one bit. And Kyre is prowling around like a hungry lion in a small cage. He can't wait for something to happen. Damn, it is a mess! Even if we could prove it, it would mean nothing but trouble for Connor. I know Kyre well enough by now to know that he would have Connor arrested one way or another, and unless Kyre gets caught holding the drug, he will probably get off scot-free," Jess groaned and was startled when Traylee laughed aloud and used her name for the first time.

"Jess, you don't know how good that sounds! I've felt like a little kid wandering around in the dark, scared to death, and all of a sudden, here's this other kid saying, 'I'm here too, wherever here is.' It doesn't seem as dark anymore. And I know that's stupid because all it means is that there are now two of us, two children who don't know what's going to happen."

"Don't lose hope, Traylee, don't! We'll find a way," Jess said urgently. "And I can't think of anything I'd rather have than your friendship, your trust."

"Friend, a nice word," Traylee said softly, and Jess knew that even without light, his eyes were shining.

She swallowed hard before she could continue. "Friendship means honesty, but this is hard to say because I don't know quite what it means. You haven't mentioned the

Englishman even though I asked, so I will, and I'll admit I've got some special feeling for him. I know he's dangerous. I've known since the first time I saw him, but that doesn't change anything. I care about him. I can't bear the idea of him being hurt again. But I don't even know what his part in all of this is, do you?"

"No, Jess, I don't," he said gently. "No one seems to know anything about him. He hasn't worked with anyone here before. But he knows a lot about the jewel trade, and he's been trying to get in. He comes with some high sounding references from some big stolen goods dealers in Europe, so his credit's good, but Tarkington doesn't want to share, especially since he's branching out. That's why the man was beaten, to warn him the territory's taken. Some of the men aren't so sure. They'd just as soon go for the best money as long as they can stay alive and out of prison. I think they're waiting to see which man wins. And so far your man hasn't done so well, but he's tough enough so that the boss man's not going to kill him until he knows whether he's got friends around who might take offense."

Jess couldn't prevent the break in her voice, the overwhelming sadness she felt. Whatever way it ended would be bad. "I knew he was involved; I just kept hoping it wasn't true. You want to protect Connor, and so do I, but I want to protect Win too, and it sounds like a bad bargain altogether."

"I know," Traylee admitted helplessly, but then his voice grew more sure. "But there are two of us now, remember? I know we're thinking outside the law, but that's where love is sometimes, so we'll just have to do the best we can. But you know I'd choose Connor over anybody else, don't you?"

"Yes. And I can't help it, I'd choose Win."

"Bless you, I like the truth. And I like being alive too, so I'd better be going," he added, his voice light in spite of the gravity of his predicament.

Jess remembered his risk with a start and said hastily, "Yes, of course. You know how to reach me. Please do if you discover anything. And how should I contact you if I need to?"

His trust was complete enough so that he did not hesitate. "Just leave a message for me at 'The Black Diamond.' It's a black nightclub, and I work there most nights at least part-time. They're pretty good about getting messages to me. And, Jess, take care. I don't have enough friends to waste them. Just tell me if you happen on something, don't do anything about it yourself."

"I'll try, and it shouldn't be too hard since I'm basically a coward."

She opened the door carefully, and they both stood listening for a moment before they went swiftly down to the water's edge. Jess helped Traylee launch the boat and waited until she could no longer see the dark shape or hear the oars working before she fled back to her room.

The timing was perfect because she heard Ann and Dana come in just a few minutes later, and it was some comfort to know they were next door. She wanted nothing more than to collapse in bed, but she was afraid, not wanting to be alone and unconscious in sleep in case Kyre came back before Sally did. If he even tried the door, she would summon all available help. The switchboard was off, but her lungs were in working order.

She sat on the edge of the bed, holding herself rigidly upright, getting up to pace the room when the urge to sleep got too strong. She did not turn the light on, and her tired eyes conjured strange, billowing shapes in the darkness. "Please, come soon, Salky," she pleaded aloud. She did not know when she slipped sideways to lie half on half off the bed, sound asleep.

Someone was in the room, someone was touching her, urging her to wake up, and she came to in screaming terror, the sound filling the room until a hand was clamped over her mouth and the voice reached her, "Jaybe, it's all right! It's me!" and she focused on Sally's white face.

"God almighty, who were you expecting?" Sally asked with a shaky laugh.

"No one, must have been a nightmare, probably a good thing you woke me up." A nightmare which goes on and on, even in the sunlight.

A soft blush touched Sally's cheeks. "I wouldn't have

bothered you, but I couldn't wait 'til morning to ask you. How would you like to be a bridesmaid at a small wedding right before Christmas?"

Jess shot off the bed and hugged her. "Congratulations! When, how, et cetera. Tell me all."

"Just a lovely little speech about the only reason for marriage being a desire to be together for the rest of our lives, that nothing less than that should ever be cause for marriage, and that he would like to see me for the rest of his life, did I have similar feelings? Did I! Do I! I'm going to write a song called 'Did I, Do I, I would, I will' to be sung in two-part harmony." She pirouetted around the room, unable to contain her joy. "Oh, Jaybe, I wouldn't have minded going on any way he chose forever, but an offer of marriage from him is an absolute gift of trust after what he's been through. He won't ever be sorry. Our life together will be joyful." She said it as though it were a solemn vow, and Jess believed her. *Sean,* she whispered deep in her mind, *I know you're glad. You taught her how to love, and now she has someone who needs that desperately, and he'll take very good care of her.*

"I know what you're thinking," Sally said. "I've been thinking the same, even Tom shares it. He knows about Sean, and tonight he said he will be forever thankful to him, even though he never met him."

"But he has. People meet Sean all the time through you, through me, through all the people he touched and gave part of his spirit," Jess murmured, curling up on her bed, and was asleep again, this time deeply, peacefully.

12

O, I have suffered
With those that I saw suffer! a brave vessel
(Who had no doubt some noble creature in her)
Dashed all to pieces!

Jess awakened in the morning to the sound of Sally singing even louder than usual, still overflowing with joy from the night before. It took her a minute to remember she belonged to two worlds now, one full of innocence and gay holiday making, the other full of danger. She groaned as she got out of bed; she wished she could sleep on and only wake when all the problems were solved.

They were ready to go to breakfast when Elizabeth Cooper knocked on the door, and since neither of them were friendly with the blonde, they simply stared at her in surprise, letting her nervousness fill the silence. "Please, Miss Banbridge, ah, Jess, could you wait a second. I'd like to talk to you."

Jess regarded her uneasily, wondering what she was up to, wondering if she had discovered something about the ruby, and Sally made no move to leave. Elizabeth's voice grew firmer. "Alone. I need to talk to you alone."

Sally wrinkled her nose in distaste at the imperious tone, but Jess said quietly, "It's all right, I'll catch up with you in a bit. You mustn't keep Tom waiting." Sally shrugged and left them, her straight back and marching step telling exactly what she thought of Elizabeth.

"Come in," Jess said none too graciously and closed the door behind them.

"Jess, stay away from Kyre."

Jess stared at her incredulously. They'd hardly said two words to each other, and now without preamble, the woman was ordering her to clear the field. It made no difference that she had no intention of getting close to Kyre again; the woman's rudeness was infuriating. "Why should I? Don't you have a husband stashed away somewhere?"

Elizabeth flinched, and her voice quivered, but she faced Jess squarely. "Yes, I do, or at least I did when I left the States. This has nothing to do with Jonathan or with me. I don't want Kyre, and I don't want you mixed up with him either." She buried her face in her hands and moaned, "Damn it, I've done so few things right lately, and now I'm making a mess of this, too. I'm warning you away from Kyre because he's dangerous. I don't have solid evidence, but I know it. You probably know by now that I went out with him last night. Well, he spent half of the evening looking around to see if you were in any of the places where we went, and he spent the other half talking about you. He didn't want to be with me at all; he wanted to find you. It gave me the creeps to listen to him. He talked more as if he'd like to break your neck than make love to you, and he kept laughing it off, but I think he meant it. He's obsessed. He must be to have spent the time with one woman talking about another. One thing I know too much about is men."

She paused for an instant and then looking at Jess with tear-bright eyes, she said, "Everything you think about me is true. I married Jon for money. He's twenty years older than I am. He knew my motives, but still he said he loved me, at least in the beginning. I've made sure our roles were clear. I am the perfect hostess. He is the perfect businessman. Our marriage is more like a business deal than anything else. I've gone on trips like this before, and he's never objected until this time though he knew I'd cheated on him—been unfaithful is too nice a way to put it. Last night I suddenly wondered what I was doing with Kyre, a dangerous, mean-minded, overgrown boy, when I could have been with Jonathan."

"Whom you love very much," said Jess with a gulp, still stunned by what she was hearing

Elizabeth froze for an instant, and then she nodded slowly. "Of course I do. I don't even know when it started, but it's irrevocable now. It's a fitting punishment for what I've done to him, but I can't bear it. He asked me if I wanted a divorce before I came on this trip. He's finally had it, and maybe it's too late to put things right, but I'm going home today to try. I'm going to start by telling him I'm sorry and that I love him, and I'm hoping he'll take it from there. In a way I ought to be grateful to Kyre; he's an ugly human being hiding in a glamorous body, and he made me realize that Jonathan is beautiful all the way through. But I don't want to leave before I'm sure you've got your eyes open about Kyre."

"Elizabeth, I'm touched by your concern, and I thank you. But don't worry. I've already decided I've seen quite enough of Kyre for a lot of reasons. I won't get anywhere near him without an escort." She wished she could tell Elizabeth she probably already owed her thanks for saving her life, however inadvertently, the night before, but there wasn't any way to explain.

The woman looked relieved but still thoughtful as she headed for the door. "I've got to get packed and organized. I believe you when you say you don't want to see any more of Kyre, but just remember, that doesn't fit with his plans at all."

"I'll remember. Good luck, Elizabeth."

Jess heard her running steps going up the walk. Jonathan, be home and be ready to listen when she gets there, she prayed. She thought of Ann and Elizabeth, both so different, yet so similar, both trying desperately to come to terms with their lives. And she herself fit right in there with them. She suspected they had confided in her because they sensed she was as troubled as they. But she was not only troubled; she was terrified at the idea of Kyre stalking her, and her footsteps were a trudge compared to Elizabeth's.

Jess greeted Tom first, congratulating him for being wise enough to love Sally. He looked completely relaxed and happy as he said, "I'm very pleased you'll be a member of the wedding."

Sally had saved a place for her at the table, and Jess gave thanks that at least Kyre wasn't there. But Win wasn't either, and that did nothing to lighten her spirits. She had to talk to him, whether he wanted to or not.

Sally could hardly contain her curiosity. "Okay, give— what was that all about?"

"I can't tell you unless Elizabeth gives me permission, but I can tell you that she is, under all that guff, a very nice person."

Sally looked at her round-eyed and gave a low whistle. "And you call me sweet! Well, I never. I think the island crazies are getting to you. But then, we're suffering from them too," she admitted and planted a light kiss on Tom's cheek.

Jess wondered why she couldn't fall in love with someone as steady as Tom. *Damn you, where are you, Win?* She started to ask Tom if he knew where Kyre was and then thought better of it when she realized that Tom obviously knew less about the man than she did. And the less interest she showed in her enemy, the safer she would be.

She and Sally had their final doubles match to play after breakfast, and their opponents, Sharon Kadas and Ellen Frieberg, were waiting for them on the court when they got there. Even the warm up was brisk, and Sally whispered to Jess, "We've got some strong trouble here, think we can handle it?"

"Sure, no problem." *No problem as long as I can keep my mind on the game,* she added silently.

There were few weaknesses on Sharon and Ellen's side. Ellen's serves were hard and accurate as they had not been on the day of the ladder match against Jess, and Sharon was one of those back-breakingly consistent players who seem capable of returning any shot with the same steady rhythm. Jess knew that if she went walk-about in her head, she would put Sally at a complete disadvantage, and so she settled down to play with a will, thinking each shot through with fierce concentration.

Their rallies were long and pleasing enough to watch so that they attracted several spectators, and both teams moved well at the net, engaging in furious volleys.

They had a set apiece when Jess heard the tapping, and this time instead of falling apart with fear, she felt such a wild pulsing joy that the adrenalin rushed through her, allowing her to move easily to a shot which should have been out of reach. He was all right, and he had come to find her. It was not just chance which brought him here; she was sure of it. She wanted the match over; she wanted to win it, but most of all, she wanted to be with him. "Win, Win," she said and giggled, causing Sally to glance at her. "You are nuts, Jaybe, but I don't mind as long as you play like this."

They won the deciding set six-four, and there were cheers and congratulations from the crowd for all of them. Jess nodded and thanked people vaguely as she headed for Win.

She felt suddenly shy as she stood before him. She had so much to tell him—warnings and love words all mixed—but how could she when his face was so stony and forbidding? She reminded herself she had vowed to end that, and she decided to plunge right in and say whatever came into her head, but he spoke first.

"Congratulations on your victory," he said gravely, and she knew he was not talking about the tennis game. It was as though he had said, "I lose." The joy surged through her again, and she did not look away as he watched it dawn on her face.

"Will you go sailing with me?" he asked, and her joy dissolved. Why that of all things? Did he know then? Was this a way of testing? One hell of a way. He was watching her with a puzzled frown, and for her sanity, she had to believe he knew nothing of the past and was misinterpreting her hesitation.

"But your ribs, I don't think you ought to do anything

that strenuous," she protested, trying to control the quaver of fear in her voice.

"They will be quite all right. I don't plan to sail to
America today. We'll stay in the waters of the Great
Sound."

She held her voice steady. "Yes, I'll go. What time?"

"As soon as you can change into something which will
offer you more protection on the open water," he said
austerely, and Jess wanted to smile at this evidence of his
awareness of her body in the scant tennis dress, but her
humor dissipated as the words rang in her head, "Protection on the open water," and were answered, "There is no
protection there, none at all."

She left him abruptly and went to change. If she did
not move quickly, she would lose her courage and refuse
to go. She was relieved when Sally came in as she was
dressing. "Will you do me a favor, please? Tell Dana I
forfeit our ladder match. She can exchange her position for
mine on the board. We were supposed to play at two
o'clock, and I don't think I'll be back."

Sally looked at her in wonder. "Jessica Banbridge
forfeiting a tennis match? I can't believe it. What in the
world is more important?"

"Winston St. James is taking me sailing."

Sally's mouth formed a perfect, soundless "O," and
she sat down hard on the bed.

"You look like a fish," Jess commented unkindly.

"I feel like one, completely out of water," Sally retorted.
"Jaybe, are you sure you know what you're doing? Sailing?
And with that man. You haven't seemed very friendly
since that night. You're not being forced to go or anything,
are you?"

"No, I'm not being forced. And yes, I know what I'm
doing, for the first time in a long time I know what I'm
doing," Jess said slowly. "I'm scared—I admit it. This will
be the first time since that day. But don't call Win 'that
man' anymore, Salky, don't. I was wrong about him. At
least I hope I was because I think I love him. No, I don't
think I do, I know I do. I'm sorry, am I making sense?"

"I'm reading you loud and clear. And if he makes you

happy, then I'm all for him. But if he makes you sad, he'll hear from me, I swear he will." Her voice was so fierce that Jess wanted to laugh and cry at the same time. Even though Sally looked the part of the frail, wispy blonde, she was no lightweight when it came to defending someone she loved.

"Trust my judgment," Jess said, and Sally looked at her intently before she nodded. "Always, Jaybe."

Win had a taxi waiting when Jess met him on the road, and she was thankful the drive into Hamilton was so short since he seemed determined to maintain grim silence and she kept dismissing possible opening gambits as inadequate—how could you make small talk with a man when what you really wanted to do was ask him to open his heart and let you in? She watched him covertly, noticing how long and fine his hands were, remembering their strength, loving the stark lines of his face more each minute. Her abstraction even drew a small, reluctant smile from him when he had to tell her that they had arrived unless she preferred to ride around in a cab all day.

She did not come to fully until she saw the boat he'd hired. What did you expect, she asked herself wryly, a hundred-foot yacht with a full crew? A thirteen-foot sunfish is perfectly adequate for two—if the water stays calm, if he's a good sailor.

He was good; she knew it immediately by the calm, authoritative way he handled the boat, and though she saw him wince once at the pull on his rib cage, his injuries did not impair his skill. And his eyes glowed briefly with approval for the way she had gotten settled with perfect balance and a minimum of fuss. She was glad he could not hear the quick, cowardly tripping of her heart.

There was enough of a breeze so that they were quickly away from the main harbor and heading into the waters of the Great Sound. They watched the ferry chugging merrily along toward Somerset, and Jess wished fervently she were safely on its comforting bulk. Even though his voice was as impersonal as a tour guide's as he began to relate various tidbits about Bermuda, Jess was

glad Win was finally talking; she had begun to wonder if
they were going to spend the whole day in silence.

Within sight of one shore, he pointed out a curious
little house with slots in its walls and a pyramidal roof
crowned by a ball and explained it had once been a
buttery to keep perishable foods cool. And he said that the
long, dry stone walls which were so numerous were called
"slave walls" because of the labor which had built them.

"It looks so mild and peaceful, but the history of
Bermuda is full of dark deeds and slave revolts—a governor who performed such kind acts as hanging a man for
stealing a bit of cheese and made another man a slave for
not reporting gossip, and there was a slave woman, Sarah
Bassett, who led a plot to poison the masters. She was
burned at the stake, admirable woman though she was.
Even some of your American Indians were brought here
as slaves after being taken prisoner during colonial wars.
And during your Revolution, Bermudians are said to have
turned the tide in your favor by supplying General Wash-
ington with some badly needed gunpowder. The East End
was loyal to Britain, the West End favored the rebels, and
one night some west enders raided the royal gunpowder
magazine in St. George's and rolled the casks right down
to Tobacco Bay and an American frigate which just happened
to be waiting. The governor slept through the whole show.
And of course, these waters are full of sunken ships, ships
broken against the coral reefs within sight of the 'Isle of
Devils' where birds and wild hogs made enough noise to
terrify the most stout-hearted sailor."

She tried to listen calmly. On dry ground she would
have been fascinated by what he was saying, but here she
was all too conscious of the wind freshening, coming in
stronger gusts. She concentrated on the incredible clarity
of the water, liquid turquoise studded with coral beneath
them. Schools of rainbow fish swept in sinuous curves
beneath the keel, their silent passage amplified by the
sound of the boat cutting water. Tiny islands with tufts of
emerald foliage and the white wash of seagulls dotted the
way. She concentrated hard, trying not to jump everytime
the sail snapped in the wind, trying to see only the beauty,

trying not to think of sunken hulls, trying to pretend she was not vulnerable.

She felt failure beginning in the cold which touched her softly at first, growing icier by the minute, sweeping through her until one hand could not feel the other. Her heart thudded so loudly she could no longer hear the sail. *Stop it! Stop it, Jess, you're going to make a fool of yourself*, the saner part of herself screamed hopelessly against the rising wave of terror.

The dream, clear in her eyes, not blurred by sleep. Their faces, mother, father, brother, all three, all their handsome features bloated, ravaged, then dissipated by the sea. She could see her mother's long, black hair spread in a cloud under the water, tangling with the slimy green sea plants; sharks hit and tore her father's body mindlessly; her brother's slim body broke easily against the rocks; crustaceans spread delicate, fanlike arms to welcome in the easy meal. She did not hear Win's exclamation, "What in the bloody hell, are you going to be ill?" She heard her own voice, grotesquely hollow, chanting the old sea song: "Full fathoms five thy father lies; of his bones are coral made: Those are pearls that were in his eyes." She could see the gray, half shining stones in sockets which had once held bright blue life. She heard a high keening wail and recognized it as part of herself and was helpless to end it.

The slap landed squarely, shutting off the sound, and she was being shaken so hard in Win's fierce grip that her teeth jarred together. She looked for a fixed point in the whirling universe and found his eyes, sea green with light, steady, all mockery and refusal gone, leaving only compassionate concern for her. His look was the final undoing of the rigid control of the past two years. She collapsed against him and sobbed, not hysterically, but with relief that the haunting was ending, the grief was being acknowledged.

He was not made helpless by her weeping. He held her firmly with one arm, minded the tiller with the other, and whispered, "Tell me, Jess. Tell me."

"They loved to sail, all three of them, my parents and

my brother, Sean. I was the odd man out. I always
preferred to play tennis. I never went on the boat if I
could find an excuse. I didn't like the feeling of being at
the mercy of the sea. My father used to say he couldn't
understand how two such sea-crazed people could have
produced such a landlubber.

"That day there were some good tennis matches
scheduled at a club not far from Marblehead. I almost
persuaded Sean to go with me; he was a good player, but
he could never resist a chance to sail. It was getting
toward the end of the season, and so he went with them. I
said good-bye that morning, and I never saw them again."

She saw things clearly now, as clearly as she ever
would. Before she had not been able to think beyond her
family's departure from Marblehead; she had seen the sea
opening up immediately beyond The Neck to swallow
them. Now the childish nightmare was replaced by an
orderly progression to disaster. "All three were prudent
sailors and good swimmers. But the weather had been
uncertain, and maybe they were overconfident with eagerness
for a last long sail. They didn't go out with their usual
group of friends. Some other boats did put out, but they
came back early. There was a freak storm, but I think
something must have gone wrong with the *Athena* before
that. Maybe they were already helpless when the storm hit."

Jess' voice faltered, and Win's arm tightened; he
knew as well as she that there was something more to be
said. "Pieces of the boat were found, all sorts of equipment,
but nothing of them, not one thing, not a scarf, a
hat, a jacket." The full horror of the nightmare lay between
them.

He did not try to reassure her with glib phrases about
clean burials. She felt the slight shudder of his body, the
physical acknowledgment of the shared vision. When finally
he spoke, his voice was soft, as though he were giving a
strange benediction. "I know, Jess, I know. Only one in
love with the sea can accept her as the final place. There is
no comfort I know of which will ease the fear of drowning.
But I don't think any death, any burial, in any place can
be accepted as long as it includes the body. It is a brutally

comforting fact that drowning is one of the least painful ways to die. But whether you will ever be able to accept that is up to you. The thing you must accept is that once death comes, the body contains nothing except a faint, physical resemblance to the one loved. All the things which made that person precious to you are gone—gone where, gone anywhere, only God knows, but the body is no longer important. The sea took the bodies of your family, but that's *all* she took; knowledge of them, memories of them, most of all, love of them, all of those things are still yours."

His voice died for a moment before he could go on. "What I don't understand is why you agreed to come with me today. Were I in your position, nothing on earth would have persuaded me to go."

She felt so relaxed, so warm, so safe pressed against the hard strength of his body, it was an effort to talk. She knew with a sure instinct that the way he held her was not the way of a man giving comfort to a distraught stranger; it was the way of a man holding a woman who is precious to him, a way of speaking love without words. She had nothing left to lose, everything to gain. Her voice was lazy and slow when she spoke. "If you were in my position, Winston St. James, you would have done exactly what I did because there is nothing worse than giving up time which might have been spent with someone you love. I learned that much from that day. There is never, never enough time for love."

Close against him, she could hear the sudden wild pulsing of his heart. She turned her head and closed her eyes as his mouth came down on hers: strength and fear, angry surrender and enormous vulnerability, endless hunger, and love above all else.

The boat lurched, and she didn't even care.

Win drew away, and his voice was shaky. "Good sailor that I am, I find it difficult to manage the boat and you at the same time, my dear."

"My dear"—how different it sounded when he said it. Uncle Arthur used it often; Elsie Clinton, old woman and crook besides used it; Kyre had said it, but no one made it sound as Win did.

"There are a thousand likely spots along the shore-line. I'll put in. I think we have a few things to . . . um . . . discuss," he said, failing utterly in his attempt to be firm. Jess gave a throaty laugh and curled closer, her eyes closing sleepily. She could hardly believe this added facet of the miracle—she felt so peaceful with him, able to close her eyes without fear of rude waking even here on the sea.

13

I,
Beyond all limit of what else i' th' world,
Do love, prize, honor you.

Jess awakened to the sound of Win's laugh, a lovely sound first time heard. "I'm happy to see that I am such fascinating company, my whole crew has fallen asleep. Look lively now, I've chosen the perfect beach."

Indeed he had. They got the boat in easily, and Jess sighed with pleasure as she looked around. The sand was faintly pink, and the small, half circle of beach was ringed by a rocky cliff and heavy foliage, making it nearly inaccessible by any means but the way they had come, and they had it all to themselves.

Jess stripped off her blouse and slacks and plopped herself down on the warm sand clad in a blue bikini made of a minimum of material. She heard Win's gasp, and she looked up at him, teasing, and said, "Scared you, didn't I?"

"Scared is not the word I would choose," he said slowly, and his eyes caressed her until she could feel shivers of delight as though he were touching her physically.

She bent her head so she would not have to look at him, so that she could think clearly. There were things she had to say. "Look, Win, I've never done this before, and I'm not so wanton that I approve. You have Margaret, and no matter her faults, you belong to her; you'll go back to her. I'm an artist, a book illustrator actually, and I like my work. I've got to go back, too. Then it will be all over. But, please, just give me these few days. Uncle Arthur meant it to be. I want it to be. I want you so much, I think I must be possessed to settle for so little, especially since you are a . . . a criminal." There, the word was spoken.

He was beside her in an instant; his arms held her tightly, and his voice was a moan against her throat. "Jess, my Jess, I don't deserve such love." His mouth found hers, kissing her tenderly, slowly at first, growing more and more demanding, and she answered him gladly and without reservation, letting the world and its problems whirl away in the joy of her mind and body. His kisses grew gentle again, touching her closed eyelids, tracing the pattern of her face, savoring the sun-warm skin in the hollow of her throat, moving. . . .

He released her so suddenly that her eyes flew open to stare at him in hurt wonder.

"Christ, sweetheart, don't look at me like that!" he protested. "It's just that I've lied by not telling you the whole truth. I've told you what Margaret's like, but I haven't told you what I've become. I knew she had a kind of illness, and I thought I could change her, but in fact it worked quite the other way. After five years of marriage to her, I had learned to hate, had forgotten how to love. She wasn't even discreet. She seduced men I knew well, men I considered friends, and she didn't care whether I found out or not.

"I divorced her. It was the only way, but putting her out of my life didn't really change anything. I have been as sick as Margaret, perhaps I still am."

"Divorce?" Jess croaked. How could so ugly a word sound so beautiful? "You mean you're not married to her, to anyone anymore?"

"No."

"Oh, Win! Why didn't you tell me that to begin with instead of letting me commit myself to sin?" She tried to laugh, but it was a bad attempt.

"Don't you see, I was warning you away! If I did what was best for you, I would still be warning you away. I thought I could do it, thought I could right up to the moment I saw you last night. The black dress helped, I admit, but it was the look on your face that finished me. I walked for hours after that. It didn't help. I carried you with me every step.

"Jess, it is a terrible sickness when one decides to hate instead of love, when one decides never to be vulnerable again. All the things that make it worthwhile to be a human being dry up until there is nothing left, no joy or sorrow, only a great empty place of hating, and even that's a dead thing."

Jess clenched her hands together until her nails bit into her flesh. For a moment, her eyes were so blurred with tears she could not see him. She wanted to hold him close and comfort him, but she knew he needed to finish saying, just as she had, all the things which he had kept in silence for too long.

His voice softened with the mention of his uncle. "The other half truth I told you was about the wager. It was not made until after I was divorced. Arthur knew what I was becoming, what I was. He has a way of knowing all too much." Jess nodded in complete agreement. "He tried various courses, chiding me gently, arranging gatherings where I would be bound to meet women who had characters the opposite of Margaret's. He hoped I would come around with just a bit of help from him. But then, about two years ago, he lost patience.

"I can laugh about it now and be thankful," he said, his eyes glowing as he looked at Jess fully again, "but at the time I was furious. He asked me to meet him for luncheon at his club in London, something he does quite often, so I suspected nothing out of the ordinary. But nothing was ordinary from the time I walked in, and I remember it all as though it had just happened.

"His club is typical of the old guard's haunts. The main room is a horrible dark cave with mounds of overstuffed furniture, and Arthur was waiting there for me, in a corner, like a spider.

"The first thing I saw was the ring, the Barton ring, the one you have. He was turning it round and round in his hands. 'See this?' he barked, and I told him I could scarcely miss it, he was making such a point of it. That was about the last thing I said until the lecture was over.

"He said that though I had always known the ring was to go to me at his death, I hadn't known that he had planned to give it to me as a gift for my bride when I chose her, that is, until he met 'that Margaret woman.'

"'Nephew,' he said, 'I would have died clutching this ring and taken it to Hades with me before I would have let that harlot have it. I kept it, but I did not lose hope for a long time. I was convinced you would find a suitable woman to share your life, in spite of your first mistake. It seems I was wrong. You have developed all of the characteristics of a misogynist, a bad first for both families. Brigands and rakes we've had, but never a woman hater that I know of. The world is full of lovely, talented, and compassionate women, but you've gone deaf, dumb, and blind. You've reduced your emotional life to something below the level of a newt. And I won't have it. I'll wager this ring I can find someone for you, and when I do, I'll put her in your path wearing this ring. I will give myself five years since that is how long we had to bear your choice. If in that time I don't find her, or if you find her before I do, the ring is yours.'

"At first I couldn't say anything at all, and then I said a great deal. I told him he was mad for a start, raving mad, and then I told him there was a fitting word for men who procure women for other men and that that would undoubtedly be a first for both families, too. It didn't make any difference to him; he just sat there twirling that damn ring. I stalked out intending never to see him again, but of course, I couldn't stick to it. A few months later, there I was, visiting him at his club. But neither of us has ever mentioned it again, and I thought he'd given the whole thing up for the mad idea it was, perhaps even engineered the scene in the first place for no other reason but to make me feel something, even anger."

Win took a deep breath before he continued. "So you can imagine how I felt when I saw a member of a chattering group of American tourists, a tall, beautiful woman with midnight hair and deep-blue eyes wearing the Barton ring."

"Yes," Jess agreed dryly, "I can imagine, despite that flattering description. I've been imagining ever since yesterday."

She laughed. "Win, don't look like that! You didn't hatch the plot, Uncle Arthur did, and you didn't go along with it, I did. I didn't know it involved you—I didn't even know you existed—but I figured I wasn't to be the sole victim. Yesterday I finally understood what he meant when he said he trusted 'uncle' would be the proper title in the future." She told him about Arthur's advent in her life, about his mention of the sea change and Miranda in the note that had accompanied the ring. And she told him honestly about Larry and saw nothing but understanding in his eyes.

"You see, I knew from the first that Uncle Arthur had something in mind, but I trusted him. And I must admit I was awfully curious besides."

Win shook his head wearily. "Everything is backwards. You trusted him on the basis of what little you knew about him; I didn't trust him though I've had a lifetime of his wisdom and kindness, and I've never known his uncanny ability to judge the worth of people to fail. With all of that, I thought at best you were a heartless little bitch out for a bit of sport, at worst a calculating woman who had done a confidence job on my uncle. You don't even look shocked. I have a nasty feeling that that says something about how truly hopeless I must seem to you."

"Wrong! I'm not at all surprised you thought those things; in your position, I would have thought the same. But I'm being terribly presumptuous because I'm assuming you changed your mind about me along the way. True?"

"Not very far along the way either. I think it started about two minutes after I saw you on the steps for the first time. A warning voice spoke right then, telling me you could not be all the beautiful young things you seemed to be, that if I believed you were, I would be as foolish as my old uncle. Yes, I've done a lot of talking to myself to no avail. Every time I saw you with that Tarkington man I wanted to kill him. And when I was injured, my instinct was to go to you for help. And I knew that even when you learned my name, it meant nothing to you. I'm fairly thick, you see, but it did begin to dawn on me that Uncle Arthur might not have told you much. He has always had enormous power to turn people in his own direction when he cares to. But what I could not understand, cannot understand even now is your involvement with Tarkington and various other shady characters."

"Shady? Isn't that the pot calling the kettle black?" Jess' voice was steady, but her pulse beat a quick tattoo—others, not just Elsie, he had to be talking about Connor and Traylee.

"Love you, I do, but I still see Caliban with a cane and an English accent. I know you're trying to buy in, or whatever it's called, to Kyre's operation. Please, please don't do it! He's evil all the way through. There's got to be something else you can do. Let Arthur help, please!"

His reaction stunned her. He roared with laughter and swooped her into his arms again. "Darling, you are such a busy little snoop-about, I'm surprised you haven't found me out. Damn my suspicious nature, until yesterday I even suspected you knew and were still deciding which side to choose. It's against all regulations to tell you, but you of all people have a right to know. I'm a police officer."

That did it. The lords and ladies and large estates fit with Uncle Arthur and thus fit with Win's aloof British manner, might even fit with stealing jewels from that same milieu—but a cop?

She pulled away from him. "A bobby?" she asked, her voice squeaking.

His face was suddenly grim, and she didn't understand that at all. "Not exactly, but that's close enough. I'm a detective superintendent, a member of the London Metropolitan Police Force, Criminal Investigation Department. You're more likely to call the Metropolitan 'Scotland Yard'. I'm part of a squad that was formed four years ago to recover stolen art and antiques. In this case, I'm using information provided by my own department and by Interpol. Contrary to films, Interpol doesn't have its own agents crossing borders and trampling on sovereign rights; it's more of an information-gathering agency whose manpower is provided by the nations concerned." His clipped description of his position, defensive and sullen, how had she deserved that? She knew suddenly that she hadn't. She recognized his Margaret voice.

She slipped into the circle of his arms again, putting her own around him, ignoring his lack of response. "Hey, if this is going to go anywhere, you'll have to stop waiting for me to turn into Margaret. I'm not your ex-wife. I'm Jess Banbridge. And the operative word is love, remember? I said it first. I gather Margaret didn't like your work. I haven't any prejudices that way, I promise. I'm just surprised. Your fault I've judged you a crook. I've just accustomed myself to accepting you as the black sheep of Arthur's family, and I find instead you're a flatfoot, excuse the expression. Do you blame me for being confused?"

He laughed suddenly. "No, I don't blame you. It's been a sore point between Arthur and me ever since I made the decision to join the force. I read history at Oxford, and he expected me to become a don. He's very generous, and I am his heir, but I wanted to do something useful and active—sounds awfully pompous, doesn't it? But I would hate to be in the position of waiting for him to die. If I had my way he would live forever. He accuses us of thwarting his philanthropic impulses. My parents are just as stubborn about not letting him accept their responsibilities. I expect a lot of it is silly pride."

"I don't," said Jess. "I couldn't bear it if you were any other way."

His arms came around and held her so tightly, she thought he must be making up for lost time. She hadn't the breath to talk anymore, and Win's own voice was strangled. "Jess, my own Jess, I love you."

They lay in each other's arms on the warm sand. And when they found speech again, they talked of themselves, asking questions of each other eagerly, making up for time unshared, skirting the main issue between them. But finally Win drew away and said gently, "I'm still on duty, and we have a great deal to discuss. I need to know what you know, and I need to know how you learned it."

Jess had known this was inevitable, but she hadn't wanted to face it. She loved Win; she wanted to help him. Her relief that he was on the right side of the law was boundless. And as she had warned Traylee, she would choose Win over everyone else. But Traylee trusted her, and that made her responsible for Connor too, and she did not want either of them in trouble, no matter that Connor was a thief.

"Please, a swim first, then I'll tell you what I can." Give me time to think of a way.

Win nodded slowly. "All right. I could stand a cooler temperature, too." He grinned crookedly, but Jess knew he understood her delaying tactics all too well.

Win had worn swimming trunks under his pants and shirt, but when he took off his outer clothing, Jess saw the tape and gasped, "I'm so sorry! I forget all about your ribs when I touched you. I must have hurt you!"

"I assure you, you did not, though I deserve it." He kissed the fading bruise on one of her arms. "I will be most grateful when these are gone; they remind me all too clearly that you have good cause to judge me less than a gentleman."

She kissed him for answer and giggled. "If we keep this up, we won't ever get to the water." She meant it, too; his body was a beautiful temptation, all long bones and hard muscle from broad shoulders to narrow hips and long legs, a body lean and capable of great strength, scarred here and there and more beautiful than Kyre's plastic perfection. Her eyes widened as she saw it; had she not been so concerned with his ribs she would have noticed it immediately, for it was hard to miss.

"I . . . I know you don't need the cane, but it looks as though you should. What . . . what happened?" she stammered, staring at the deep and still red scar which ran an ugly gash across his left kneecap and partway down his leg. No wonder he didn't wear Bermuda shorts.

He shrugged in dismissal. "It's fully healed now, and

the scar will fade with time. I happened to be in the wrong place at the wrong time, and someone took offense."

"That was on purpose?" Jess gasped in horror.

"Well, yes, though the man had meant to use it on a crate of stolen paintings, a crowbar is fairly purposeful. But don't look like that, darling, a good surgeon repaired it perfectly. I haven't needed the cane for a long while. I just brought it along as cover on this job because people tend to discount those with physical disabilities, even partial ones. A man who limps doesn't seem much a threat to anyone."

"You did to me," Jess said, forcing a laugh when her real impulse was to be sick. Her mind could picture all too vividly the iron bar smashing into Win's leg, gouging out skin and muscle, breaking bone. She was getting far too clear a picture of what his job could mean. She turned and fled into the water while Win confined himself to the shallows to keep the tape dry.

The cool water felt heavenly, and she willed herself to be mindless as she swam, but all too soon Win called her out. "Enough, back to the beach, my girl."

They sat facing each other, and she could not keep her eyes from straying back to the scar. "Don't torture yourself, Jess," Win said quietly. "I must seem a clumsy chap to you, but honestly, I've had less than my share of injuries. I'm usually careful and lucky. I just pushed the crowbar man and here in Bermuda, Tarkington too far. I didn't realize Tarkington's temper was that short. He's got a nice little operation, and the last thing he wants is a partner."

"And I've made it worse," Jess said flatly, and she told him about Kyre's threat and her own belligerent admission that she knew what he had done before and would kill him if he hurt Win again.

Far from being angry or worried about it, Win laughed in delight and kissed her hand in mock gallantry. "That's for being my fearless defender. I will request that Her Majesty award you the Order of the Garter." But then his face sobered. "You will, of course, stay away from him until this thing is over?"

"You bet I will! He's the last person on earth I want to see!" She shivered, remembering the hide-and-seek game of the previous night, a game to be avoided in the future even if she had to hang on bodily to other members of Jet Sets for protection. She was glad Win didn't know about it.

"Are you ready to tell me?" he asked and it was impossible to miss the firmness under the gentle note.

She spoke hesitantly, trying to give him the maximum information without betraying the Jamesons. She explained how she had noticed the difference in the stones, how she had taken the necklace to the jeweler, how she had judged Elsie's ignorance of bird life and proximity to Elizabeth indications of the old woman's involvement in addition to the damning glitter in her eyes at the sight of precious objects; she told of how she had noticed the bruises on Kyre's hand the morning after Win had been so badly beaten; she mentioned the house near Church Street where Elsie went under suspicious circumstances, and then she stopped with a nervous gulp—the only reason it was suspicious was because Connor had gone there, too.

Her eyes were full of misery when she raised them to Win, but he said nothing, only watched her, waiting for her to trust him fully.

"I told him I'd choose you," she said sadly, "but I won't tell you the names. I can't, they trust me, too." She was careful not to use names, but she told him everything else about her meetings with Traylee and then drew a deep breath before she told him about the drug shipment. "You probably know they're all waiting for something, maybe you even know what it is, at least what we think it is."

"Yes to the first question, no to the second," Win said curtly.

"Well, I can hardly believe any of this, but my friends think it's cocaine, a large shipment, and that it's coming in by plane to be picked up at sea by boat."

He didn't look surprised. He merely nodded and said, "It makes sense. Tarkington is a very greedy man, and the narcotics traffic is lucrative to say the least. No wonder he didn't want to cut me in. Jess, I want those names."

"I can't tell! The older one, he's been involved, he's broken the law, I know all that. But he's dead set against drugs, and that's why he's been following Kyre, threatening him, trying to see if he can get enough of the men to oppose the plan, trying to see which side the old lady is on. He's grown up a hard way, but he has his own set of rules, and he sticks to them. He didn't have anything to do with beating you up." The wild, pleading note, her voice, Traylee's voice.

"I am utterly astounded by the extent of your knowledge. That an amateur should learn in a few days what has taken several professional agencies a couple of years to piece together is nothing short of a miracle, and I'm proud of you. But it must stop. You are an amateur, and amateurs get hurt playing with professionals. It would take very little effort to break your pretty neck. Jess, I love you, but I'm a police officer, and you are withholding valuable information. That's a criminal offense. You're an accessory to the crime."

"I know." Her voice was hardly more than a whisper, but her will was as strong as his. "Give me a little more time. I think I can persuade my friends to cooperate willingly. The most important information is theirs, not mine, and basically, they're on your side in this, and it would give the man a break as far as punishment goes, wouldn't it, if he helped you?"

"Yes, it probably would, but it's out of the question!" he snapped. "Do you think I am going to let you go wandering about, dealing with people like that? You haven't been listening, have you? I love you. I don't want you to be killed!" Win reached for her and held her hard against him but all she could hear was Traylee's voice, "I don't want you dead. You're all I've got."

She pulled away, and the lie was firm. "I wouldn't be wandering about. My young friend is supposed to call me sometime tonight. I'll ask then. If I haven't arranged it by tomorrow, I'll tell you the names."

"Short of turning you over to my colleagues, I haven't

much choice, have I? It's blackmail, you know, a sweet way to love." The steel was back in his voice, and Jess couldn't bear it. He had such a long way to go to learn to trust again, and she was spoiling it. The tears slipped down her cheeks unbidden as she searched desperately for some way out.

"Don't cry, darling, don't," Win begged, brushing her tears away with an unsteady hand. "I think your loyalty is misplaced, but I can understand it. I love you most of all for your fierce heart. I'll give you your twenty-four hours, but you are not to make any contact save by telephone, agreed?"

"Agreed." Her voice was muffled as she nestled against him. *I'll try, I really will,* she promised silently, *but I know I can trust my life to Traylee and even to Connor, and I will if I must.*

"Just a minute," she said, pulling away suddenly and regarding him intently. "I've told you not everything, but close to it. You've told me nothing. How did Arthur's plan work so well, and then why did he warn me against it? And come to think of it, since you are a policeman, why didn't you just go get regular medical attention that night instead of risking so much by coming to me? If you claim professional silence, I'll sit here and scream until the harbor patrol or whatever comes to my rescue."

He looked at her a long time before he spoke. "Most of the information I have is classified, and I have made it a rule never to discuss such things with anyone. I certainly never did with my wife. But if I can't trust you, then I'm lost in any case, personally and professionally." Jess' throat closed with gratitude for the ultimate gift of his trust, but she did not have to say the words; he could see it in her face.

"The most innocent part played in all of this belongs to my uncle. He is in fact a shareholder of the Queen's Gate, as you well know I am not." Win smiled at her briefly in tribute. "He arranged the special rate for Mrs. Allenby's group, and when I told him I was coming out, he was delighted, and of course, he then made certain you came too. It wasn't his fault he didn't know I was on duty and not on vacation; I didn't tell him. We seldom discuss the particulars of my assignments. He is too nervous of my safety. I found the most casual tale would distress him, and so it's easier for both of us if we don't talk about my work."

Jess touched the scar on his leg. "I sympathize with Uncle Arthur," she said, and he grinned at her. "You would. The two of you have a lot in common. He can be as nosy as you are. I assume he's found out about this. I can imagine how he felt when he discovered he'd sent you into the middle of a police case. He's a close friend of one of my superiors, and I expect he began having second thoughts about why his nephew was taking a vacation all of a sudden. I haven't wanted to do much beside work for a long time."

"We'll just see about that in the future," Jess murmured as she kissed him.

"Good lord, woman," he said awhile later, "I'm glad I don't normally have to give reports with you around. Where was I?"

"Uncle Arthur."

"Yes, of course, he certainly has had more than a little to do with this." His fingers traced the delicate angle of her jaw. "Coincidence, fate, whatever one calls it, did play into his hands because, had I not been working on this case, I wouldn't have come to Bermuda and Arthur might have had a much more difficult time making his plan work. It is really not so odd that Tarkington and Mrs. Clinton chose an excursion such as this one. It seems they've been doing it for years, choosing harmless, wealthy groups to travel with, though usually they haven't been in the same place at the same time."

"Yes, I know," Jess admitted.

"I see," said Win, "then I expect you also know from your friends that the men they've recruited have little cause to cooperate with the authorities."

The way he said "your friends" with such automatic contempt made her angry, but she kept her voice even. "Please, stop doing that! You don't know them; I do, and in spite of everything, they are my friends."

His voice was as quiet as hers. "All right, Jess, I

apologize, and I'll try. But everytime I think of them, I think of you in danger, and that is not getting any easier to bear. Truce?"

"Truce." War with him was never going to be successful when he looked at her like that.

"As a matter of fact, I admit it was through one of these people we got our first solid clue. A man died in Nassau, in the Bahamas, and it might have gone down as just another waterfront incident—quick tempers and a quick knife—except that his wife wanted revenge badly enough to overcome fear for herself. She didn't know much about what he'd been up to, but she knew it was illegal, lucrative, and dangerous enough so that he had wanted to get out for a long time despite the money. She reported that once when he had been particularly incoherent on rum, he had babbled about the Devil buying his soul for the pretty green stones. And the Devil was a white man."

"It's a good description of him," Jess agreed grimly. "And he's very effective in his choice of whom to tempt."

"Yes, but unfortunately the world seems to have more than its share of people like Tarkington, and the description might not have meant much had not one officer been so alert. He remembered a report he'd read about the increasing number of specialized thefts on the international scene, thefts involving well-known paintings, jewels, and other objets d'art. There are any number of collectors who are fanatic enough to pay high prices for stolen articles. Though the Bahamas are self-governing in most aspects, England still retains responsibility for the police, and the officer sent a humble inquiry to headquarters to be directed to my squad and to the office of Interpol. He asked if the murder might have anything to do with a larger picture, adding he had to admit he knew of no missing jewels in his area and it was all very confusing, but he was curious.

"We were more than curious. We were thankful because it appeared to be the lead we'd been waiting for. For nearly two years Interpol and when it concerned British territory, my squad had been tracing a strange pattern. Wealthy clients would arrive at the jeweler's to sell some valuable trinket or to have it cleaned only to be told the stones were paste, good quality paste, but worthless nonetheless. The green stones the man had spoken of were emeralds, and the woman had already discovered they were missing. When we checked with her, we found she had indeed taken a holiday to the Bahamas. However, she had met a score of people of various nationalities and remembered little about any of them, so she wasn't much help. But one common factor did emerge when we checked back with other victims, and here Interpol served as an invaluable liaison since they went through the same process with authorities and victims of countries other than Great Britain—we found that almost without exception the people who had suffered the theft of major gems in the past two years had visited or lived in the Caribbean area or Bermuda, and many of them had spent a good deal of time in some exclusive section in or around your city of Boston.

"Having the area narrowed down somewhat was a help, but not enough since it still involved thousands upon thousands of people. Two things happened to break the case. The first was a trap we set, the second a trap which was set inadvertently and worked for us.

"The police have often been accused of being less than a step away from the criminals, and in a sense, that's valid. In order to work effectively, we must know how the criminals work. And there are favors exchanged, a little less pressure here or there in exchange for information which might lead to the capture of bigger game. That's how I acquired a list of disreputable references for my assignment here, and that's also how we set the trap. One of my men spent months setting himself up as a buyer of stolen goods, particularly jewels, and some very dubious characters helped spread the word that he paid well for purchases. It was a gamble, of course, since the stones might well have been out of circulation already, but we guessed there must be some cooling-off period involved in the scheme, and the gamble paid off. Tarkington sold him the emeralds at great cost to the British taxpayers six

months ago. And he has been watched ever since by your
government and mine. He was not arrested because it did
not seem possible he could be working alone, especially
because he himself did not have the extensive social
connections necessary.

"The second trap was set for us by Mrs. Clinton's
daughter, Janet. The worst mistake Mrs. Clinton made
was to underestimate her. I expect mother has a lot to do
with it, but I've read the report, and that young woman is
a walking nightmare. She's in her midtwenties and has
been in and out of trouble with your police since she was
fifteen. She's been living with a man who has several other
bad habits in addition to her. They always need money,
and Janet has found several ways of obtaining it, but she
seems to prefer stealing. She and her mother hate each
other."

"Damn! I swallowed it, the whole thing," Jess swore.
"I nearly wept for the old woman when she told me the
tale of her wayward child."

"So have a lot of other people, otherwise she would
have been caught long before this," Win said kindly and
ignored Jess' snort of self-disgust. "But it seems old mother made a serious mistake—she left some of the stolen
jewels in her house, probably waiting for a way to get
them quietly to Tarkington. Her housekeeper still has
some feeling left for Janet, and she let her in and fed her
one day while mother was out. Janet helped herself to
several things including some of the jewelry. Apparently
the housekeeper denied Janet had been there, or perhaps
Mrs. Clinton never asked—one can hardly demand the
return of stolen articles. It must have been a pretty scene
when she told Tarkington what was missing. But neither of
them took any action; the last thing they wanted was to
attract attention.

"Janet, on the other hand, knew nothing about it, and
fortunately she took the jewels to a pawnbroker who,
though he isn't noted for his honesty, has a healthy respect
for the police. He called them, and they picked Janet up
for questioning. She protested she was just inheriting
things ahead of time—clever idea that—and her mother

had been holding out on her. Though her reasoning was crooked, her story rang true. She really did believe the jewelry belonged to her mother.

"Again, there was luck. The police checked it through to higher authorities instead of simply returning the stuff to Mrs. Clinton. Everyone was struck by the same incongruity which had made the pawnbroker so skittish—why should costume jewelry, worthless metal, turn out under a glass to be set with magnificent stones? Your FBI isn't a member of Interpol, but they maintain liaison posts in major European cities, and they got in touch. Interpol sends out circulars describing jewelry, paintings, and such when there is reason to believe they've been smuggled out of the country where they were stolen. Of course, they couldn't identify all of them, but there were a couple of peculiar cut which they had on report, and the whole thing seemed to tie in with our case.

"It made good sense. The woman had all the background and connections necessary to know the wealthy and their jewelry, so it was fairly clear she was the brain behind the operation. With a little checking, a couple of other things came to light. She had been rich, then poor, and for heretofore unknown reasons, she was well off again, and she traveled a good deal, mostly to the Caribbean area and to Bermuda. She's been under surveillance ever since.

"Tarkington and Mrs. Clinton have been very clever. They—" His voice stopped abruptly, but Jess didn't need his silence to know something was wrong. She could see his muscles cord, and she could feel his tension as though it were her own. He was suddenly a sleek, dangerous, and unfamiliar animal, ready to spring. She barely had time to recognize his alarm was caused by another sailboat heading for their beach before he was in front of her, blocking her view of the boat, shielding her, she realized, from its line of fire.

"Stupid of me, I haven't a weapon, didn't think I'd need a gun for lovemaking with you. If anything happens, run, get into the water as fast as you can, and try to make it around the island to some place where the foliage is heavy enough to cover you. Don't wait. Promise?" His voice was as calm and matter-of-fact as though he were giving yesterday's weather report. Her voice was not. "Yes," she whispered, knowing she would not leave him, and the words were a dry rasp.

The threat was over as quickly as it had begun. The two in the boat with their short blond hair were a look-alike couple of honeymooners in search of the perfect beach. They were even prepared to meet new people and share the sand, but Win was not, and Jess listened in growing amazement to the accent he was using; it was so overly British it would have pleased Noel Coward, and it was not at all like Win's normal speech. "Terribly sorry, old chap, but this beach belongs to Lord and Lady Crenshaw, private you know. We're their guests, so we can't extend an invitation."

Aside from storming the beach, there was nothing for the couple to do except sail away, and Jess managed to wait until they were out of earshot before she started to laugh. "You are awful! That accent and Lord and Lady Crenshaw no less! I saw their faces. Nine out of ten Americans are completely undone by an English accent. It's a national curse. And your battered body probably convinced them you're a troublemaker." She knew she was laughing and chattering to cover the nervous reaction which was hitting her, and Win knew it, too. He held her until she stopped shaking, murmuring, "It's all right, Jess. I'm sorry I frightened you. I'm becoming as worried about your safety as Arthur is about mine."

Jess let it go at that. She didn't want to explain that the change in him had scared her as much as any danger from the people in the boat. The men she had known had little experience with violence beyond hard tennis games and weekend sailing; if they had fought another human being at all, it had been in long past school days and even then had been ineptly done and for inane reasons. Win lived constantly with the threat of violence, and there was nothing inept about his response to it. No one could win the contest every time—his body showed the rounds he had lost—but he had won more than his share because he was trained, ready, and dedicated, a man of power, a man of violence.

Her tension eased suddenly. The acceptance which had begun earlier grew stronger. She would live with it. It was part of him. She did not want him to change.

She drew away from him and met his anxious look with a smile. "I believe you were telling me about how clever Kyre and Elsie have been when we were so rudely interrupted. I'd like to hear the rest, please." Resolutely she kept herself from glancing nervously out to sea.

She saw the relief flood into his face; he had known her doubt, and now he saw her undiminished acceptance. So strong in other ways, so vulnerable in this—the responsibility was hers now.

"Yes, they have been clever." His voice steadied. "They have seldom stolen the jewels outright unless the piece was so exotic it couldn't be duplicated. And the substitution of paste is tricky because it means two things—Tarkington must bring the paste copies with him, and when the substitution can't be made at the scene because of intricate settings, he must steal the article, make the switch, and replace it without getting caught. Actually, he is well-qualified. His Boston firm is legitimate, and he travels to Europe often under the cover of business. He knows a great deal about antiques, especially about antique jewelry. He showed promise as a jewelry designer when he was at university. Many of his instructors were disappointed when he gave it up for a more stable profession. They're going to be more disappointed when they discover he didn't give it up at all, merely put it to a different use. I expect when he and the woman worked separately, he simply carried the paste copies in; even had they been found, he couldn't have been arrested for possessing costume jewelry. And when Mrs. Clinton arrived later and left wearing the cheap settings bearing genuine stones, she was hardly the type of woman who would be suspect. Demure old ladies of sixty or more seldom hold much interest for customs' officials. We did not know at that time that Mrs. Clinton and Tarkington had first become acquainted for similar reasons. While

Mrs. Clinton's husband was busy disposing of her fortune, she sold most of her gems. Tarkington got rid of them for her, quite legally, and substituted paste. Undoubtedly they recognized a common bond of greed even then.

"But had we not been so fortunate, we would most probably still be regarding the case as a hopeless maze, and the best luck of all came when they both made plans to come to Bermuda. The airlines kindly supplied us with daily passenger lists beginning with the day Tarkington bought a ticket. You were a suspicious last minute addition to your tour, damn that scheming uncle of mine! I assume Tarkington and Mrs. Clinton being in the same place together is a result of the power play over the cocaine deal."

"Yes, that much I can confirm. My friends say the old woman is against it."

"She'd better be careful then. Perhaps it will never be proven, but I am convinced that if Tarkington did not murder the man in Nassau, at the very least, he ordered it done. He is not a man of delicate sensibilities, Jess. He wouldn't scruple to kill a woman if she were a danger to him. And that includes you."

Jess shuddered, thinking of the two men Traylee had said were missing, and licked dry lips. "I believe it. I have no intention of giving him a chance. But you still haven't told me why you didn't go for proper medical care."

She saw his guilty look, and she knew. "Why, talk about taking risks! You didn't go because a report would have meant more men assigned to the job, having it taken out of your hands. Of all the silly, egotistical idiots!" She was furious because she was so afraid for him.

"Things are a bit touchy here. The Bermuda police are very competent, and unlike the force in the Bahamas, they are independent of Great Britain. Only the Home Office's request and the fact that I was involved in the case in England with information from Nassau besides made it possible for me to work on it here. Even so, the Commissioner here was supposed to have been informed of every development, and I was to have worked with a detective sergeant. I have been a bit greedy, but too many police officers have a tendency to put criminals on their guard."

Jess still regarded him skeptically, and he shrugged and admitted, "All right, that too. I didn't have so much to live for then. But I will call in assistance; I'll have to since there's to be some sea action, and it's now basically drug squad work."

She caught the glitter of excitement in his eyes, and she kissed him. He held her tightly before by silent, mutual agreement they put the boat in the water and headed back. They were both weary from so many emotional upheavals and from the intrusion of so much violence. Their time would come when the case was closed.

The wind was fresh, and Win sailed the boat skillfully, but already his mind was completely back into his work. He looked carefully at every boat they passed. "It's off season and cruising the Atlantic can be hazardous now, but there are still far too many ships coming in and out of these waters. We need the name of the craft."

"I'll ask my friend when he calls." She just barely prevented herself from saying, "When I see him. It's worth a try anyway."

"Yes, it's worth a try," Win agreed. Though he did not complain, Jess saw him move restlessly to accommodate the growing pain in his side. He looked so tired and far away, she was even more committed to her plan, but she had one more thing to tell him. "The ring, I'm sorry, it's gone. Unless you took it back, they have it." She stopped, unable to admit how easy she had made it for someone.

He understood her all too well, but his voice was gentle. "I haven't got it. I noticed you were no longer wearing it. I don't blame you, and in any case, the ring has done its work, turned curse to blessing. Perhaps we'll have it back, perhaps not, but you are not to feel guilty or break your heart over it."

"I love you," Jess said, and for a moment, Win's full attention was hers again.

14

*Now would I give a thousand furlongs of
sea for an acre of barren ground—long heath,
brown furze, anything. The wills above be done, but
I would fain die a dry death.*

It was late afternoon when they got back, and Win
insisted on walking with Jess all the way to her room,
though she protested that Kyre wouldn't try anything
while there was still daylight. "Anyway, I think he'll leave
me alone as long as I stay out of his way."

"I'm not taking any chances," Win said grimly. "I'll
come by to escort you to the pub, too."

"Help! I'm being held prisoner at the Queen's Gate,"
she cried, only half in jest.

"You are indeed," he agreed, and Jess' heart skipped
a beat. Despite finding comfort in his protective attitude,
it was going to make it very difficult for her to arrange a
meeting with Traylee.

When Sally came in, she said smugly, "I know all
about Elizabeth's husband. She told me before she left.
You missed it, you should have seen her face! If any man
of any age can keep his hands off a woman who looks that
young and beautiful, there must be something wrong with
him. Congratulations, my matchmaking friend." Jess hoped
Jonathan wouldn't keep hands off, and she hoped with
equal fervor that he wouldn't notice the ruby glass until
the real stone could be returned.

Sally took a closer look at Jess. "And speaking of

young and beautiful, I was just going to ask you about your day, but I don't think I have to. So the Englishman has it?"

"Yes, the Englishman has it, my God, does he have it! I just gave my world into his keeping, and I haven't any regrets. He'll give me room to be, he'd hate it any other way. And I'll give him room too, I will." Her voice was firm, and she did not try to shut out the image of the terrible scar or his battered side. She would have to accept those and their causes as he would have to accept the hours when she forgot that normal routine called for a meal or sleep and drew a picture instead.

"Well, aren't you going to ask me to be in your wedding? Turnabout's fair unless you have some sneaky idea for a run-away, to-hell-with-the-world plan."

"We didn't talk about marriage," Jess said. "Win's had as tough a go with it as Tom has, and you know I've never had terribly positive ideas about it. I love him. He loves me. We want to be together. That's enough. But I would say yes, wouldn't be able to say anything else if he did ask," she added wryly.

"Okay, Jaybe, I can handle that, just as long as you're happy. Two more questions, and I'll quit. Tom and I are going out to dinner tonight with dancing afterwards, would you and Mr. St. James like to go with us? And secondly, would you like to tell me what's been going on, aside from your falling in love with a foreigner?"

"I would like to say yes to both," Jess said quietly, "but I can't, not yet. Tomorrow night may be completely different, soon anyway. Will you have patience with me, old friend?"

"Of course I will," Sally agreed, but Jess was sorry about the worried look on her friend's face. What a relief it would be when she could tell her, to have the whole thing over, Win's case closed, the threats and violence reduced to the level of a fantastic story.

Jess was already dressed when Tom came by, but Sally was still in the middle of her preparations, and Tom threatened to take Jess out instead.

"Her Englishman might object to that," Sally warned

him, and after a first flash of astonishment, Tom wished
Jess well. "We've all fallen under the spell of the enchanted
islands," he said with satisfaction, and Jess was not surprised that he made no mention of Kyre; he was aware a
frost had set in between Jess and Kyre.

"Doesn't he look cute in that fatuous smile," Sally
quipped.

"Forty years with you, and no doubt I'll look suitably
grim," he shot back as they were leaving, and Jess would
have given much to have been able to spend the evening
with them in Win's company.

She picked up the phone as soon as they were gone
and asked the switchboard operator to call The Black
Diamond for her. The operator hesitated and asked, "Are
you sure that's the club you want, ma'am? It isn't a tourist
spot."

"It's the one I want," Jess replied firmly and suppressed
her annoyance at the unspoken objection in the woman's
voice—it was none of the operator's business if she wished
to call a black nightclub.

A soft island voice answered with the name of the
club, and Jess asked for Traylee, gripping the phone hard,
praying he would be there, feeling dizzy with relief when
he came on the line.

"Traylee, it's Jess. I've got to see you and your
brother, particularly your brother, tonight."

"Don't know, things are happening," Traylee said.
"But maybe he'll be here tonight, say half an hour before
our last meeting time. You could try, but it's risky. Boss
man's on the move."

Eleven thirty, half an hour before midnight, at the
club with Kyre on the move somewhere and Win totally
ignorant of her whereabouts—the whole plan was terrifying, but she couldn't see any other way. Even if she could
persuade them to come to the Queen's Gate, it would be
too dangerous; Win would surely discover them. "I'll be
there," she said before she could change her mind.

When Win came for her, she was composed enough
to smile at him, and there was no falsehood in the kiss she

gave him; she had to fight her impulse to cling to him and beg him not to let her go.

When they entered the pub, there were a few raised eyebrows at the sight of them together, but everyone was too polite to comment aside from Ann who whispered, "I'm happy because you are," as they passed her.

Jess knew from Traylee's words that Kyre would not be at the Queen's Gate, but she wondered with some misgiving why Elsie was also absent. She hoped it wasn't because the old woman had decided to work with Kyre on the drug deal after all. She pretended not to notice Win's frequent surveys of the company or the small frown that made the grooves of his face cut deeper. She wanted to touch him and smooth away the lines of pain and premature graying caused, she knew, more by the bitch who had been his wife than by the worries of his job. "Why, I don't even know how old you are!" she said in sudden wonder.

"I'm thirty-seven. Is that too old?"

"No. I suspect it's even rather young for a detective superintendent, but it's perfect for me. I'm twenty-six but giddy. I need an older, mature man to give me a balanced outlook." She tried to keep a straight face but failed, and they both laughed in realization of the picture they had just presented, grinning at each other like infatuated sixteen-year-olds. Jess was understanding Sally and Tom better every minute, and she vowed silently that no matter what she became, mistress or wife to Win, she would do her utmost to make his days so joyful that he would look less his age instead of ten years older.

They shared a table with the Kadases, and neither of them could help but relax in Joe's friendly presence. Sharon accepted Jess' change of companions with a knowing smile, which said she now truly understood why Jess had been so unhappy with Kyre.

Sharon and Joe were so obviously happy together, and when Joe ordered a bottle of wine, his first toast was to his wife. "My wife, my love, my joy," he said without embarrassment.

Jess found Win regarding her gravely, as though the toast were his, proposed to her, and she met his eyes bravely in spite of the inner voice wailing, "Why can things never be as they seem? I'm lying to you, Win, smiling at you, loving you, and still planning to go and see the Jamesons tonight."

Things worked too easily. When she excused herself after dinner, refusing coffee and reminding Win she had a phone call to wait for, he agreed readily. He did ask if he could wait with her, but he did not protest when she refused, telling him she would feel too constrained, too afraid of betraying her friends before they had a chance to give the information willingly. "I'll ring you as soon as I've gotten my call," she promised.

"All right, but if I haven't heard from you by the time the exchange closes, I'll stop by."

"What if I'm asleep?" she asked weakly, so little time to get back from the club if she ever got there in the first place.

"I'll disturb you," he said, and under other circumstances, Jess would have been amused by the wicked gleam in his eyes. He made her wait outside while he checked the room, and then he kissed her long and thoroughly.

She roused herself and went inside when she could no longer hear the tapping. Soon even that masquerade would be over. "Let it be soon, let it end well," the words hummed in her head as she changed into dark slacks and a jersey. She couldn't help the white of her tennis shoes; she had no shoe polish, and she needed quiet walking shoes because she was going to have to sneak out and probably walk the whole way to Hamilton. It was nine thirty now; if she left by ten thirty, she would have time. She listened at the door for a long time, and she heard it more than once—the tapping, Win on patrol. She smiled grimly to herself; though he undoubtedly had an eye out for Kyre, his main purpose was to make sure she did not leave, and worse, he was justified in not trusting her. He must be very busy, making his rounds while still checking back at his own room to see if the phone was ringing, not wanting her to know he was suspicious. It was complicated, but it would work for her—she guessed he would wait the maximum time before knocking on her door.

She heard the tapping again shortly before her departure time. She waited until she could hear it no longer before she opened the door very carefully, closing and locking it behind her. She was committed now. She could hear nothing besides the lap of water, distant voices, and the thunder of her own heart as she went up the stairs and stopped before she stepped onto the road. She willed herself to know where he was, to pick up the slightest noise. He had left the light on his balcony out, or perhaps he had unscrewed it again on purpose, and she could not tell if he stood there in the shadows. She shivered as the cold sweat broke on her skin. It was horrible to be hiding in terror, waiting for the chance to flee from the man she loved.

She heard it, the faint tapping at the top of the stairs. He had been standing there, and he was coming down now. She took her chance, trusting he would be concentrating for a few seconds on the dark stairs. She stepped quietly onto the road, and body hugging the building, she moved along it as swiftly as she dared and ducked into the next stair opening. Her heart was going so fast she had difficulty breathing without gasping audibly for air, but no shout rang out, and she heard Win go down the stairs toward her room.

She was on the road again, walking swiftly and then running into the darkness, not stopping until she was on the main road leading into the city. There were no sounds of pursuit, and she drew a deep, jagged breath and rested a minute before she started walking again. She met no other foot traffic until she reached the first buildings on Front Street, and though a couple of young men eyed her appreciatively, no one gave her any trouble. But she felt terribly vulnerable. Traylee's words kept coming back to her, "Boss man's on the move." That could mean anywhere, including Hamilton. No mention of Elsie. The old woman she could handle, but not Kyre. She hurried her steps toward the center of Front Street, and she grabbed the first taxi available.

"I want to go to The Black Diamond, please," she said.

The driver was an old man. His tightly curled cap of hair and his small beard were streaked with white, and his brown skin was as lined as fine wood. His eyes were sad and wise, and even in her distress, Jess ached to capture him on paper. His voice was soft but precise, as though he spoke to a wayward child. "Little one, you don't want to be going there."

"But I do! I must go there; it's more important than I can tell you. I'll be all right, I've got a friend who works there, and he's expecting me." Wild with pleading. *Oh, Traylee, we've got to work it out so we won't have to be scared anymore.*

The old man nodded slowly. "I'll take you. But know I believe white woman, black man, trouble, trouble all around."

Jess let him think what he would about her relationship with her friend, but she could not resist answering him as they drove. "Trouble usually comes from those who enjoy making it. The main difference in people isn't the color of their skin or whether they're male or female, it's whether they enjoy good or evil." More clearly than ever before, she knew what she said was true. She would trust Traylee and Connor with her life—she was going to do just that—while she knew Kyre, a white man with a background far closer to her own than that of the Jamesons, would kill her without a second thought if he had to.

"I'm old. You're new and young. I won't live to see it, but I hope you do," the driver said.

They followed an up and down road through back streets Jess had not seen before, and when they arrived at The Black Diamond, the old man refused to take any money. "Don't take money for trouble," he said.

"Will you take my thanks, then?" Jess asked, offering her hand, and the man shook it firmly and smiled at her. "I'll watch you to the door." Jess, grateful for this added bit of comfort, turned and waved to him before she went inside.

At first her senses could take in nothing save the loud

pulsing beat of the music—soul straight from the States. The club wasn't all that large, and the dance floor took up a good half of the floor space, leaving the rest closely packed with tables and chairs and booths along the walls. The club was crowded, and the air of the people was happy as they danced or sat at the tables trying to carry on conversations on a different frequency from the music. A no-hassle place—hers was the only white face.

A tall man materialized at her side. "I am the manager. May I help you?" he asked politely, but his face was a mask, his eyes wary. "Perhaps you have come to the wrong place?"

Jess saw other people noticing her presence now; she watched their conversations die, their faces taking on the same reserve as the manager's.

"Please, I'm looking for a friend. This is the right place. I was to meet him here, though I am a little early. His name is Traylee Jameson." In spite of her efforts to hold it steady, her voice was quivering. The man's eyes flickered at the mention of the name and searched her face intently, but he made no move to find Traylee, clearly judging she could mean nothing but trouble, just as the old man had said.

She was beginning to feel desperate, and when Traylee came up beside the man, she had to restrain herself from flying into his arms.

"It's okay, Jim, the lady is a friend of mine," Traylee said, and Jim's face relaxed, glad to have the problem out of his hands, but Jess heard him whisper to Traylee, "Strange friend. Better take care."

Traylee led her to a booth along the far wall, and Jess heard several comments in their wake, most of them uneasy, some unpleasant. She couldn't blame them; she was off limits, and her color made her a threat to them, to Traylee, even though she did not wish it so. *Maybe I won't live to see it either, old man,* she thought dismally, but when they sat down, Traylee's smile reassured her. "You are one brave lady, glad to have you on my side," he said.

Her eyes were growing more accustomed to the murky red light, and she saw that the walls were hung with posters of black leaders and artists from all over the world. Martin Luther King and Jimi Hendrix were side by side on the wall beside their booth. She looked at the pictures sadly—both dead now.

"Jess, we're not here to worry about race; we're here because we're friends—with people we love in trouble. Right?"

She was struck anew by Traylee's maturity and wisdom, both so much greater than his actual age of twenty or so. Strange to have him reassuring her with the same argument she had given the old taxi driver. "Right. Do you want to talk about it now or wait for Connor?"

"Wait for Connor. He's reluctant, you know that, but he'll be here. He promised." Connor's promises to Traylee were obviously regarded as the word of God.

And suddenly he was there, his enormous bulk towering over them as he looked first at one face then at the other, his scowl giving way to a reluctant grin. "You two figured out yet how to save the world?"

"Not yet," Traylee replied promptly, "but if you'll sit down, we'll discuss it."

Connor sat so that he had a view of the room, his back to the wall, and his eyes did a quick survey. We all do it, Jess thought, all of us in this game, constantly watching for enemies.

Apparently Connor was satisfied with what he saw, or did not see, and he turned his full attention on his companions. "All right, give, what're we here for?"

Jess looked at Traylee, and he nodded for her to speak first. "I expect Traylee has told you what I know and how I found out."

Connor agreed grimly, and Jess felt a wave of fear— he would be a dangerous enemy, but she had known that from the first meeting with him, and her voice was steady as she continued. "Well, I've found out a couple of things since then, and they're important to you and me. I could wait, and we could trade information bit by bit, but I came here because I trust you and I want to help, so I'll tell you what I know and hope you'll return the favor."

All of Win's painstaking undercover work, she was

going to blow it now, and if it didn't work for the best, she would have his contempt in place of his love forever, but she didn't hesitate. "The Englishman, Winston St. James, the one with the cane, the one who is supposedly trying to buy into Tarkington's operation, he's a cop."

They did not look as shocked as she had thought they would. "I thought it once, but he's good man, he's good, he got through that, had us all convinced, all us dumb black bastards and even our fearless white leader. This is a nice setup. You got him waitin' outside with an army, cause that's what it'll take," Connor snarled.

"No," Jess said quietly. "If he knew I was here, knew I've told you who he really is, he'd wring my neck. He thought I was going to do it all by a phone call, just get some more information for him, and even that he didn't like, called it blackmail. I haven't told him your names either."

"You into this dude, you love him?" Connor asked sharply. "Your face tells, so talk straight."

"Yes, I love him, and I'll tell you as I told Traylee, if it gets down to that, I'll choose Win over both of you. But Traylee's my friend, and I hope you are too, and I don't want to choose."

She watched him struggle with his deep distrust of her race, and she watched as his equally deep sense of fair play won. Traylee had not been wrong in his judgment of his brother's character. "What'd you have in mind?" Connor asked, and this voice was as quiet as hers had been.

"The authorities have been on Kyre's trail for a long time. They know about the jewel-thieving operation here and in other places, and they know the old woman is involved, too. They suspect a murder committed in Nassau was Tarkington's doing. But they didn't know about the cocaine until I told Win. And now he needs to know the pickup time, the ship's name, the location. If they catch Kyre with the shipment, they can nail him. And if you help supply the information, it will lighten your punishment. Connor, they're going to get that man and everyone else one way or another, and this way you have a better

chance. From what I hear, you're in more danger from
Kyre than from the police."

"Him I could handle, but he don't work that way, not
alone. An' I still don't know how many are for me, how
many for him. Money's powerful. Don't even know where
the ol' woman's gone to."

"But you do know about the boat, don't you?" Jess
asked urgently.

"Yeah, I know, one man he not sure, playin' both
sides, talkin' here, listenin' there." He ran his hand over
his face tiredly. "I don' know, whatever I do, goin' to be
bad. I go to your man, I turn over brothers to th' law."

"I know. It's ghastly any way you look at it, but
sometimes you have to make a choice between evils. Tell
me, and I'll take the information back, or if not go to Win
yourself." She described where his room was at the Queen's
Gate. "Or call him, anything, as long as you let him
know." She could feel Traylee pleading silently in unison
with her, asking his brother to save himself.

"Not enough time, not near enough," Connor murmured distractedly, and Jess' heart lurched against her
ribs. "You mean it's going to happen soon, tonight?" she
croaked and she didn't need Connor's reluctant nod to tell
her it was so. "Then you've got to tell Win!"

She received no answer. Connor went suddenly rigid,
every muscle tensing so that she could see them stretched
like steel cords in his face and arms. He was half out of his
seat by the time the man reached their table. He was
small and moved furtively like some burrowing animal
caught in the open, and when he was close Jess could see
the sweat shining on his face. His skin was muddy gray
with fear, his eyes huge and terror-filled, but he retained
something of his humanity in his concern for Connor. "He
outside, got others, come for you, got to get movin', thinks
you talk," he gasped, and Jess had no trouble at all
understanding the jumble of words. Her fear matched his.
She sat paralyzed as the little man disappeared in the
crowd. They were all as good as dead if Kyre knew they
had been together. She saw three burly men come in the

front entrance just as Connor herded her upright. "Move!" he barked. "Traylee, back door, head for it!"

They pushed their way through the crowd, overturning chairs in their wake, following Traylee. He led them through a swinging door, and they were in a hall, passing doors marked for utilities, finally going through the one at the end to stand blinking in the sudden darkness of an alley.

They heard them before they saw them, a tight knot of men coming down the alley toward them, and they bolted in the opposite direction, Traylee gasping, "There's a fence this way!"

"Man, we climb it! Some o' these dudes, new, don't know!" Connor hissed back.

The footsteps were thudding behind them now as they ran, and when Jess saw the fence, she knew it was hopeless—a high, solid board fence she couldn't possibly climb. Surprisingly it was Connor who grasped her hand. "Hang in there, we lift you over."

"It's no use!" she panted. "They're right behind us! Both of you, go, get help, it's my only chance. No use three dead. If you care, goddamn it, go!" Her voice ended in a scream as their pursuers neared enough so that each face was distinguishable even in the dark. She heard the impact and scrape as Connor and Traylee vaulted and pulled their way over the fence, and she saw the man beside her grab Traylee's leg as he clung precariously to the top of the boards. Without thinking, she sank her teeth viciously into his wrist, feeling his grip loosen, hearing Traylee drop down on the other side, tasting salt blood before the man cuffed her hard on the side of her head, making her see bright explosions of light and then nothing.

She heard the voices and kept her eyes closed. "We lost them, but we'll go after them when you're gone. No guns, no noise," one man reported, and another asked, "What you want done with her? Kill her, dump her?" And she had no problem at all recognizing the next voice, even with her eyes closed. "No, she's better use alive, for a while anyway."

Her eyes flew open to find Kyre staring at her. He reached down and grasping her shoulders, stood her upright with careless strength. She shuddered at his touch, and he laughed maliciously. "You didn't find me so distasteful once; you'd better get used to me again. We have hours yet together, my dear." *My dear.* In all probability, she was not going to live to hear Win say it again. She swayed, and Kyre's hands bit into her shoulders as he gave her a shake. "Are you going to walk out of here with me, or do you want me to knock you out again and carry you? No one's going to ask, and even if they did, I'd proclaim my undying love for my drunken girl friend."

"I'll walk!" she spat at him, rage and disgust giving her strength. She had to believe that Connor and Traylee would get help and not just hide out somewhere. It was her only chance, that and doing what Kyre commanded, gaining time any way she could.

They left the alley and went to a car parked a little ways down the street. Jess looked around wildly, wondering if anyone would come to her rescue if she screamed. Kyre saw her intention. "Don't try it! I'll strangle you before the sound leaves your throat," he said pleasantly as though he were carrying on a normal conversation, and Jess swallowed hard. He didn't even have the excuse of being truly mad. He was cool and purposeful, dedicated to greed and devoid of any other feeling.

Most of the men melted away into the shadows, but two stayed with her and Kyre, and the four of them got into the car. Three strong men against her, the odds on her escaping were remote. She reckoned there had been at least seven besides Kyre, and she wondered how many of those were newly recruited for the drug run. She wondered if any of them were on Connor's side. She and Kyre were sitting on the back seat, and she stole a look at the two men in the front. Illuminated by occasional flashes of light, their ebony faces were expressionless, graven images of men committed to violence and death. One of them must have felt her stare, for he turned slightly in the passenger seat and looked at her, but his face did not change; no warmth touched it at all.

They wound down toward the harbor, and the man driving paid careful heed to the in-town speed limit, taking no chance on drawing needless attention from an officer. When they finally stopped, they were at a boatyard. It appeared totally deserted, and Jess felt what little hope she had draining away and did as she was told without protest.

Everything was well planned. Of course, it would be with Kyre in charge and so much at stake. There was a motorboat tied up and waiting for them, but before they got in, Kyre tied Jess' hands behind her, binding them so tightly that the rope began cutting into her wrists instantly. "Now you'll think twice before you try to throw yourself overboard. It's difficult to swim with no arms. I don't want to have to watch you every minute," he said.

He got in the boat, and then the man who had sat in the front passenger seat picked Jess up and handed her down to Kyre who deposited her none too gently on the floor of the boat. She couldn't be sure, and she could scarcely credit it, but she had the oddest sensation when the man picked her up. He said nothing, and his face changed, but just for a second, it had seemed that he had pressed her close, given her a little reassuring hug. Even though she didn't see what he could do without getting both of them killed, she prayed he was one of Connor's friends and on her side.

The boat began to move, swift and evilly quiet, and as she struggled to a sitting position, her body brushed against it, and she saw the figure which shared the floor with her. No wonder Elsie had been missing at dinner. Jess screamed, forgetting everything except the sheer horror of seeing Elsie's crumpled body and staring eyes, dead, quite a long time dead.

Kyre slapped her so hard, her head snapped back painfully on her neck and her teeth cut the inside of her mouth, but the sound stopped. "Interfering old bitch, I should have dumped her long ago," Kyre said.

Only once did they see a boat which might have been of any use to her, but their pilot saw it while it was still far away and cut the motor, and they began to drift in

darkness. The powerful engines and the running lights
passed them at a good distance, never even veering in
their direction. Jess tried to draw some small comfort from
the fact that at least Kyre's man knew these waters well
enough so that they would not be cracked against coral
and spilled into the water while her hands were bound.

They seemed to go on for hours, and every minute
was taking her further away from help, from Win. She felt
heavy with unnatural sleep, with the shock of capture and
the proximity of death. Her mind kept drifting as though
it were going out with the tide, and it was hard to
concentrate on anything, but she knew when the sea got
rougher as they left the Great Sound. She closed her eyes
and tried to picture Win laughing, but it was all wrong; he
was weeping, his face grotesque with grief, and Uncle
Arthur was there too, his face just an older version of
Win's, his grief as raw and young as Win's as they mourned
her death.

No, not yet! her mind screamed in panic, and then
she saw him as his face drifted into her vision, hazy at first
then sharp in every detail. He was smiling, and his blue
eyes were very bright. *No, not yet, Jaybe.* She heard his
voice very clearly even as his image faded, and she relaxed
her tense muscles against the wet floor of the boat and let
herself go blank, let herself rest for whatever was to come.

She didn't open her eyes again until she heard Kyre's
satisfied, "There she is, right on time," and then she
watched the sleek white lines of the schooner grow more
definite with each second.

Even in her terror, Jess had to admit the beauty of
the craft. The *Circe* had to be some sixty feet long, trim
and capable of great speed in skilled hands. And skilled
they were, the two white men who managed the ship.
They had the four from the motorboat aboard in no time,
and though Jess felt as if she had been hauled up like a
sack of potatoes, she was thankful to be in one piece. She
shut her eyes and tried not to hear the occasional thud as
Elsie's body was hauled aboard ignominiously by rope.

One of the men called Kyre a foul name and told him
they hadn't bargained on two extra passengers, but there

wasn't any rancor. He was just needling Kyre for the inconvenience. Kyre replied, "Come on, Tyler, don't I always work things out? The old lady's no problem. She signed her own death warrant, left a note telling our dear tour directors that she was going home, not feeling well, et cetera. She meant it, too. She was running out on me. It won't be until at least next week that anyone figures out she's missing, and they won't be able to connect it with anyone."

You're wrong, no matter what happens to me, you're wrong, Jess thought. She was glad some instinct had warned her not to threaten Kyre with the fact that Win was a policeman, not to warn him, thereby giving him a chance to change his plans. Let him go on thinking Win was a crook with a purpose as twisted as his own.

"This other one, no problem either." Jess held very still, listening to him talking about her. "The last people she was seen with were two black men I'd like to put away anyway, and I've got witnesses. I'll use it. Bad scene, two black men in a black club with a white girl."

Jess was sure she heard it, a low throated growl of anger from her maybe friend. *Don't do it, don't give yourself away,* she pleaded silently.

Kyre and Tyler went on discussing their plans, making no attempt to speak softly—why should they? they planned to dispose of her anyway. Jess shivered, but she could not help listening in fascination, and her respect for Connor grew with every word. There was so much money involved that her mind could scarcely comprehend the figures, yet Connor had not been swayed into the drug traffic by it. Tyler was Kyre's partner, the other man on the boat was just a flunky. Tyler and Kyre had worked, planned and invested in the cocaine venture together; Elsie had refused. They considered it a good deal to have paid less than $5,000 a kilo for the cocaine in Bogotá, Colombia, especially since every gram of the fifty keys was guaranteed to run about ninety-seven percent pure. Together they had paid close to $250,000 for the stuff, so no wonder Kyre thought murder such a small price to pay when he was gambling everything he had begged, borrowed, and mostly stolen on this deal.

She came out of her daze to hear the doubt in Tyler's voice. "Guaranteed, that's a funny word for this business."

"No, not in this case, it isn't. The source is reliable, can't afford not to be. And I snorted a couple of lines when I made the deal. It's good, pure Colombian flake. The Snowman will take it all. He can hardly wait to get his hands on it, and at thirty thousand dollars a key, he can have it." The electric note of greed in Kyre's voice made Jess' neck prickle.

"We could make more if we stepped on it ourselves, even if we just cut it once with lactose." Tyler was so reassured, his own greed was growing.

"No!" Kyre's voice was tight. "The Snowman gets it as is, and we stand to make over half a million bucks each. He can cut it as many times as he wants. I figure by the time everyone's had their chance and it's all out on the street, it will have made about ten million. But the Snowman and his organization, they deserve the money. Hell, they'll have narcs breathing down their necks every step of the way. I don't want any part of that, and I don't want to go back on my word. I can't spend anything if I'm dead." Even Kyre feared someone.

They congratulated themselves on choosing Bermuda, far enough north to be out of the suspicious area of the Caribbean where the cocaine traffic was brisk and officials alert. Even the plane carrying the shipment would be above suspicion because after the drop, it would land carrying nothing more alarming than South American goods and foodstuffs normally imported by Bermuda and the islands of the Caribbean. The drug was a bonus package.

They checked timetables. Kyre and his two men would go back to Hamilton before dawn, once the cocaine was safely on board the *Circe*. The *Circe* wouldn't go into Hamilton until Monday, timing her arrival to coincide with the confusion of the liner, *Sea Venture*'s docking which would dump a horde of tourists on Hamilton. The *Circe* wasn't in much danger anyway. She had already passed inspection. Kyre would see the cocaine safely hidden in Bermuda save for a small amount he would smuggle back in a body block to reassure his buyer that the merchandise was as fine as promised. He doubted his departure on Tuesday would be delayed by Jess' disappearance since the police would be looking for two black men. The *Circe* would sail southward, pleasure cruising until enough time had passed to assure a cooling-off period, to assure them that no one was tracking the shipment. Then the boat would retrace her route, reclaim her cargo and sail for the United States.

"We can handle things until then," Tyler said. "We'll keep a good eye on the weather, and we'll trust your men here to get the coke aboard, but you sure as hell better be there to transfer it before we hit U.S. waters."

"That's the whole point, isn't it? Do you think I'd risk my fortune because of cold feet? I'm not the nervous type," Kyre commented dryly.

Jess was trying desperately to cling to her faith in the Jamesons, but Kyre and Tyler sounded so sure, and their plan sounded foolproof. Connor and Traylee had to be running scared. Would they risk so much to save her? The irony of it was that if they did not, they would be accused of her murder—she believed Kyre when he said he could engineer it. And even Win had said he had no cause to trust her friends. Win, by now he would be looking for her, but without the Jamesons, it would be an impossible task. She could no longer control her fear, and she began to shiver violently, her clothing wet from the boat ride, her bones cold from terror.

She shuddered even more violently when Kyre touched her. "Poor little girl, she's cold. Guess old Kyre will just have to warm her up. We've got half an hour. I'll be below, call me if they're early."

Tyler snickered. "You're a fast worker. Me, I'll take the slow time when the work's finished."

"You scum!" Jess screamed, and when Kyre hauled her to her feet, she tried to kick him, but with her hands tied she had no balance and would have fallen had he not held onto her.

"That's it, I like a little spirit. I'll bet my would-be partner liked it, too," he said and he laughed as he pushed her toward the ladder that led below. "Here, let me help you with the steps, don't want you to break your neck." The mock solicitude in his voice and the touch of his hands were sickening.

He shoved her ahead of him into the master cabin, and she lost her balance and fell, knocking the wind out of her lungs. She lay sprawled and panting on the floor, not even conscious that he had reached down and cut her bonds until the blood seared like fire back into her wrists and hands. She sat up shakily, rubbing her hands together, watching Kyre fearfully as he twirled the knife.

"You can take your clothes off willingly, or I'll cut them off, but that might leave some nasty marks."

She stared at him, immobilized by the snake light flickering again in his eyes. He moved so swiftly that she didn't know what was happening until the knife flashed down, baring her to the waist, leaving an oozing trail of blood droplets where the knife had broken skin. "Is that enough, or shall I do the rest? I'm in a hurry."

"No, I'll do it," she said dully. She felt so numb she could barely make her hands work to take off the rest of her clothes. This would gain so little time, and one way or the other, she was going to die. But maybe if she pleased him—her stomach heaved at the thought—maybe he would make a swift death.

Kyre advanced on her, unbuckling his belt with one hand, his eyes taking in every detail of her slender body. "Oh, my, yes, we will have a nice time. Played hard to get, didn't you? Stupid. I always get what I want."

She moaned Win's name without thinking, and Kyre lunged, all calm menace forgotten, screaming obscenities at the Englishman, screaming that the man had gotten what he himself wanted without effort.

Jess reacted instinctively out of her mindless terror, stepping aside at the last minute, putting her leg out, sending him sprawling against the wooden rim of the bed.

She heard the impact of his head hitting the hard frame, the knife clattering on the floor, even as she was fumbling with the lock. She was out and running down the companionway when she heard his howl of rage. She ran smack into the solid chest of the man from the passenger seat. He gripped her arms for an instant. "Go, momma, up an' over th' side. They ain't got time to look," he commanded and half lifted her onto the ladder.

She scrambled up the steps and was across the deck and diving into the water even as she heard shouts ring out. She entered the water cleanly and swam under it until her lungs were bursting with pain, but even then she made herself surface quietly, not taking a deep breath until she was far enough away from the ship. A light went on, beam searching the water, and she dove again and swam further away. When she surfaced, the light was out. Just as her benefactor had said, they could not afford the time to look for her, nor could they afford attracting attention with a searchlight. She was safe at least until the drop was made; they could not even risk the noise of the motorboat for fear it would drown out the sound of the plane. Afterward, yes, perhaps then they would look, but they didn't really have to bother, the sea would finish her for them.

Something brushed against her leg, trailing a fanning current as it passed. Barracuda, shark, sea snake? What awful creatures lived here, swirling beneath, around, ready to strike? The blood from her chafed wrists, from the knife scratch, was it already sending signals to the predators? She felt the scream rising and clenched her teeth against it—a sea beast might kill her, Kyre certainly would.

She drifted quietly. The closest lights were mere pinpricks a million miles away. The *Circe* was fading from her vision, and she could no longer hear any sounds from it. She was cold, and then she was very sleepy as she had been earlier. She wondered vaguely how long it took to drown if you did it willingly, could you do it willingly?

Decide, Jaybe, decide now! She was startled by the clarity of Sean's voice. She remembered. It was over a silly thing which had become important. She had played so badly at the beginning of the match that her concentration was gone, all her energy was being expended on self-loathing, and she was hitting each shot as if failure were her goal. Sean was beside her at the break, making her feel more miserable. *The hell with you, Sean Banbridge, I don't give a damn whether I win or lose. It's only a stupid game.*

The rage against herself didn't touch him. His blue eyes, so near the color of her own, were dark with compassion. *Jaybe, that's your problem, you'll always care about whatever you do. Right now you're playing a lousy game of tennis, about the worst I've ever seen you play. If you really want to quit, tell your opponent. It's only fair. The way you're going now, you're making her feel ridiculous too. Look, I don't know how it happened, but you've gotten so wrapped up in the overall picture, you've forgotten what you have to do. You have to take one shot at a time, do your best, and then let it go. That's all. Decide, Jaybe, decide now! This isn't your style.*

She hadn't won; she was too far behind, but the match had been good enough at the finish to bring the spectators of the amateur match to their feet, to draw a grateful smile from her opponent. The strangest thing about Sean had been that he understood and accepted equally quitting or fighting your hardest—what he never understood was the middle ground.

The choice was the same now. She could quit, let herself drown, surrender with some dignity to her old enemy. Or she could do her best to stay alive. She saw Uncle Arthur's face and more clearly, Win's. She wanted to see them in the flesh again; she wanted above all to be with Win, for uncountable days and nights ahead she wanted to be with Win.

The decision was made. She felt an extraordinary sense of peace, and Sean was smiling his approval. She lay on her back, floating, and the sea drift rocked her gently. If she were lucky, she might find one of the absurd little islands which dotted these waters, but the velvet blackness showed her nothing save the cold, far-off brilliance of the stars. Perhaps that government ship, surely that was what t had been, all that powerful speed and light, perhaps it would come out again on patrol. She considered the major factor in her favor—people had survived the ice of northern seas; she was in much warmer water. And by day these waters were as well trafficked as the streets of Hamilton. If she could make it through the dawn, some vessel would be sure to happen along. Any vessel would do as long as it was not the *Circe*. She hadn't much sense of time, but she thought it must be past three, not so long until the sun. Had Connor or Traylee gone to Win, did Win have some idea now of where to look for her? She would trust them all, though perhaps she would never know.

Even the terror of creatures prowling the sea lessened; they were something she could do nothing about. For the first time she began to understand Sean's feeling of kinship with the sea; Sean who could not have written a sonnet had his life depended on it, but who had waxed lyrical at any mention of the sea. *Don't you understand at all, Maybe? The salt in our blood, the salt in the earth, everything coming from and washing back to the sea. She's the first and final womb, she's life even in death. I don't understand how anyone can be at peace until he feels the rhythm of the tide in his blood.*

Jess felt it until she felt nothing else, just the cradled rocking of her body, the spreading warmth in languorous limbs. She lost all sense of time and space. Sometimes her body would start suddenly, her legs surfacing again after the beginning of a slide downward, but there was no sense of panic, just an automatic balancing. Sometimes she thought she slept and dreamed, either that or her mind wandered off to more amusing things than floating. Once she heard the drone of a plane overhead, but she didn't care about it anymore. She tried to make Uncle Arthur tell her the truth about all the changes he had made in her life, was his magic and Sean's part of the same thing, the sorcerer and his spirit helper? Did he even know?

Win's voice kept shouting, "Jess, Jess, answer me!"

How like him! He was even demanding in a dream. The call came again. No, not demanding, frantic with fear. She heard the boat then, saw the strong beam of light searching the sea. Her legs swung down, and she started treading water. Water washed into her mouth, and her answering cry was gasping and much weaker than she had intended. She tried again. Better, he had heard. The boat swung in closer, and the light caught her. Someone was in the water with her, hands lifted her, someone said her name over and over.

"Sean, I won," she said and slipped into darkness.

15

*Though the seas threaten, they
are merciful.
I have cursed them without cause.*

Jess noticed many things simultaneously when she
came to. She could still feel the sea's motion, but she was
dry and warm in a boat's small cabin; the faint light of
dawn was showing through a porthole; the rope wounds on
her wrists had been carefully bandaged; and her head
ached dully on one side, strange she had not felt the effect
of the blow hours ago. She shouldn't have sat up because
she didn't have anything on under the blanket which
covered her, nothing except a meandering line of orange
disinfectant over the knife scratches; and Winston St.
James looked a hundred years old with worry and fatigue
until she smiled at him. The change in his face was so
complete, her pulse jumped, jarring her skull. She subsided under the blanket again, clutching the side of her
head.

Win's face was grim again. "If it makes you feel any
better, Tarkington has a broken jaw in addition to a lump
on his forehead which he seems to have received in a fall.
I sincerely hope he feels a bloody lot worse than you do.
He and his crew, they're under lock and key on another
cutter going into Hamilton. The Americans will probably
be extradited for trial in the United States. We found Mrs.
Clinton's body ready to be thrown overboard. I am sorry
you had to see it, but it might have been worse, it might

have been you." He held his voice steady with an effort
and continued, "We found the ruby, set in a pin as the
body of a bird. The old woman must have been wearing
it."

Jess nodded. "I saw the hummingbird pin before,
when it had a fake stone in it, but I never thought of it
again. Elsie was running from Kyre, trying to get out of
the country, poor, twisted old lady."

Win started to speak again, but she forestalled him.
"No, I have things to tell you, and I want to say them
before I forget." As clearly as she could remember, she
told him what Tyler and Kyre had planned, the strange
terms they had used, how much they had paid for the
cocaine, how much they were going to sell it for, the man
who was going to buy it from them once they got it into
the States.

"The authorities in your country will have a difficult
time arresting the Snowman, even if they do know what
his real name is. Criminals at that level are hard to touch.
They let their lackeys do all the dirty work. But we've got
the cocaine. They tried to throw it overboard, but it still
had the floats on from the air drop, and we got every bit of
it. Fifty kilos of that quality, it's a tremendous catch!" His
eyes sparkled, and Jess knew that in spite of Elsie's body,
in spite of the violence, he had enjoyed every minute of
what must have been a lively fight on the *Circe*. There was
a new bruise beginning on his jaw, and she reached out to
touch it gently and murmured at the still damp state of his
clothes, a further reminder that he had saved her, even to
the final rescue from the sea.

His control broke at her touch, and he seized her
fiercely, drawing her against him, moaning against her
hair, "You little fool! I ought to finish his work so I never
need worry again. I lost a lifetime tonight, thinking never
to see you again." He kissed her cheeks, her eyelids, her
bruised mouth, and she was as shaken as he when she
tasted the salt of his tears—not even knowing he loved her
had she known how great a part of his world she had
become in such a short time. It was an enormous responsibility she accepted joyfully.

"I found your clothes in the cabin. Tarkington, did he. . . ." Win began and could not finish, and Jess could hear the pain of the words in his throat. He cradled her head against his breast and smoothed her hair with a gentle hand.

"No, darling, he tried, but that's all. Even the sea was preferable to him." She described what had happened, and she could not suppress a shiver of remembrance. Win's arms tightened. "You know it would not have made any difference in how I feel about you, only that it would be difficult to bear the knowledge that you had come to more harm."

"Yes, I know," she said with no doubt. She stirred suddenly and pulled away so that she could see his face. "I'm so glad to be safe with you, I've forgotten everything else. My friends, is that how you found me?"

He nodded. "You were quite right to trust them, Jess. They are both on board. I had just discovered you were gone and was considering succumbing to total madness when they found me. You are a very devious woman. Connor told me everything, and we grabbed the pilot of the plane first. He was reluctant to talk until I let Connor question him. Highly unethical, but very effective. The man was closer to death than he'd ever been while flying, and he didn't like it. He was only too glad to give the location of the drop to escape Connor's fists. Both of the Jamesons came with us to help locate the ship. They know these waters well. They're good friends; they risked a great deal to help you."

"Will Connor be all right? I hate to see him put away after the help he's given."

"I think the authorities will be lenient, especially because there is shared guilt. Connor has good reasons for much of his anger and putting him in prison would be a bit like incarcerating Robin Hood, bad form for the ruling class. I shall certainly recommend leniency in my report."

Jess' mood lightened, and she giggled at the picture of Connor in forest green tights and a peaked cap. She could hear him growl in protest, and she could hear

Traylee say, "Aw, come on, Connor, white man, black man, doesn't matter. Robin Hood was a hero."

"May I see them?" she asked eagerly. "And there was that other man, the one who helped me, I don't even know his name, but I'm sure he's a friend of Connor's. Without him, I never would have gotten away."

"I'll see that it's known, and you can see the Jamesons after you put something on." He let her go reluctantly, and she smiled at the look on his face as he handed her a short, yellow slicker. "Your clothes aren't in very good shape, and they're on the other ship in any case. This is all the ship's store has to offer which will fit you," he said as he helped her into it, "and it doesn't cover half enough of your charms."

"Are you the jealous type who is going to keep me in long flannel?" she asked demurely.

"Keep you? No, my dear, I am going to marry you," he said softly. He reached in his pocket and brought out the Barton ring. "Technically this is evidence, just as the ruby is, but I have it under special circumstances." He slipped it on her finger. "Tarkington must have had an obsession about you to have risked carrying this with him," he added, his anger surfacing again.

"Win, don't. He's under lock and key, and maybe he never would have been caught if he hadn't had basic weaknesses. I just happened to be one of them. It's over now, and I'm safe. I plan to be safe with you for the rest of my life. I know you have room for me and for what I do, and I've already gotten quite used to the idea of living with a policeman who doesn't take very good care of himself." She fended him off for a second. "But I warn you, I've thought about it, and I'll make a lousy lady."

He laughed in delight and hugged her. "Lady Lousy, that will be a new one, but the family can stand it. I'm going to call Uncle Arthur as soon as we have a chance."

"To tell him his plan worked and Miranda suffered a sea change, to say the very least?"

"No, to give him hell and ask his blessing. He never had the slightest doubt about his plan working sooner or later. He would have tried again, you know," he said with resignation.

"Um, hummm," Jess agreed, tugging at him. "Let's go, I want to see Connor and Traylee. They're probably wondering what you've been doing down here with me for so long."

"I think they know," Win laughed.

When Jess emerged topside, she saw full dawn, Hamilton, some uniformed crewmen, and the Jamesons. They both came at her at once, the concern in their faces changing to broad smiles. She put her arms around them and gave them each a resounding kiss. "Bless you both for saving my life!"

"All right, baby, all right," Connor mumbled, and Jess and Traylee exchanged brief grins over the big man's discomfiture. He could handle any amount of violence, but he was utterly disarmed by gentleness. Jess looked up at him. "Are you going to be all right? That's the important thing."

"I think so, for th' firs' time I think so. I'll try. Traylee's always givin' me lip 'bout workin' in th' system," he said, the softness still in his face for his brother and for her. Jess accepted the fact that the capacity for violence would always be there, the urge to hit out before someone else hit first, but she hoped fervently there would be a place for Connor, a peaceful place inside the law. Traylee would help, Traylee would always help. She looked at him, and his eyes acknowledged their secret bond. They had fought hard; they had trusted against all odds; they had won and the wild pleading was over.

There was still so much to do. Win would have endless tasks to perform, as would other officers in widely separated places, to track down and arrest all of Kyre's network. Jess herself would undoubtedly have to testify in court. Elizabeth's ruby and who knew what else would have to be returned to the rightful owners. She would be glad to tell Otto, the jeweler, that it would be done. Sally had to be told the whole story immediately—Jess could hardly imagine how she must be feeling at this moment, wondering if her friend was with the Englishman, afraid to find out, afraid she might be somewhere else. Jess would have to make a decision about the house in Lexington, arrange to be at Sally's wedding in the United States and her own in England. She had no doubt but that it would be there with Win and his family, with Uncle Arthur. She had the seal to give Uncle Arthur, the fairy tale drawing to give Win. They were her family now. She had no one at home to give her away, and she knew with a sharp, last pang of sorrow that she would never hear or see Sean as clearly again.

Win's arm came around her and held her close against his side as they neared the dock. It was all right. She alone was giving herself into Win's keeping, taking him into hers. She no longer needed Sean to protect her. His spirit was free at last.

ABOUT THE AUTHOR

CELESTE DE BLASIS, a native Californian, lives on a ranch high in the Mojave Desert. She is the author of such memorable novels as *Wild Swan*, *Swan's Choice*, and *The Proud Breed*.